`D1578591`

### THE MISPLACED CORPSE

———

A.E. Martin was born in Adelaide in 1885 and died in Sydney in 1955. He owned a weekly newspaper when aged eighteen, then worked for many years as an entrepeneur and publicist in theatre, circuses, the movies and vaudeville. Many of the characters in his crime fiction draw on his experiences in early Australian show-business, but he always said that private investigator Rosie Bosanky came straight from his imagination.

Rosie's story, *The Misplaced Corpse*, is the first of the Wakefield Crime Classics, a series that revives forgotten or neglected gems of Australian crime and mystery fiction.

# The MISPLACED CORPSE

### A.E. MARTIN

WAKEFIELD
CRIME
CLASSICS

Series editors Michael J. Tolley and Peter Moss

Wakefield Press
Box 2266
Kent Town
South Australia 5071

First published in 1944
Published in Wakefield Crime Classics in June 1992

Edited by Jane Arms
Designed by Design Bite, Melbourne
Printed and bound by Hyde Park Press, Adelaide

Cataloguing-in-publication data
Martin, A.E. (Archibald Edward)
The misplaced corpse
ISBN 1 86254 281 3.
I. Title. (Series: Wakefield Crime Classics; no.1)
A823.2

Those who live in quiet, and, I am sure, highly respectable neighbourhoods where the stealthy footstep of the private enquiry agent is seldom if ever heard, will, I am afraid, find Rosie Bosanky a little alarming. Let me hasten to add, however, if she shocks, the most surprised young person in the world will be Rosie herself.

In handing me her story, she has stipulated that I make no alterations except to 'scatter a few stops and things'. I have also been instructed to print all French words in 'slanting type'. So where, after consideration, it appeared it would be most helpful, I have punctuated, and where I have been able to recognise Rosie's French I have slanted.

**A . E . M .**

CHAPTER I

If you was nineteen years old and the red-headed daughter of a policeman who has been murdered by a poisonous thug, I bet you would get a lotta satisfaction, too, to see your sign on an office door:

ROSIE BOSANKY

INVESTIGATIONS

I bet you would feel like me if those Nazi baskets ever came over and blitzed it; you would be as mad as hell and it would be one more argument why you would want to trample Hitler's moustache in the mud and make him give Dantzig back to the Czechs.

It is for this reason I got the office in a location where there is no hospital within miles, because I have always found in my life that, while a young girl of a modern type has to take a great lotta chances, when such is not the case it is a wiser course to follow the idea of safety first.

The idea of this office was a growing ambition in me since longer than I can remember, and though it is now a war-time period, Inspector Browne says I can be a saviour of my country to a far bigger extent in such a position than if I was a land girl digging up grapefruit for the American invaders.

I think in this decision Brownie has persuaded hisself that some day he will be able to use me as a Mata Hari. Anyway he has got me a paper which says I am a restricted occupation and I have got a high priority on silk stockings because, for such a job, to send a young girl out in the world without 'em would be like sending a tank to a battle without gunpowder.

Brownie has gotta idea, too, that he should keep his eye on me on account he was a great friend of my pappy, and it will be nice an' easy to ease round to my office in his off-hours to see about my spiritual welfare, the old wolf. I gotta keep a neat balance in my mind of Brownie as a wolf and an orphan-minder because he can be a very handy man in the life of a young girl who has just set out to be an investigator, because he can cast in her pathway a lotta work the police hounds has sniffed out, but, on account of being in a uniform, cannot run down to a satisfactory climax.

This Brownie, I think, would make up an ideal world if he was a lot of years younger and only half as ugly and still had his well-paid job; but, now, he is not the type that any young girl would pitch upon to spend an evening with on some far southern beach with the soft Honolulan waves blowing in, and, on the outskirts, a band playing the Moonlight Sinatra.

I would be the last one in the world to lead you up the garden path and I wanta say now, if you got in your mind this is a war book, you had best go and fight the bookseller for your money back because it is a book about my first case which occurred when the war was but a pup and which I gave a workin' title to called *The Misplaced Corpse*, because, if ever a corpse was misplaced it was this one I am going to relate.

But, as the song says, let us begin at the begin. My real name is Rosaleen Bosanquet, but I am a girl who likes a simple form of life and I always call it Rosie Bosanky to rhyme with swanky. If you should see me stepping out in my high heels I am five feet and one inch; and I have red hair that grows so I can run my hands through it, and I still don't look a fright, besides which it is a red of a hue which made a college boy, who I came in contack with, write a poem. I do not pretend to know a lot about poems, but he tells me it is in the class of Ovid, though, if you ask me, it was a bit personal for a poet who I only met twice and one of those times at a dark picture show.

I have a snubby bit of a nose and blue eyes and a figure which sticks out far enough in the right places because my pappy has always taught me that it is a good idea for a young girl to leap outa bed by dawn's early light an' do a lotta physical jerks, an' I dress it to get the best out of it by only just keepin' the best in it, if you get me, because, like Confucius said in his less ribald moments, a Paris gown may entice a man around a block but what's inside it will lead him round several hemispheres.

My pappy was a widower policeman who was very fond of his job and he had ideas of bringin' up a only child which woulda made a modern clinic be turned into an asylum for insane nurses, because as long as I can remember he would talk to me about the criminal classes and all the cases he had on hand and all the crooks he was sendin' to gaol an' why. Even when I was nine I knew more about Jack the Ripper than Jack the Giant Killer.

I would sit an' listen while he told me about all the nice murders that were the rage of the moment with a lotta inside information that wasn't in the *News of the World* even so that in time I got to thinkin' no more of a murdered corpse than most kids woulda thought of the wolf eating Red Riding Hood's gran'ma.

I got toughened all right. Before I was eleven I could read finger prints and knew the life history of all the public enemies, and, when I was thirteen an' was a child no longer he learned me the facts of life concerning which dame in the underworld was going with what crook and why, an' that a disorderly house was a different house to ours on a Sunday morning when no one has bothered to wash up Saturday's dishes.

At fifteen pap's keepin' nothin' back and old Brownie with who I have come in contack, thinks he is crazy to lead a young girl such a life; but pap only laughs and, next thing, when he gets a chance, he is edging me into the morgue showing me the finger marks on the strangled girl's neck or taking me to the scene of the crime where the rich banker's wife has harpooned her husband in the neck with a steel knitting needle and explaining how and from what angle it was did and why he figures it was Mrs Banker did the job, an' so forth. An', all the while, he has gotta good moral tone and I learn from what I see that there are plenty of things for a young girl to avoid unless she wants to be caught by the pitfalls of tragedy.

But, long before this, I have stayed at home keeping house because I've got practically expelled from school for writin' an essay on Seven Sure-Fire Methods of Murdering a School Mistress which were pretty good, even if only five of them were practically foolproof. I think the mistress was glad to know I might be leaving because, when my fate was kinda in the balance, I couldn't help noticin' little details like her hair turning white and how she wouldn't drink from the school tap, and hardly ever had her back to the class.

On the last day, too, when I was practically chucked out, she was too scared to go out to lunch and sat in the classroom and opened a little parcel of sandwiches she had brought from home and was just goin' to bite when I popped my head in the door and said I only came to say goodbye but, oh, Miss Metherington, didn't she think it would be wise to let one of her less favourite pupils eat some of the lunch first – just in case?

After that she put the lunch away, and I bet she had a pretty big appetite when she got home for dinner. I tell you this to show there are some people I take a like to an' some I don't, but, just the same, I am not holdin' it out as a good example, an' when I came to think of it, brought up like I was, I shoulda never been allowed to be a school kid. Just the same she should never have said I had no idea how to be a lady and that my frocks were so short she would never dream of taking such a responsibility as sending me to the headmaster for a dressing down.

When I am sixteen I go to work for a chap in an office with a beard – the chap I mean – and it's pretty dull till I learn that the petty stamps and cash is being pinched and they can't find who the hell it is. This is right up my alley, an' I get the chap with the beard and the head manager together an' I show 'em how there is a way to catch this pilferer red-handed, and this is such a ingenious way that, after the head manager has gone off to set the trap, the old Ziff is so pleased he gives me a squeeze an' a kiss which I don't like so I pull his beard an' slap his chops which *he* don't like.

Later on while things are this way between us, the head manager tells me my scheme has worked, and who'd you think it is that is the pilferer? It's nobody else but old Whiskers's son. This don't make me more popular, and the Ziff gets me alone again in his head office and, when he sees no sign that I am of a relentin' nature, he thinks it best for all concerned if I was to take a month's salary and leave at once.

I say, all things considered and the way he has behaved, I don't see any reason why I should be thrown out with only a month's wages, an' the way he has behaved an' the stink I could make, I think it's worth six months but I'll take three because I hate the place anyhow an' catchin' his son out as a petty criminal has been the only little ray of sunshine about the joint. He gives me a very sour look and pays me the money an' I hope he has learned his lesson.

I tell my pappy all about this, an' I say how about him goin' round and take a poke at this Ziff, but he says all men is wolves at heart, only in the present instant you mustn't blame 'em too much because, in a way, it's a sorta compliment; an' he says if he had to go round taking a poke at all the men who he thinks will make a pass at me in the future, life will only be one long fight.

He tells me some men has to have their appetites wet and he says, 'Rosie, you're one helluva appetiser the way you bulge out in all those places and the way you look an' all I don't suppose you can help it. It's just born in you, an' all I can do is to give you a friendly warnin' an' teach you some tricks.' He then teaches me these tricks which, as the well-known poet says, I will speak of anon.

An' then he gets leave, an' he has his life's desire an' goes over to see New York where my mother was born an' where she died, too, when I was seven an' they had to pack me back to my pappy on a ship in charge of the captain.

An' what happens in New York? Only this. My pap is in a speakeasy seein' life in the New York way. He is with some friends. It is all new to him, the quiet old dear. The band, the noise, the girls on the floor show in the near nuddy, and all. He's enjoying it up to his neck. An' then, in walks a gunman, whose name is Stalozzi, with three thugs at his heels.

My pappy watches 'em walk past him an' up to a table where a guy is sittin' with a dame. This Stalozzi says something, an' the guy at the table starts to get up. One of the thugs pushes him back and the woman screams. Another thug pushes *her* back.

My pap has got on his feet because, after all, although he's in a foreign clime an' is in a evenin' dress an' not a uniform he's a policeman just the same, an' he smells trouble. One of his friends pulls him down into his seat, an' the next moment this Stalozzi has shot three or four bullets into the guy at the table an' he is as dead as mutton.

This gunman an' his off-siders then begin to walk out. Nobody moves. He comes down between the tables, not lookin' to right or left, with one thug on either side an' one thug behind him, an' still no one moves. My pappy can't stand it any longer. As Stalozzi gets near him he stands up an' goes out to meet him. One of the thugs shoulders him, so he lands this guy one on the chin an' makes him reel. He then blocks Stalozzi's way.

And Stalozzi, who has never seen him in his life before and doesn't even know he's a policeman, just looks at him once and shoots him dead. Then he steps over my pappy an' goes on to the door. The gorilla who my dad slapped laughs.

An' not a damn one in the whole speak-easy moves till the killer has gone.

The police heads in New York write me some nice letters and send me the press clippings how my pappy met his doom, but I write back an' I say you don't have to tell me any good things about my father, I know plenty. All I want 'em to do is send me a picture of this snake who has taken his life without a rhyme or a reason, an' who they don't seem able to lay their hands on. I tell them I would like a description of him too, even to the most intimate detail, because all my born days I am goin' to remember that man an' I am never goin' to bed any night without I ask Heaven to give me a break and some-day let him fall across my path.

My dad's police cobbers get up a testimonial for me an' give me a nice sum, an' one of 'em is so sorry for me already he wants me to go live with him an' be his love. But I am fry-ing other fish an' has my own ideas. I am not goin' to take on any more jobs where old codgers like the Ziff will be squeezin' me in their private office. I can see it is a lurk which would be very easy to pull off, such as workin' about a week an' then gettin' three months salary to leave at once on account the boss's feelings being hurt. I admit I have a great temptation, but I think, too, if I had my pappy back an' was to tell him the idea, he woulda give me such a smack on the tail I would wear it till my dying day.

I fixed myself a little one room office an' paid one week's rent in advance. The agent wants a month but, when I take my purse from where it is gartered on to my knee, he says one week will do an' he'll come round each Monday an' collect. I think he's going to be a very despondent agent when he comes round an' finds I have got the money waitin' for him on the mantelpiece.

I have gotta lot of police notices about murders and rewards on the wall, an' I reckon when I open the whole room has a lot of atmosphere an' should be just the idea for a visit by anyone who wants to have someone investigated because, when you come to think of it, 'investigating' covers a helluva lotta ground.

After I get opened there is quite a bit of traffic up an' down the hall outside, but no one comes in, even if it is only to sell something, so in the end I open the door a bit an' plant my chair so that anyone could see in but not my head an' shoulders. All they'd get a eyeful of was my two legs in my best silks an' my Frenchiest shoes lolling friendly like on my desk.

In a mirror I could see who was peeking in an' at last it seems I have caught something. There is a well-dressed chap who is about thirty-five peering in. I cross my legs to give him a action view an' I see him blink, but he hasn't got the average look of a guy who is watchin' Eve make a quick change in the garden of Eden. His look kinda puzzles me but, in the end, I suppose, his curiosity gets the best of him an' he comes in, an' I think he gets a shock when he sees the complete picture, because he gapes with his mouth open.

I jumps up an' shuts the door an' pushes him into a chair because I have a kind of a intuition that this guy has gotta have his mind made up for him. He keeps on starin' a bit stupidly, but you can see it is a stupidness that is not in a moron class but is half a shyness and half a wondering what he's gonna do about something which has got on his mind.

He has got a slimmish figure with a well-cut navy blue suit that has a tiny red thread in it you can hardly notice and I bet it is a suit that woulda made my old dad have a heart failure just to see the price of; he has also got a longish nose and dreamy sort of eyes and his hair is blond and his mouth is nearly always open, which is not a great drawback because he has a set of teeth like a film star having a still made. I have a intuition to like this guy, and, just to put him at his ease, I say, 'Just take it easy. Everything is quite confidential. What is the trouble. Rape?'

This visiting client looks a bit rocked. 'Good heavens, no,' he says and, if ever I saw culture, he has got it in his voice. I bet this guy has got a family which goes so far back it would make William the Conqueror look like he was the latest thing out.

'I see,' I said. 'It's the old story then. Your wife, eh? Cleared out?'

He looks at me in astonishment. 'By jove,' he says, 'that's amazing! How did you guess? Not that I think she has, you know. What!'

He tells me his name is Adams – Roy Stockforth Adams. I see that his dreamy eyes is a soft brown and his hands have got good-shaped nails that look as if he has paid them a bit of attention without being a sis. I think he is the sort of guy that would suit some dames very well, but, as for me, if I ever took a fling into the bonds of matrimony, I think he would bore me stiff, he'd be so damn decent.

As he keeps on starin' at me across the desk I'm figurin' that if he hadn't heard something about his wife goin' off the rails, perhaps he'd never have taken a second decker at my legs but woulda passed on prim and proper, like Saint Whatshisname who had a lotta propositions put up to him in a vision but was strong enough to prefer a desert.

I've written his name down on my pad, an', as I said, it's Roy Stockforth Adams, if you please, an' he looks every bit of it, especially the Stockforth part. I asks him his age, an' he comes back, What's that gotta do with it.

'Sometimes a great deal,' I tell him. 'Not that you got anything to hide.'

He tells me thirty-five so my guess is right, an' his wife is called Malwa, which is a helluva name, an' I don't like it because all the words I know beginning with mal end up bad, like malefactor, which is a crook, malodrous, which is a stink, malediction, which is a very strong curse, and malpractice, which also has a dirty sound, besides which there is a city in Africa called Malparaiso, which is a sink of iniquity and the original old home town of white slavers, and those are the birds a girl like me would cheerfully give up some years of her life to see sitting on electric chairs and the heat comin' on peacefully so that they are cooked, like the recipe books say, in a slow oven.

I say, 'Now tell me all about it,' and he begins to stammer something about no intention to mention it, an' he thinks he better be tootlin' along. For a moment, my red hair comes to the surface, an' I'm about to ask him who the hell does he think I am that he can come bargin' in wastin' my time, when I suddenly recall how it was I set a hook for him an' I forgive him an' I say very sweet an' gentle, 'Maybe, Roy, it will help just to *tell* it.'

He melts at that an' swallows, an' I see at once that he's a kind of guy who is very prone to sentiment, an' he is now a lonely soul cryin' in the wilderness for someone to tell his troubles to. And out it comes!

He's met this Malwa somewhere in the East when on a world tour. She's a bit of a mystery, if you ask me, because there's no evidence at all that she was even born, only some yarn about her father and mother being killed in some convenient earthquake and her being looked after by some kindly nuns till she was old enough to sit up an' look round for herself for which, I think, she musta had some talent because he's found her on a tourist boat, hasn't he? and not down in the steerage neither but up on the boat deck with a full evening kit and a expensive romantic perfume.

He tells me about this perfume because it is what has attracted him in the first place when he was roaming about the top deck one moonlight night feeling a bit homesick. I can imagine this perfume, an' I bet it's been laid on to order an' in the right places, an' I guess it's the same kind as sounds so attractive in the ads in them smutty French papers where it is called 'Night of Love' or 'Harem Triumph' or some-such.

Well, Roy tells me, an' can you beat it? his eyes glisten with tears because he imagines he can still see that Eastern moon in the sky shinin' down on the sweet, sad face of this Malwa whose other name he comes to learn is Nawadi, which she has taken because I guess it has the right number of syllabus to go with Malwa and make a swing of it. He thinks he can still smell that love-dope she's sprinkled over herself, though what he's really sniffin' is my own special brand which ain't got no fancy name but has a kick of its own so that there have been times when I've been taxied home with a guy and I wish'd I'd watered it down.

To get back to this Oriental boat, however. There he is, this Roy, and there she is, Malwa Nawadi, and she relates about the earthquake, an' he tells her about his old home far away an' depicts scenes from his life since he was a small child, which makes her very sympathetic an' all, an', by and by, one thing has led to a lot more things, an' he's in her state room, an' its midnight, an' she's got on a pink negligee.

I can tell by the look in Roy's eye he can see her standin' there with the moon peepin' in the porthole and shinin' on her, an' then, quite unconscious, she passes between him an' the window, an' her form is revealed in all its lithesome loveliness, an' poor Roy is wrecked. She musta spilled the Night o' Love because she is in his arms an' there is no more talk of earthquakes or old home towns – just those sighings and gurglings which you all but, and never quite see in the movies, but which are part and parcel of the deadly routine life of a special enquiry agent.

So it boils down to he married her, an' about all she brought as a dowry between you an' me, was the Night o' Love perfume an' the pink negligee.

We got this far in Roy's life's romance when I think of the bottle of whisky I got set aside for just such an occasion, an' I pour him out a good stiff one, an' he feels better an' says what about a spot myself, so, just to please him, I say okay, though I don't like the stuff. All the same it don't do me no harm the little bit I take – in the matter of the old grey cells, I mean. It don't make me think any less clear, but the stuff is apt to work on my emotions in a way that ain't good for business.

Therefore, I only sip because this Roy, the more you see

of him the more he is easy on your eyes for all his goody-goody mother's boy manner, an' my pappy has long ago taught me a girl has to look out when a man drinks because whisky's a helluva thing to give a guy who's not used to it, in so far as in one swoop it will sozzle him up to the eyebrows an' give him a feeling that is impotent, or it will develop him into a raging lion who has just got word that his wife is going to stay still another week with her relations in a distant oasis.

I'm glad to see Roy keeps a nice balance, an' all he does is put out his hand an' hold mine where I have placed it on the desk. This gives him confidence, so he goes on an', just for a second, I believe he's goin' to try and reconstruct the honeymoon, but he sees I have raised my eyebrows so he skips it an' tells how he and Malwa sailed over the water, an' everything in the garden's lovely, though he finds out pretty soon she's got some expensive ways that the kindly nuns couldn't have learned her.

'I hope,' I say, 'that she didn't spend more than you could afford.'

This is my neat way of working round to what does he amount to in round figures and is he worth while to be a client of Rosie Bosanky who, after all, has got to make her way in the world and can't afford to fritter away her talents. No talents no talent, as they woulda put it in the dear, dead days of the ancient Bible.

'Oh, no,' he says, 'nothing like that, old dear; only after all, you know, whether you've got pots of it or not, dash it all, money shouldn't be thrown down the gutter, what?'

I say he's very right. I can't imagine anyone being so crazy as to throw good money down a gutter. I draw him a very pretty mental vision, an' I bet it is so realistic he can see just how good a way a man could spend his money on a woman without throwing it down the drain.

'Ah,' Roy says, 'but I didn't begrudge Malwa pretty clothes and things. I paid all the bills when they came in. But every now and then she wants a special cheque, a few hundreds for this and that' – things she don't specify an' which she don't wear, day or night.

'I see,' I tell him. I am beginnin' to wonder more about this Malwa Nawadi piece who, I figure, has some secret in her life. I am very pleased because secrets are what I am in the business to sniff out.

I say off hand, 'Would you be considered a wealthy man, Mr Adams?'

And he says just like it was nothing, 'Oh, I suppose you'd say so. About £60,000 a year.'

If there'd been a couch in the office which there wasn't because when I started my business I made up my mind that whatever sleeping I do I'll do in the old flat – I say if there'd been a couch, I could have swooned on it.

I squeeze his hand just to let him see I got his interests at heart, and say, 'Now, tell me, Mr Adams, what are your suspicions?'

'Suspicions?' he says. 'I'd hardly call them suspicions. Mind you, when it gets right down to bedrock I don't think for one jolly old moment that Malwa would let me down. No, no. They're not so much suspicions as jolly old anxieties.'

I think, Well, jolly old suspicions or jolly old anxieties, they will cost him just as much. He lets go my hand and dives into his breast pocket and brings out a letter an' shoves it over to me.

'I received that this morning, Miss Bosanky,' he says. 'My wife has been away and I've been sleeping at the club. It was waiting for me this morning and ever since I read it I've been a bit crazy, walking about, looking for someone to talk to. I came up here to see a pal and he was out and then I saw the sign on your door. I don't know exactly what made me come in.'

I have a good idea but I don't rub it in. I take a squiz at the letter. It's anonymous and it tells him his wife has done the dirty on him and it can be proved. She told him she was going to So-and-So and would be staying at the Palatial Hotel, didn't she? Well, she wasn't there last night, but he could trace her all right, because, if he took the trouble he'd find that a Mr and Mrs Adams had stayed at a hotel in Brighton on the night we have just slept through. It has all the hall marks of some friendly stickybeak.

I ask him where he got this letter because it hasn't got an envelope, which he says he must have destroyed, an' he says it was at his club, an' then, no it wasn't. He'd toddled out to his house an' it was there in the letterbox. He remembered because when he took it into his den to open it, the paper knife he uses for such an occasion is missing. He don't like this because it is an Eastern paper knife Malwa has given him for a keepsake in her early married life.

I ask him has he rung the Palatial Hotel, an' he says he has. They know her quite well there, an' she hasn't been on their books for some days. I then ask him has he rung up this pub in Brighton, an' he says of course not, because he doesn't believe the letter which he gives me to believe is an odious letter and stinks in his nostrils. I ask him would he mind if I give a ring because it will be just as well to clear everything up and he says he don't like it, but go ahead if I think it is okay.

After a bit this Brighton pub comes on an', casual like, I ask can I speak to Mr Adams. Oh, they say, what a pity Mr Adams has gone out. Okay, I say, can I speak to Mrs Adams. They say hold the line and then they come on again and say she has gone out, too. I say thank you an' hang up because I do not wish to be too anxious with these hotel people. I have a intuition at the moment it is better not to wake them up that there is anything fishy about their Adams couple.

I think it is a funny thing for a man to pinch a guy's name in addition to his wife; but of course this Roy is not the only Adams in the world. In fact it was one of them in a singular tense who set the ball rolling.

I tell Roy that she was there all right, but he won't have it. I can see he is the sort of man who, even if it was true, he wouldn't believe it, an' I begin to worry what sort of a case is this where a man is a client an' won't believe the evidence I get for him. I think perhaps Roy is under an impression he has just come in for a sympathetic chat an' will shortly take up his hat and walk out an' I have got nothing more for my trouble than the pleasure of his company, besides which he has had a whisky an' I will also have to pay a long-distance call.

I think it is a time when I have to use tack. I say, 'Listen, Roy, we gotta clear this thing up. We gotta clear it up because you gotta live your life with a peaceful mind. You say you don't believe Malwa is off the rails. Okay we will work on those lines. But she's not at the Palatial an' there's a Mrs Adams down at Brighton.

'Maybe it ain't Malwa. Okay. But she ain't at the Palatial; then where is she? You told me something about handing her some cheques every now and then, but you don't know what for. Do you know what, Roy? I gotta intuition that this Brighton business, an' her not going to the Palatial, like she said, has got somethin' to do with those cheques.'

I got nothin' of the sort. I think it is a plain case of this Eastern dame runnin' loose. But I can't just let a client worth £60,000 p.a. fade away before my eyes. I get a break because he says, 'By jove! I wonder!'

I take him up quick. 'Maybe there are some letters or something in her room that would give us a lead where she's gone.'

'I wouldn't dream of such a thing,' he says.

I take a firm hand. I also take his hand. I say, 'Roy, there comes a time in the life of every man when he's gotta make up his mind whether he's a mouse or what the scientists call a *hobo sapiens*, which means a wise guy. You are in love with Malwa. She has gone off somewhere, God knows where, an' you have a chance in a life time an' a damn good excuse to find out something that has begun to cast a cloud on your brow. Anyhow, you gotta find her. She may be in danger.'

This gets him. 'Yes, yes, of course, you're right,' he says. 'But I hardly like the idea – '

'You don't have to do nothin',' I tell him. 'Only show me where you live.'

'But,' he says, 'what if she's come home?'

'All the better,' I tell him, but I hope she won't be – not yet, anyway.

He makes up his mind. 'All right,' he says, 'but aren't I putting you to a great deal of trouble?'

'Not a bit,' I say. 'After all, that's what I'm being paid for.' I take my hand away very gently an' pat him on the cheek. He takes it like a gentleman that I'm not listening to his troubles for the good of my health, an' I have a great weight lifted off my mind because I have registered a business arrangement between us an' not just let him imagine this is a office where no bills ever go out.

'Just a moment,' I say, 'till I powder my nose.'

I get my hat which is a saucy little devil of a thing though it *was* cheap. I stand in front of the mirror, an' then I freshen up with my lip stick an' open my bag and take out my special brand of scent and dab a bit on my ear lobes and here an' there, an', before I put it back, I stick it under his nose.

'Like it?'

I see him go a bit woozy because, as he has already told me, he is very prone to perfume, an' he is not even quite recovered when I have put it back in my bag. I pull up my skirts an' give my suspenders a hitch, not that they really need it, but just to keep him interested in the old firm of Rosie Bosanky, an' then I say, 'All set.'

He opens the door an' don't go out first so I got more evidence that he has a lotta class. I think what a lucky girl I am. I have my new office open only one day an' hook me a client who is a gentleman who is what is called a cuckold and who has £60,000 a year as well.

We take a taxi, an' it is a longer ride than I have ever been with a metre ticking, an' I have a little bit of worry trying to spot how much the metre is registering, an' then I think what the heck because I am not paying for it anyway, and Roy Stockforth Adams wouldn't notice it so much as I would a run in my stocking.

I am that relieved that I don't mind when I get a sneaking feeling that whether he is a cuckold or not, an' no matter how much his mind is filled with anxieties, this Roy Stockforth has got his hand on my knee. But it is only in a uncle-ish sorta way, as you might say. I tell him what nice hands he has, an' I pick up the one he has forgotten he has on my knee an' start examining the cut of his manicure, which is my delicate way of bringing to a close a beginning which you never know where it might end. Besides which, you can't treat a client who has £60,000 p.a. in the same category as a guy who mightn't have anything at all an' might even have such a mean disposition that he would tell you you could walk home.

By an' by we are travellin' up a long drive with trees on either side which are kinda mournful, an' would look very nice for a fillum set for a Bela Lugosi in a thunderstorm, but now it ain't a thunderstorm but a day like the poets rave about, an' you can leave your gingham parked in the hall stand. The only sound is the one we are makin' as we skim up this long drive. It's as peaceful as a cemetery an' just as excitin', an' I can't help saying' to Roy, 'Do you mean you *live* here?'

'My God, no,' he says. 'At least only now an' then. It's the old home, an' I gotta keep it on account of the will. But just now it's closed up an' the servants away on holiday.'

'On full pay?' I say, facetious.

'I suppose so,' he says, which is the kinda remark I like because it shows that this Roy isn't standin' over his £60,000 p.a. with a Tommy gun but is prone to leave details to his minions. I make up my mind then an' there, if this Malwa dame has been up to anything, an' even if she ain't, this is one time in my life when I don't mind bein' a minion, too.

Roy tells me he shut the place up about a week ago when

his wife tootled off, an' there won't be no one there at all unless she's come back sudden an', even then, she wouldn't be stoppin', an' it would only be to load up a new trunkful of unders and overs.

I am hopin' that the dame is not there because I'd like to have a peek inside the sorta house a guy with this large amount of income has to live in. I realise, though, I am takin' a chance with my red hair an' all, an' the thoughts I've maybe caused to arise in this Roy; but I take a sly peek at him, an' his eyes are so soulful, I think, Heck! he ain't no Clark Gable in a film romance who'd slap a girl down in his own mansion.

Even if he's got ideas, I think I can distort 'em for him because I can see he's chockful of this chivalry, like this standin' aside at doors for a girl to pass, an' even if he has got primitive passions too, he has got 'em under control, which is a good way for a guy to be, though it must lose him a lotta fun an' cause him nights he can't sleep for ponderin' what mighta been, whereas the other kinda guy has forgot the past an' would have to look up a dictionary to find out what a word like remorse would mean.

By an' by we swerve round a corner, an' there, sure enough, is the old ancestral hall. There are two storeys an' a front door you coulda drove the taxi through, an' there are some tall, thin trees growing against the walls right up to the top windows.

When the taxi's gone, Roy fishes out a key, an' we toddle inside. It's the biggest hall I ever see, an' me an' my pappy coulda lived in it an' partitioned it off an' sublet to any neighbours who could live without fightin' an' then had plenty of room to swing a coupla cats.

'This is the library,' says Roy Stockforth, and there's a room like the policemen's club only no spitoons an' no policemen, only big chairs covered with dust cloths an' enough books to stock up a dozen circulatin' libraries, though no one would read 'em because they're all bound the same way and pretty dull lookin' too, with no coloured jackets or nothing.

He shows me some other rooms, an' they're all solid looking an' so big, I guess, if only two people lived in 'em at once,
they'd have to carry on a dialogue with a megaphone.

We go upstairs at last an' come to the main object of the
visit, which is this Malwa's boudoir, but first Roy puts his hand
on the knob of another door an' says, 'This is my particular
room. You may care to see it.' An' then, believe it or not, he
adds, 'I have some rather fine etchings I'd like to show you.'

You coulda knocked me down with the well-known
feather to hear him springin' that old one, and then I see
he's on the level and either he don't read *Esquire* an' listen to
bawdy jokes or he don't pay no attention. He's as innocent
as a babe unhung.

I pop my head into this room of his an' it's a duck. Not
very big, an' it's got chairs that look like they *like* to be sat in,
an' there's a settee affair which looks like it had seen a bit of
life in its day, an' there's a shelf or two of real books with
lively covers on an' some pipes on a rack an' cigarettes an' a
drink wagon an' a fireplace you could sit in, an' I bet my
young life I could pass a hour or two here in good company
with my shoes kicked off, etchings or no etchings.

And speaking of etchings they were there all right. He
starts to point 'em out, but I shut him up by saying I ain't
here today for a lesson on art but to find out about his wife,
an' he says, 'Yes, of course, of course, by jove,' an' just in
case this etching business is not on the level but is the usual
lead-up I say, 'But I should love to see these etchings some
other time.'

I expect him to brighten at this like most guys would and
come back at me with, 'That's a promise,' an' try an' nail you
down to a date, but he don't do nothin' of the kind. He just
gives me the double 'Of course' again and goes to the door an'
holds it open for me like the gentleman I told you he is.
Strange how this bit of business gets me. I feel kinda touched.
I suppose it is because, if any of the guys I been around with
had remembered to let me go out first, it would have been

with a definite object in view which could not be classed in the realms of chivalry.

We begin to tootle along the big hall an' he is a bit in the lead an' he does not see me stoop quick an' pick up a small article from the floor. It is a damn strange thing to me to see even a speck of dust or a cigarette butt in a hall in a mansion like this let alone a return half of a railway ticket which this is.

I say, 'Ever been to Brighton?'

'Good God, no,' he says, which is a speech which proves that east is east and west is west like Shakespeare said, an' the way Roy says it I know he is either a better actor than even Lon Chaney or he has nothing to do with this ticket I have found. I drop it into my bag.

Roy stands outside another door like he was a prophet about to enter a inner temple.

He says in a hushed voice, 'This is Malwa's bedroom.' He hesitates for a moment and adds 'I say! It's hardly cricket, what?'

I think, Well, from what evidence we have collected so far it don't look like Malwa's been playing cricket either. I make up my mind for him by pushin' the door, but it don't open. I say, 'It's locked.'

'Locked?' he says. 'That's funny.'

I ask him why.

'Well,' he says, 'I've never known Malwa lock it before. She is rather carefree about such things. Well,' he goes on, 'it looks like we had all our trouble for nothin'. We can't get in.'

I see by this he ain't gotta key to the room, an' if there's another he don't know where it is. I wonder whether there is some reason why he don't want to go in the room other than he don't think it's cricket. But I don't want the case to be at a dead end so I say, 'Can't get in nothin'!' Outa my bag I yank a key that'd open the Bank of England if I had a little patience. I give Roy a demonstration how good a pupil I was when I was learned the art by my pappy who was taught by all the best burglars. He stands by with his eyes nearly popping out of his head.

'By Jove!' he is saying. 'By Jove! Well, I never. D'you mean to say you can open any door with that gadget thing? This is most frightfully exciting.'

It's funny how a little thing like opening that door had spunked him up. I think to myself, I must remember to put a special item on my account sheet for this breakin' and enterin' because this Roy looks like he would expect to pay real money for such a job.

An' then I open the door an' look in, an' the room is a honey. It's lika film fan's dream of sleepin' in Hollywood. It's so big I guess it would save your feet if you skated from the bathroom to the bed. This bed is way over from the door, an' the light is not so good there. I've begun to make the grand trek an' am half way before I can believe what I think I see.

Roy has stayed put on the doormat as if he don't want to invade the sacred precincts. I think back what it was he said when I used my little gadget on the door. 'This is most frightfully exciting.' I remember the way just manipulating a simple lock like that has got him all het-up.

Well, if he was lookin' for excitement he was goin' to get it good an' plenty for, lying on his back on his wife's downy bed, was a guy in his pyjamas.

All right and improper in its way, all things considered, but the thing that was wrong was that you could see at a glance that this guy was dead as mutton, an' there was a knife sticking in his neck to prove it.

—

CHAPTER 2

I think to myself, as I get a close-up of this guy on the bed, that I am a very lucky dame because all on one morning I have come across a rich client with a naughty wife and a corpse caught red-handed in her bed. It looks like it's a nice case for a young girl to start off her professional career with, an' I figure I'm set for life. I bet if next week I try an' float Rosie Bosanky Investigations into a company I will be rushed like a south sea bubble, an' I'll begin to eat regular, an' the first thing you know I'll have that hat I see in M'lle Fifine's for seventeen guineas, which is made for me if ever a hat was, an' when I see it for the first time in my life, I am sorry I am a good girl with moral principles.

I'm standin' there by the bed half thinkin' of the hat at Fifine's an' which way I'll wear it, a little cockeye or not, an' half thinkin' what a sleek lookin' sheik this guy on the bed is, when I hear a hoarse sorta sound in my ear, an' I look round an' there's Roy peering over my shoulder an' pointing, an' the hoarse sound I hear is the gah-gah noises he is makin'.

All of a sudden he whirls round an' makes a dash for a door, which is the door of a bathroom, an' I can hear him in there vomiting his disgust at the sordid things of life in the raw. So while he is busy, an' in no fit mood to be asked questions, I take a close-up of the bird who is dead.

I can tell by the feel of him that it was quite a time since he was feelin' a good deal better. I make a practical rough test like my pappy has taught me in our little dalliances in the morgue, an' I figure how long he has been deceased. The bed clothes has been pulled back to his waist line, an' his head's on the pillow, an' he's a good-lookin' guy in a cheap, oily sorta way with a darkish skin, an' what strikes me is the cute way his hair's done, just like he musta been sittin' up in bed with a brush an' a mirror gettin' himself all slicked up to be murdered.

This guy looks a bit strange to me because guys sleepin' in double beds ain't usually so spick an' span but is inclined to get their hair rumpled like. I ain't been to movin' pictures for nothin', an' the times I seen Melvyn Douglas in his pyjamas you couldn't count on both your hands.

There's no more nasty sounds from the bathroom, an' presently Roy Stockforth Adams comes out looking like he is Hamlet's ghost. I take him by the hand and lead him back to his private room an' pour him out a good stiff drink from a decanter on his cabinet. I let him take it neat because I am not afraid now so to do because there is nothing like finding a corpse in his wife's bed to rob a man of his stamina and relieve his mind of wicked thoughts an' designs, even if he's a real wolf.

When Roy's got it down he looks at me an' whispers, 'Who is it?'

'Don't ask me,' I say. 'I'm a stranger hereabouts. *You* tell me.'

'I've never seen him in my life,' he says.

'No?' I says. 'Well it looks like he's been acting very famil-iar. Now, listen, Roy, you gotta be a man. You gotta face the facts of life. You gotta keep your head, too, because it ain't a nice thing for a husband to have a dead man found in his wife's bed.'

Would you believe it, all he can say is, 'No? I suppose not.'

But he doesn't get me. He doesn't catch on that what I am tryin' to indicate in a delicate way is that, before long, this deserted mansion will be lookin' like old home week. There will be coppers crawlin' all over the joint, an' if I know my detectives, their prize suspect No. 1 will be this same Roy Stockforth Adams who is sittin' by my side like mumma's timid pet lamb, because the way all coppers' minds works is that a man who is a husband and quite likely to come home unexpected is most probable to get very annoyed if he finds a strange man in his wife's bed whether she is there or not. And for all he is a gentleman even a nice guy like Roy might act similar.

I wonder whether I can trust this Roy. Maybe he is a Othello in sheep's clothing. It might be that he has got me here at this dump to suit his own purpose, an' I'm the mug in a frame-up of some sort.

But he doesn't look clever enough to work out a plot, though, I tell myself, you never can be sure. I have sat in a train and seen a man who looks like he has the brains to have a Winston Churchill for a rouseabout and, next day, there he is on your mat selling a new line of egg-beaters.

I suddenly think of the knife that's sticking in that sheik's chest, an' I remember what Roy has said about missing his Eastern paper opener, an' I ask him sudden, 'What sorta paper knife was that one you missed? What sorta handle did it have?'

He tells me, an' asks, very innocent, 'Why?'

'Only this,' I tell him. 'If you wanta know where it is, it is sticking into that sheik in Malwa's boudoir.'

He gives one look at me an' says, 'Oh, my God, Rosie,' an' next minute he has sunk his head on my bosom an' has got his arm about me, only it is like I was his mother, an' this is a very new experience for me, so I stroke his blond hair an' act like I was a madonna an' Florence Nightingale rolled in one.

I know it's not an act because his hands is quite passive though he has got 'em where they coulda been what is known by the word provocative. If there are any young, innocent girls of a modern type who are reading this, it would be a good plan for them to note down that there is practically no occasion in life where a man can be relied on to stay put, an' even in the very shadow of what you could have a justification for calling a sombre tragedy, some men will act just as if it is of no more importance than you have taken shelter from a thunderstorm in a haystack.

After a while Roy has calmed down an' I say, 'There, there,' an' he looks up into my face, an' I give him a sort of night-nurse kiss, which hardly leaves any lipstick, so light as thistle-down is it. I jump up and dab my hanky on his lips just in case, an' say, 'Now you must be a brave boy an' come back to the boudoir because, if I'm gonna be any help, there's plenty I wanta know.'

You can see I've fallen for this Roy's manner. He's impressed me that he just couldn't do this nasty bit of work even if it was a case of *flagrant delicto*, though I keep tellin' myself that you never know in these crimes which are what the French call passion crimes. But Roy has got £60,000 p.a. and, as a hard-working girl investigator with a livin' to make, as far as I am concerned this must give him the benefit of the doubt.

I lead him by the hand like he was a small boy an' out we go and across the hall and into Malwa's fairy bower, an' again I'm thinkin', If a dame has got herself hitched to a guy who can give her a sleeping palace like this, why does she want to go off the deep end with a sheik like is now dead in her bed an' who, you can see at a glance, for all his oily hair, ain't in the same grade as Roy an' don't match up with this high-class dump he has to live in accordin' to the will.

Roy swallows hard an' woulda fled, I think, if I hadn't held his hand firm an' dragged him over by the bed, an' then he says, sudden, 'I ought to be ashamed of myself. You're such a little thing, Rosie. And me, a great hulking brute frightened to look on death!'

Well, he's right about me being little because I could fit under his armpit but he's not exactly big in a Walter Pigeon way, an' he ain't by any means hulkin' an', after all, I reckon he hasn't had the same advantages as me in being able to tootle along to the morgue with his pappy an' view the remains. I guess if he had one little peek at the collection of photos of corpses I have seen and heard about, which I got stuck away in my office desk, there wouldn't be a bathroom outside a Turk's harem big enough for him to show his distaste.

So I soften things down for him, an' tell him all I want is for him to take a deep breath an' have one good squint at the guy in the bed, just to make very sure he ain't never seen him before; an' he is very brave about it, an' he has a steady look, an' he says, 'I could have sworn I had never seen him before and yet there is something familiar. Maybe I have seen someone like him on the films at some time or another.'

Now I know this may be right because often, in the street, I pass a guy, an' say to myself, I know that bird, an' I can't think where I've seen him before, an' it worries me all day till I get it. He's a double for some nasty piece of work I have seen on the fillums. And I think this Hollywood must be a wonderful place where a director can just put his head out of a studio window an' whistle an' get himself a actor who is a dead ring for a blackmailer or a dope, like he would call for a taxi cab.

'If I've ever seen him,' Roy tells me, 'it must have been a long while ago because I'm not even sure.'

'Okay, Roy,' I say. 'Keep thinking. Try an' remember all the people you've seen Malwa with one time and another,' and then he turns his head away, because he's gotta lotta modesty this Roy, while I pull back the bedclothes off the oily sheik and start in makin' a real close-up. I'm so business like that Roy, says maybe he better sit down somewhere and wait till I'm through, an' he thinks then, shouldn't we telephone the police.

Well, of course I've had that in mind, too, but I say to him to wait a bit because they'll be with us a long time once they have heard the news, an' a little waiting won't do anybody any harm.

'But, Rosie,' he says from the distant boudoir couch on which he has sat hisself, 'while we are lingering here, the man who did the dastardly thing will be getting away.'

He's still not wise to it that the police will think to their-selves that the one who did this dastardly crime, as he puts it, is His Nibs hisself. He's just chockablock with the idea that it's a horrible affair an' is still dizzy in the nut. So I tell him not to worry, all in good time, but I ask casual, 'What makes you think a man did it?'

I can see his eyes protrudin'.

'Good heavens,' he says. 'It never struck me, but that's nonsense. No woman would –' His voice trails off, an' I can tell that he is a guy who is prone to put a woman on a pedestal, which I have found is a very good thing in books, perhaps, but, in real life, such as it is lived at the present pace, it is not a wise thing to do because I never yet met a woman except a tightrope walker who was any good at heights.

He sits for a moment starin', an' then his eyes fall on the corpse again an' he gets up suddenly an' comes over to me.

'By jove, Rosie,' he says. 'I've just spotted something. I've just thought of it. This chap in the bed is wearing my pyjamas.'

I'm hard-boiled, but, darn it, I think this a bit thick, an' I don't like the sheik who is dead any better. I don't hardly believe it either because the way my mind has worked up to now is on the single track that this sheik has not got hisself where he is because he was a unexpected visitor who had to be loaned his host's nightshirt when pressed to stay till next day. I have just had the simple idea that he has come to stay the night for his own fell purpose, in which case only a heel would pinch another man's pyjamas. I think maybe this sheik is a heel. I give him another look. I think he *is* a heel.

Roy points out to me he can prove the pyjamas belong to him because of his monograph which is embroidered on the right breast in a very classy manner. If I don't mind looking he says I'll find a tailor's tab on the back of the neck inside.

I don't mind lookin', an', sure enough, there's the tailor's name Roy had mentioned, an' I am settlin' the dead guy back where I found him when I notice another thing an' that is he has been very careless about doin' up his pyjama coat because the button holes an' the buttons don't match. I mean they are not goin' hand an' glove, as it were. He's put the buttons into the wrong button holes so that there's one too many buttons at the top an' one too many button holes at the bottom.

Now this I figure might be done by a man in a hurry to get to bed for one reason or another, but somehow it don't match up with this stiff who is so careful and pernickety about his hair-do. But I don't spill what I see to Roy who has gone back to his boudoir couch an' whose mind is complicated enough as it is.

I carry on. I have my microscope, an' I go over that bed like I was lookin' for gold, an' I give the pillow an encore because, if anything was doing like the police will think, it's kinda rum to me.

The more I study it out after I have noted these things I have mentioned, like the guy having his hair done so pretty, and bein' in Roy's pyjamas an' not doin' them up right, the more intuition I have got that this Roy Stockforth Adams is a guy who, in the very near future, is going to be very much maligned an', though he don't know it, he's a very lucky guy that he has a Rosie Bosanky to keep her both eyes on his interests.

When I've finished with the microscope I pull the clothes back half way up where I found 'em an' I call Roy to come over. I look him right in the eye an' I show him my hanky which I have got ready in my hand, an' I say, 'You're sure that thing sticking into him is the knife outa your den?'

'Yes, Rosie,' he says. 'Absolutely.'

'Well,' I says. 'I'm goin' to wipe off the fingerprints, an' I make a move towards the bed.

He grabs me by the arm an' swings me back an' I fall right up against him an' face to face. I can tell you when he lets himself go without knowing it this Roy ain't so meek an' mild. He gets me by the two shoulders an' grips me an' I guess he don't know how hard he's holdin' on, but somehow I like him like this.

He says, 'For God's sake, Rosie. You can't do that.'

I say, 'Why not? They're your finger prints, aren't they?'

'No,' he says. 'No – at least. Why, what do you mean? You don't believe –?'

'I mean this,' I tell him. 'I don't believe you croaked him. But, all the same, your fingerprints could be on that handle. You've been using it to cut papers an' things, ain't you?'

'Of course,' he says. 'But –'

'But nothin',' I say. 'Someone coulda easy stuck that sheik an' still have left your fingerprints. There's some crooks has been brought up slick enough to pull that off. Don't you see it will look bad for you –'

I wouldna done it, of course, but I pretend I'm goin' to wipe the handle with the hanky, but he won't have it.

'No, Rosie. You're a trump. I do appreciate it really,' he says, 'but, dammit, Rosie, I've got to take a chance. I didn't do it, so perhaps there might be other prints besides mine.'

Like hell there might, I think. If all the things I am thinkin' are right, there's something so fishy about this murder the neighbours oughta be complainin' about the smell.

Just the same, I tell myself, I mustn't let my intuition ride me lika hobby horse. I take old Roy's hand an' I pat it. I say, 'I want you to take this in the spirit in which it is said, Roy. I don't want you should blow up. But you gotta face the facts of life. There is a possibility about this murder I don't think has ever entered your innocent mind. But we gotta face it.'

He is puzzled. It is stickin' out a mile.

'I can't think of one, Rosie,' he says. 'Tell me.'

So I tell him an' is he rocked? I tell him in four words.

'Malwa mighta done it.'

'Malwa!'

He goggles at me, then closes his eyes and sways a bit and, for a moment, I think I am goin' to have a faintin' client on my hands. He pulls hisself together, however, an' says, 'No, no, Rosie. Not Malwa.'

'Listen, Roy,' I tell him. 'I ain't sayin' she did. I'm only sayin' what is a possibility. You say she couldn't do it, but you don't know where she is or what's been goin' on. There's somethin' funny been in the wind about those cheques. Anything might have happened. An' I'll tell you something. Almost anyone feels like doin' a murder some time or other, an' some of 'em do.'

He shakes his head. 'Not Malwa,' he says.

'All right,' I say. 'You say not Malwa; but I say, *maybe* Malwa, an' she mighta done it with a damn good reason. But, if you're so sure, then we don't need to worry about her fingerprints bein' on the dagger.'

With this remark I say some tactful words about powdering my nose and exit to the adjoining bathroom. I could spend a lotta time in a bathroom like this one, which is in pink marble with a tub let in the floor, but I got no leisure just now because I have made up my mind to watch old Roy's reactions. He is standin' by the bed lookin' down at the corpse. As I peer through a discreet crack I see him look round over his shoulder. Then he goes closer to the bed an' pulls out his handkerchief. He is stretching out his hand when I open the door of the bathroom an' give a loud cough. Roy jumps like he has been shot and then pretends he is using his handkerchief to blow his nose.

I have gotta strong realisation that I have a very funny case on my hands. I start out on what looks like it would be a nice straightforward divorce, an' now it's a murder, an' my client is goin' to be Suspect No. 1. Moreover, I am of the strong opinion that my client is innocent up to the hilt. But there is a problem in addition, which is that whatever he may say against it this client has got enough suspicion that his runaway wife did this crime he is ready to commit a felony an' wipe her fingerprints, if any, off the fatal weapon.

I wonder how it will pan out in a business way, because if I try an' get this Roy outa the soup, it may be only to get his wife, Malwa, into the frying pan. And this is not goin' to be popular with Roy who is the one who will have to foot the bill of costs. Besides which he is the sorta guy a girl would like to keep for a friend which could hardly be if she had been the means to get his wife hung.

Roy is lookin' very pale, an' I think it best to steer him back to his den where I can telephone to the police hounds, an' dose him up with a strong whisky from his cutglass decanter, which I bet cost him a pretty penny.

When we are there he says, 'Well, here we go, Rosie,' and picks up the telephone.

I say, if it's all the same to him, I'll speak, because I know lots of cops, an' I can tell it them in their own language, an' there's one head cop I know in particular who was a friend of my pappy and woulda done anything in the world for him. And this, I recall to myself, would include holdin' his daughter's hand outside the morgue one night just in case she should be frightened of the dark while pappy was goin' into some details with the copper on duty – only the way he held it put me wise to how much a man's friendship is worth to a man who has a daughter like I am with red hair and a lotta appeal.

Knowin' what I do about what he'd do for my father an' a lot more about what he'd do for me if he got half a chance I can sort of talk to this head copper like a bosom friend. His title is Inspector Browne but while he was holding my hand outside the morgue he told me always to call him Brownie.

I ring him up, an' I am very careful to ask for Inspector Browne because he is a type of man who would be very delighted for a young girl to call him Brownie outside a dark morgue but would think it would be bad for discipline if he was handed that title in his regular office hours.

The message comes back who the hell is it, but that is not the copper on the 'phone, it is Brownie shouting from some-where near by. So I say, sweet as pie, 'Tell the inspector it's Miss Bosanky, but if he's too busy –'

Old Brownie comes on fast enough when he gets the message. I'll say this for the old devil, he's persistent, an' he's never give up tryin' an' wantin' to act like a father to me, only he's got the most queer ways of showin' his paternal feelings an' takin' a next-of-kin privilege.

He says, 'Just a moment, Miss Bosanky,' then I hear him tell someone to take a message somewhere, an' I get it that he's clearing the office decks so he can have a nice confidential gossip. After a bit he says in a cooing voice, 'Hello, Rosie dear. How you doin'?'

I pretend I am disappointed in him.

'I think you mighta popped round and wished me a God speed when I opened my office today,' I say.

'I meant to, Rosie,' he says. 'I did indeed. But you know how it is. You get snowed under with routine. But I'll be round. How you makin' out?'

'Good,' I tell him, 'considerin' I only hung out my sign a hour or two ago.'

He thinks I am being facetious.

He says, 'You gotta be patient.'

'I'm all right,' I tell him. 'I gotta coupla cases already.'

'You don't say,' he cries. 'Splendid, Rosie. I'll pop round an' talk 'em over with you.'

'You're tellin' me,' I snap back, an' then he says, 'What kinda cases?'

I tells him they're sorta linked up. 'One's findin' out what a lady's been doin' behind a gentleman's back.'

'I see,' he says. 'Watch your step. Keep your nose tidy.'

He means play the game an', when I keep on sayin' nothin', he says, 'What's the other case?'

'Just a murder,' I tell him, casual.

You can hear his head hittin' the roof at the other end.

'*What*!' he yells, and Roy gives a jump, too, because even he can hear it. I guess he is thinkin', If Inspector Browne hollers that loud when he just has the news handed him in a nice quiet ladylike style, how will he holler when he knows there's a strange guy in his wife's bed with his own pet slitter stuck in him?

I think I'll calm Roy down by the way I talk back to Brownie an' let him see that even coppers are human, an' just because they gotta uniform or a badge is no reason why a decent guy like him should get the wind up.

I say, 'Don't you dare screech in my ear like that, Brownie.'

But all he says is, 'Did you say *murder*?'

So I holler back just as loud, 'Yes, I did say murder. M. U. R. D. E. R. Now have you got it, or can't you spell?'

There's a bit of a silence, an' I smile over at Roy just to give him confidence because he is a bit trembly; then the inspector says in a hoarse, choky voice, 'Listen, Rosie. I know you're always hell bent for pokin' your nose in what don't concern you. Your old dad – rest his soul – brought you up all wrong, but he was my friend, Rosie, an' if I find you've been sticking your smeller into anything dirty I'll come round an' smack you on your pretty little pink pants.'

Them psychologists will tell you he's gettin' a second-hand kick outa this kind of talk because never in his life has he got a good reason for believing my pants is either little or pretty or pink, an' he ain't got one tittle of evidence that they ain't baggy an' flannelette, which God forbid because, even on a cold day, I can't bear the feel of it, an' it always makes me think of the little boy at the party with velvet pants an' some-thin' happened.

'Now *you* listen, Brownie,' I come back. 'You ain't talkin' to no wayward kid in the juvenile court. You're talkin' to Miss Rosie Bosanky of Bosanky Investigations, an' she's tellin' you that there's been a murder done in the house of her valued client.' I give a killing glance at old Roy an' go on. 'Mr Roy Stockforth Adams.'

'Who?' Brownie says, an' I get the idea he thinks I'm kiddin'.

I repeat the name while my client's Adam's apple is pop-ping up an' down like one of them celluloid balls you see bouncin' about on top of a fountain for an advertisement.

'Never heard of him,' Brownie says gruffly, an' that just

shows you how, even with £60,000 p.a., you can go through life unheralded an' unsung. Not I reckon that Roy ain't goin' to be known far an' wide as soon as Brownie gets it into his thick nut that he is hearin' something from real life, an' that it ain't just his old pal's kid daughter pulling his leg. I can hear him breathin' hard because he's tellin' himself, an' very rightly so, that murder's not a thing to joke about. I can almost hear him thinkin' to hisself that the red headed little hussy's not under the age of consent any longer, an' maybe what she's sayin' smells like it was the truth.

At last he says, 'Listen, Rosie. Try an' remember. This is a police office. Forget for a moment I'm Brownie. Talk to me like you would to Inspector Browne, an' for God's sake tell me *is* there a murder or ain't there, an' where the hell are you speakin' from.'

'Now you're talkin', Inspector,' I say. 'The murder has been done at the home of Mr Roy Stockforth Adams and the address is – wait a jiffy.' I get it from Roy, and Brownie notes it down. I go on. 'The victim is a unknown man and he's –'

'Never mind that,' Brownie shouts. 'You stay there. An' who's that you're talkin' to?'

I tell him.

'Well, tell him to stay there, too. Tell anyone to stay there. I'll be right over.'

Even before the receiver's down I can hear him shoutin' where the hell's his hat.

Roy asks me, gentlemanly, would I like a drink, too, but I won't partake. Instead I say, 'Tell me about Malwa. What is she like to look at?'

He goes to a drawer an' pulls out a picture, and this Malwa is the goods all right. She's got all I got, an' then some, because while I am a pocket Venus, she's full grown an' full blown, an' what gives me a surprise is that she ain't got that in her face what I've ben expecting. She don't look like a dame who would do the dirty on a guy like Roy with £60,000 p.a.

even if it was only £30,000 an' out of that he's gotta pay taxes.

She's got a brand of elegant gentleness about her, an' she's got a flair for wearin' the kinda clothes I can't afford an' wouldn't suit me if I could.

I get to thinkin' hard about that sheik with the sleeked oily hair, an' I say, 'Excuse me a moment,' an' Roy says, 'Why, of course,' because he thinks I want to go to the hoojah-kapippy, an' I can see him strugglin' with himself tryin' to make up his mind whether it's delicate to get up an' open the door on such occasions an' tell me it's the third door on the right round the corner, or whether he should stay put an' pretend he hasn't noticed.

Anyway, I guess he's forgot there's one in this Malwa's bathroom off her boudoir, an' I wouldn't be knocked off my perch if it was put to him in a court of law on an oath had he ever been inside it, except to be sick in this very morning, he would have to swear so help him God he hadn't.

I trot back to the room of death an' take another peek at the dead guy. I lift up his head an' sniff, an' it's a smell I tell myself I don't want ever to meet again, but I'll know it if ever I have the misfortune. Then, when I'm holdin' his head up, I give the pillow it's been restin' on the once over, an' then I look at the guy's face, an' I think of the picture I see of this Malwa, an' I think it must be a funny world where a dame that looks like her could fall for a sheik that looks like him.

But then, I tell myself, it *is* a funny world anyway, an' it's all a stage where men an' women are only players, an' it takes all sorts to make it up, as some poet wrote, though I found that out long before I heard he had said it, an' that weren't from no poetry book but by sittin' in the back row at the police court an' sometimes being glared at by some old-maid p.m. who'd just made a speech about he wouldn't give orders to clear a court but hoped all decent dames would take a hint an' leave the precincts.

I look at this guy's legs, an' while guys are not like dames, an' the less you see of their legs the better, I make one little find which may be nothin' or maybe will be a clue of some sort. It is a corn plaster the corpse is wearin' on his big toe. I yank it off because it is nearly off anyhow, an' I see it has got a tiny little trade mark on it which says it is a Carew corn plaster, of which I have never heard, because through good circulation and doin' early mornin' exercises I have never had a corn in my born days. I put the plaster in my bag with the railway ticket, though what the hell they mean, or what I am goin' to do with them I haven't a idea in the world.

When I get back to Roy he has worked his nerves up like he was in a hospital an' it was gettin' near time for his operation. He keeps thinkin' he hears the sirens of the police cars comin' up the drive. But we gotta few minutes yet even if the gendarmes break all the traffic laws that was ever made, an' I got time to ask Roy did he ever scrap with Malwa.

'Oh, no, *no*, Rosie,' he says. 'Most definitely not. By no means. We didn't have any words – ever.'

'Well,' I say, because there's no more time to beat about the bush. 'Was she a lovin' wife an' how often, an was it lately?'

He goes all pink, an' I am very discreet an' turn away, an' he says in a choked voice, 'We used to see each other occasionally, but of late months she seemed always to have something on her mind. It was a kind of barrier between us. I used to wonder had she fallen in love with someone else.'

I tell him I'm glad of this information but, if I was him, I wouldn't tell it like that to the cops. Not to Inspector Browne especially.

'Why, surely he wouldn't dare ask such a personal question?' he says.

'He'll dare all right,' I warn him, 'if he thinks of it.'

'Shall I tell him about that ghastly letter?' he asks.

By gum, I'd nearly forgotten it. 'No,' I say, 'not yet. Give it to me.' He hands it over.

'Were you really surprised to receive it?' I ask.

He looks at me, and he has a queer expression but he says, 'I was surprised as the dickens, Rosie. I might have thought in my nasty way that Malwa was thinking about some other man, but I thought if she began to care enough for him to –' He gulps.

'I know,' I say.

'– that she'd tell me about it so we could have things fixed up decently.'

I pull off my toque an' throw it on the table an' sit down an' run my hands through my hair. I am not afraid to do this because it never makes any difference an', just now, I wouldn't care if it did. There's a helluva lot about this affair that I don't get, an' I bet it's goin' to keep me awake.

We are on a settee affair an', when he sees me worried, Roy says, 'I'm awfully sorry to have dragged you into this, Rosie.'

That makes me laugh. 'Don't be silly,' I say, a bit hard-boiled. 'I'm actin' for you, ain't I? I've gotta be paid. You know that, don't you?'

He gives me a little frightened look.

'Oh, of course, of course,' he says hastily, 'whatever you say.' Which is pretty good hearing for me. He goes on, 'I'm most frightfully grateful, Rosie.'

I jump up an' kneel alongside him an' take his two cheeks between my hands. 'You're a dear,' I tell him, 'an' you can believe it or not I'd stick to you if you didn't have a banknote to your back.' And I mean it.

I am in a very sociable position to give him a kiss he could put in the scrapbook of his memory and take out an' it would be like lavender an' old lace when he was an old man ninety years of age. But he has got this anxiety complex so bad I can see even a kiss like my friend's special is not registering like it has been in the habit of, so I say, 'But that's the last time you call me Rosie today, Roy. You must practise saying Miss Bosanky because this head copper, who is coming to visit us, is a friend of my pappy's, an' he can't bear to see anyone talkin' on intimate terms with an orphan.'

He says very nicely, 'I'll remember Miss Bo-sankay,' giving

the accent which I am entitled to by right, and I wet my hanky with my tongue an', with a delicate, bird-like motion, I wipe the lipstick off his lips. Then we have to run downstairs because Inspector Browne an' his horde of trained policemen is screaming up the drive.

———

CHAPTER 3

Brownie has brought with him a tall, dark sergeant who is a new one on me. He is a handsome devil with a small black moustache an' a look in his eye. He don't look so much like a policeman as something that has come outa the crooners' union because, if ever I see pent-up emotion, he has got it in buckets slumbering behind those eyes, which looks like they musta been smudged in, an' which are apt to have an effect on a untutored girl which would be what could be termed deleterious.

I am glad to see this bird. He is a nice set-off to old Brownie who is fairly bristling with importance an' who is not pleased, I can tell, to see his offsider give me the once over. I bet my life, if he had his way when I am workin' on a case, Brownie would like for a offsider a man who has once had his face caught in a mangle.

'Thank heaven you are here at last, Inspector,' I say.

Brownie don't fancy the 'at last' crack much, an' he says sharp like, 'Now then, young lady, what's all this about?'

If there hadn't been others present he'd have put a fatherly arm around me an' said, 'Now, Rosie, tell Brownie all about it.'

I introduce him to Roy. 'This is the owner of this palatial home, Mr Roy Stockforth Adams,' I say, an' Roy puts out his hand an' is a bit flabbergasted when Brownie don't take it but barks, 'Where's the body?'

I jerk my thumb towards the stairs, an' he says, 'Come on,'

which means me an' Roy, I guess, and off we go with Brownie in the lead. At the foot of the stairs, both Roy and this handsome beast, who has come with Brownie as an offsider, step aside because there's not room for three to go up at once without crowding, an' it's a case of after you, my dear Alfonse, an' I can see that this sergeant has class, too, an' I'm dyin' to hear if he talks like he looks.

I say, 'The Inspector is too excited to remember his manners, but I'm Rosie Bosanky.'

I hear Brownie snort.

'Sergeant Clancy, at your service,' Handsome says, an' blow me down if he doesn't give a ballroom bow.

'Meet Roy Adams,' I say, an' he gives my client a disciplined nod. 'After you,' he says. He has got a voice with a lotta appeal in it. It is a slow kinda voice with a Gary Cooper accent when he is in a passive mood, an' I think I would not be averse to hearin' it engaged in some more subtle dialogue than 'At your service'.

He waves his hand to the stairs, an' Roy an' me goes up, but I ain't so dumb that I don't notice this Clancy lingers a bit, pretendin' he's giving some order to one of the coppers in the hall, so that, by the time he starts to follow up, we are quite a piece ahead, an' I am in a very nice position for a interested party to observe.

I do not have any idea of embarrassment because I am one of those girls who is always prepared for this sorta conduct on the part of men who I have got used to seeing magnetised by my Betty Grables. Once even, in a underground train, I was sorry to see almost a fight because a guy who had got a good position had his view blocked by a strap-hanger who had come in late.

Brownie is glarin' at us from the landin', an' not lookin' nearly so cheerful as he musta looked in the dark that night outside the morgue when he held my hand to comfort my feelings.

'Now where?' he snaps.

I lead the way and Fancy Clancy follows just behind us. I open the door of Malwa's boudoir an' let 'em go in. The inspector stands lookin' round the vast domain with its fussy furniture and its soft wallpaper with a tiny rose pattern you could hardly see without specs. He gives it the once over with his eyes and the twice over in that part where there is a swell picture of a lotta dames caught in the nuddy by a passing warrior. He digs his flat feet into the rich carpet an' he says, 'Whose room is this?'

I can't help sayin', 'Surely it is the maid's,' an' I hear Fancy Clancy titter, but before Brownie can come back at me, Roy Stockforth has said innocently, 'Oh, no, no, Miss Bosanky. This is not the maid's room. It is my wife's.'

Brownie gives him a nasty look as if he thinks he might be in the joke about it bein' the maid's room, an' then he marches over to the bed an' stands lookin' down at the corpse.

'Who's this guy?' he asks and glares at Roy, and my client says, 'I haven't the foggiest.'

Brownie gives him another sour look an' comes again: 'This is your *wife*'s room?'

'Yes, of course.'

'And this is your wife's bed?'

'Naturally, old boy.' Roy don't mean to be familiar. He has got a natural *bon hommy* manner.

'An' you don't know this guy?'

Roy shakes his head.

'Maybe,' Brownie goes on, 'you gotta idea of his name?'

'Not the remotest.' This is just the same as not the foggiest.

'Where is your wife?' Brownie barks.

Roy says he doesn't know.

'Is she in the house?'

'Oh, no. Most definitely.'

'When did you see her last?'

'About a week ago. She went off on a holiday.'

'Alone?'

'Oh, quite.'

'And you stayed here?'

'Oh, no, no. Definitely not. We shut the old house up and gave the servants a holiday.'

'On full pay,' I put in, young and smarty, and I wished I hadn't.

'On full pay?' Brownie repeats, as if he has got on to something. 'Whose idea was that?'

'Oh, no one's in particular,' Roy says. 'It's the regular thing, y'know.'

Brownie goes closer and peers down at the knife which is sticking into the oily sheik. He points to it. 'Take a peek at this,' he says to Roy. 'Ever see it before?'

'Oh, yes Roy says at once. 'Yes, indeed. Of course. Most definitely. It's mine.'

I can tell you I have never seen such a guy for emphasising ideas which might get him hung.

'It's yours, eh?' Brownie looks across at Handsome Clancy behind Roy's back an' winks. I can see his mind has worked just like I expected. He's got Roy good an' hung already on the motive of jealousy.

Handsome begins lookin' round the room. He pulls open drawers an' tall boys, an' then toddles into the bathroom. Brownie is pullin' back the bedclothes an' givin' the corpse a close up. I can tell he thinks this is one of those French passion crimes when, of course, anything may have occurred. I hear him give a grunt, an' I don't know whether he was hopin' for the best or fearin' the worst. Roy has gone an' sat hisself at his wife's dressing table. By an by Clancy comes back an' says, 'There's no sign of his clothes, sir.'

'Clothes?' Brownie says.

'He's in pyjamas,' Handsome says, an' I think he sounds like he has to have the patience of Jonah to be a offsider to the Inspector. 'He would hardly have come here wearing them.'

I coulda slapped myself. I'm a bum investigator, I tell myself. I think of all sorta things, but the one that is the simplest to think of outa all I give a miss.

'Maybe he undressed in another room,' Brownie suggests, an' takes a bit of starch out of this smudgy-eyed sergeant.

An' maybe he did, I figure. I have got a intuition that Malwa would be a dame who would be in the soft cushions an' shaded lights class, in which case, if this is what old Brownie thinks, there would be a certain amount of what is called by a French word, *finess*. There would be no question of hangin' a man's pants on the gas bracket.

I tell myself if I had a sleepin' palace like this one I wouldn't have the view of a pair of trousers an' braces clutterin' up the place, even if I am married to Alexander the Great, because, to a woman's idea, this is a view which is prone to bring a thing down from the sublime to the ridiculous. I put it down in my mind, therefore, that, if Malwa has played a leading role in what has been goin' on, this oily sheik's outer garments will be discovered in some other part of the house.

An' there's another thing! Some chaps is delicate in this way though I don't think the sheik who is dead looks the kind. I don't think he'd be a flash dresser underneath, either. He ain't got that look like the fellow in the advert you see in *Esquire* where it gives the advice that a man should always look his best under all circumstances, an' then there's a picture of a guy found wearin' someone's pink panties for particular persons bein' caught with the colonel's wife.

Brownie goes to the door an' calls a cop, an' I hear him giving instructions for a search of clothes such as the dead sheik would most likely have wore. An' then a doctor breezes in an' says nice mornin' ain't it an' I don't think I have had the pleasure, so, of course, Brownie has to tell him who I am, an', by the way he looks me over, I know there's one more joined the pack.

The inspector beckons Clancy, an' Clancy ushers Roy before him, an' Brownie takes my arm in his hand, an' we all go over to Roy's den an', like the gent he is, Roy gives us a drink.

Brownie asks a lotta questions as to how I came to discover the body, an' my relations with Roy, an' then a lot more personal questions which he directs at my client. I make him mad as hell when I tell old Roy he needn't answer 'em unless he wants. I think if Brownie wasn't so confirmed a friend of my old dad he'd tell me to go jump in a lake.

After a bit he goes out an' has a pow-wow with the doctor, an' I can hear the photographer boys an' fingerprint guys on the job an', by and by, he comes back and then the copper he sent to search says they can't locate any clothes such as the sheik in the bed mighta wore. They've checked up all the suits an' things in Roy's bedroom, an' they have all got his tailor's brand on 'em. The copper further says they have searched every room except the one we're in.

'All right,' Brownie tells him. 'We'll deal with this,' an' makes a sign to Clancy.

Clancy looks at Roy an' says, 'Have you any objections, Mr Adams?' an' Roy says no definitely, not at all, by all means, go right ahead, an' Handsome starts tumblin' things around. He goes through everything till he comes to a bottom drawer in a bureau which is locked.

He says, 'This drawer is locked, Mr Adams. Would you let me have the key?'

I say, 'For heaven's sake, Handsome, what is this? What's in your mind? I can understand a guy bein' delicate about undressin' in front of a comparatively strange lady, but I can't see him comin' into a private den an' takin' off his pants, an' things, an' lockin' 'em in a bureau. It don't sound like the act of a passionate lover.'

Clancy grins at me. 'I guess you're right,' he says. 'It was just routine.'

But Brownie says, 'I wish, Rosie, you'd keep your trap closed.'

'You wish all you damn please, Brownie,' I say, hot under the collar, 'but you got no right to bust open any drawers. My client has gotta clean record, an' an Englishman's castle is his home.'

Clancy smiles at this, but, me, I don't feel in a smilin' mood because I have the idea that something is bein' put over my client who, I think, if you asked him nicely would put his head in a noose an' pay for his own scaffold. You will note, perhaps, that both Brownie an' me have forgot we are official an' are hurling at each other the time-worn personal names.

Brownie says, 'I gotta lot more powers than you think Rosie. An' what are you gettin' in such a stink for?'

I say, 'My client maybe has some private matters in his locked bureau which have got no more to do with this case than the Karl Marx Brothers.'

'What sorta private matters?' Brownie says.

'How should I know?' I ask. 'Every man has got some secret he wants to keep sacred from the world at large, not because it ain't on the level, but because he is indulgin' his fancy, an' only he knows why such is the case.' This speech to me has a very good sound an', just for a flash, I wonder whether perhaps I shoulda paid more attention to education an' trained up to be a lawyer. But Brownie ain't impressed.

'Oh, rats!' he says.

'Not rats, Mr Inspector,' I says, but he has give me a lead. 'Maybe he collects white mice.'

I turn to give Roy a nice smile, an' I am surprised to see he has turned a sunset pink. Brownie has noticed it, too. He says, 'Well, I put it to Mr Adams. Does he object to telling us what is in the drawer?'

Roy swallows hard. He says, 'Oh, in there? Well, I don't usually say anything about it. People have a habit of laughing. I don't know why. I – find it – er – rather stimulating, don't you know, especially when one's left a good deal alone in a big house like this –'

Brownie interrupts. 'What the heck are you talking about? Come to the point.'

'Philately,' Roy says.

'Phil who?'

'Philately. Stamp collecting. I'm not particularly good at

it – not much more than a beginner in a way. I've been goin' in for British Colonials, sort of specialising –'

His voice trails away. I'm feelin' sorry for him because I can see what these hard-boiled coppers can't, an' that is exactly what he has painted for us in our minds. I can see him very lonely in this big house in which the will says he has gotta live, an' longin' to go in an' chat to this Malwa, an' her not wantin' to talk to him on account of the unseen barrier which has sprung up between them, or gone out or something, and him havin' to turn to these British colonial stamps to pass the time.

Maybe it don't sound real to you, but then you ain't seen this Roy, an', when I got a mental picture of him in my mind, I begin to think that the guy who wrote that sad composition, 'The Mansion of Breaking Hearts', has a good insight into human life.

Brownie says, 'Is that all you keep there? Just stamps.'

Roy answers, 'Yes – just my albums and some spare cash.'

'Cash? How much?'

'Oh, I wouldn't know,' Roy tells him. 'I just keep it there handy for an emergency. Malwa might want some. You know how it is. But there's never much. Not more than a hundred.'

'Not more than a hundred!' Brownie scoffs. 'How much is there *now*?'

Really, I haven't the foggiest,' Roy says, an' I can see Brownie don't believe him because he's got the brain that can't tell there's a difference between a guy with £60,000 p.a., an' a policeman with a pay envelope. They has a different attitude towards £.s.d., an' you could use as a parable the case of a good little girl in a orphanage who would treasure up a pair of silk stockings with a coupla runs in 'em an' a bad hussy who has took the wages of sin in sheer silk an' has so many pairs she can afford to toss 'em carelessly aside on the washstand railing.

Brownie says, an' it rather surprises me that he doesn't pursue the question, 'Okay, Mr Adams.' Then he says to me, 'Let's go an' have a look round, Red.' We go outside, an' he turns an' says something in a undertone to Handsome who stays behind. Roy starts in bein' a Cook's guide while we look round the joint.

It is so big that even in what is known as the servants' quarters you'd need a magaphone to tell the milkman to leave a extra pint.

But it's *too* big. Even if I was married to this client Roy an' his wad I couldn't stick it. There ain't nothin' personal about it. Nobody could get into anybody's way. I think you could roam about this house an' meet someone by accident, an' you would have to say: 'Doctor Livingstone, I presume?'

I take a twig at Roy's bedroom, an' it's a barn. I can see him in a vision takin' off his pants after a hard day at the club, an' standin' in that room like he is in the middle of the Sahara desert. An' I can see Malwa in her big boudoir, a solitary figure in a vast expanse, takin' – well, it don't seem what holy matrimony is meant for an' while I don't hold for crowded up flats, there's a lot to be said for a good middle-class double bed with nice springs an' last in puts out the light.

When the tour's over an' we've returned to the hall upstairs, I am wonderin' whether the whole idea of this great trek wasn't just Brownie's plan to get me an' Roy outa the way, because Handsome is standin' outside the den door. He nods to Brownie who grins.

'Go inside, Mr Adams,' Brownie says in a vocal tone like he was selling Roy the Tower of London for twice what it was marked up at. Handsome steps aside to let him pass and then follows him, but Brownie catches hold of my arm and holds me back. He whispers, 'I hope you ain't gettin' too fond of your client, Rosie, because I think you're goin' to be separated. Do you know what I think? I think he's going to get hisself good an' hung.'

'Oh, yeah!' I say. 'An' do you know what I think? I think you're nuts.'

He laughs quite good-natured. 'But then, Rosie,' he says, 'we ain't shown you yet what we just found.' He steers me through the door, an', as I go in, just to show his triumph, he gives me a patronising little smack on the fanny.

Clancy is lookin' very grave. I like this stranger when he's grave because it shows he ain't devil-may-care through to the core, an' there comes a time in every girl's life when she can't be on the *Quay Vive*, an' she likes to know that the guy she is fond of at the moment is ready to call it a truce, too.

I think Clancy has the look of a man who is kinda sorry a decent looking bloke like Roy Stockforth Adams has been caught with his pants down.

Spread out on the bureau is a suit of clothes. They are a sea-sick green, with a red stripe, an' they look like the sort of reach-me-downs a flash piano player might wear at what is called a honky-tonk, which is as good a name as any for the sort of place I mean, but it don't make it any sweeter. This suit is so loud it would drown a swing band.

Handsome is still lookin' kinda sad and reprovin', but Brownie has got a face like a cat with its first mouse – greedy an' glad together. He has a tone in his voice which, even with your eyes shut, you would know he is rubbing his hands together. He says, 'So you found it, Clancy. Where?'

Clancy says, 'Underneath Mr Adams's stamp albums.'

'Well, well,' Brownie says, 'and what does Mr Adams say to that?'

'I don't know what to say, old bean,' Roy says. 'I'm utterly thunderstruck.'

'I'll say you are,' Brownie says. 'You wanted to mislead us about the drawer, didn't you? You had 'em hid there.' Roy looks at him as if he can't believe his ears.

'Oh, no, no constable,' he says, getting Brownie's goat more an' more each minute. 'Indeed, I'm as astonished as you are.'

'I ain't astonished,' Brownie snaps, 'an' I'll tell you something more, Adams. You got plenty to tell us an' it better be quick.'

'But – but,' Roy begins to stammer. 'What can I say, old

boy? I really know no more than you do.' He looks at the suit like it was something that might crawl off an' he would have to put his foot on it. Then he turns to Clancy an' says, 'Did you really find this thing in my drawer, sergeant?'

This sergeant business is not doing him any good with Brownie who he has called a constable. You gotta know Roy to understand that this is not to hurt anyone's feelings. It is just that he don't know any different an', even me, unless I had been told, I woulda thought, too, that this Handsome was the boss, because you don't have to be a psychoanalyser to see that Brownie is a hundred per cent mediocre.

Clancy says, 'Yes, Mr Adams. The suit was there all right.'

'Oh, then, of course, there's no more to be said,' Roy says, an' knocks the inspector off his perch because he's expecting to be accused of a frame-up. 'If this gentleman' – he looks at Clancy – 'says it, it must be so. But I still don't understand it.'

Handsome smiles a bit an' pulls open the drawer. 'They were at the bottom under this cash box and the stamp albums. And, by the way, there was no money in the cash box.'

'What's that?' I say, because Roy has told us plain as daylight he had stowed some dough in the drawer for an emergency.

'Don't get excited, Red,' Brownie says. 'It just weren't there. It weren't true what His Nibs said.'

A very slow flush begins to spread over Roy's face. It is like dawn breaking in technicolor only in slow motion, an' he says quite haughtily, 'Look here, constable, if you mean to insinuate –'

This is just the kinda talk Brownie likes. He's got a reason for talkin' back, see, and he interrupts. He shouts, 'What I mean to insinuate, Adams, is that your wife was playin' round with that sheik in there, an' you come back last night an' caught 'em red-handed an' pushed that dagger in the guy's neck.'

This speech is followed by a silence which you coulda cut with a knife. I watch Roy's face. All its colour, which was the result of indignation, has faded out an' he has become a ghostly white. I can see he's been shook to the soles of his feet at what Brownie has just unloaded, an' the reason is that the poor dear sap has never thought for one little minute that he's their Suspect No. 1.

That, leastways, is how I figure it, but Brownie's idea is that anyone who turns pale is as good as in the dock, an' he has got a grin on him like a Cheshire cat, he's that pleased.

Roy's mouth opens an' closes like a goldfish's, an' his eyes goggle, too, but he can't utter a word. If ever there was a time when a guy had his breath took away this is the time. An', while he is still strugglin' to use his vocabulary, Brownie comes again.

'I bet your wife was there with that guy. Now you tell me, an' tell me quick what you have done with her, or is there another body?'

If he means that this Malwa has been in that bed in the sleeping palace I think that that's plain screwy; though, maybe, a man like Brownie wouldn't know it an' it would have to be pointed out.

Because I'm a fussy kid when it comes to upholstering the old frame, I gotta intuition Malwa ain't been in that room last night at all. Me, myself, I gotta get dressed in a little two-by-four bit of a place, an' I bet my life I can't get dressed in a hell-fire hurry without leaving some signs that any dame who ain't blind would notice. An', mind you, if a dame had to get herself dressed an' there were a gentleman who had been murdered just behind her I think she would be more prone to leave a lot more evidence of a hasty flight.

And there's no signs at all in this boudoir because I've nosed round, an' I *know*. And there's another thing. That bridal bed weren't no bridal bed at all on the night of the murder, anyhow, because, except where this dead guy's got his greasy head on the pillow an' that part where he's parked his frame, there ain't any signs of occupation.

I've been over it, too, as I told you, with my little microscope, an' I ain't been lookin' for bobby pins or anything so obvious, but I figure with my evil mind if this Malwa has been playin' kiss in the ring, there'd be some little clue like a hair out of her head, for instance, but there ain't anything.

I'll bet all I know that Malwa was not in the bed at all the night the sheik got his. An' that makes me wonder why he has picked this particular bed to sleep in, an' why the heck he locks his pants in Roy's bureau under his philately albums. Whether Malwa's been in the boudoir or not, it's a scream of a place to park 'em.

I think I would give a helluva lot to find this dame Malwa an' have a short conversation.

What I would wanta know first is where she was the night the sheik gets stuck, an' does she know him, an' how much. All I got at the moment to save Roy Stockforth's neck is a railway ticket an' a corn plaster, which may not be worth the paper they're written on, an' a lotta ideas that make sense to a dame but mean nothin' in the life of a copper, who all his life has worn trousers.

Brownie's idea is that, if a guy is in a lady's bed, it is *prima facie* evidence that they'd been playin' kiss in the ring, an' I gotta admit if this were just a case of Roy wantin' evidence for a divorce he'd hold a pretty strong hand, an' little Rose Bosanky would be for him a hundred per cent. But this ain't nothing to do with co-res. It's murder with a capital M, an', if you ask me, a pretty dirty sorta murder at that.

All these thoughts are passing through my mind while Roy is sittin' there gapin' at Brownie who, you remember, has been askin' him to tell pretty damn quick where his wife is, an' hintin' that perhaps he has done her in an' rationed her out and left her body in different railway cloak-rooms.

When the inspector finds Roy is so incapable of speech he gives a nasty laugh an' says, 'Okay, Adams, if you *won't* talk. You may be sorry. I'll leave you to think it over.'

He looks across at me an' grins. 'You better come with me, Miss Bosanky. I don't want you should be putting any ideas in his head.'

It's a hell of a hide he's got orderin' me round, but it suits me at the moment, so I hop up an' say, 'Okey doke,' an' Roy looks at me kinda pleadin', as if I was a mother desertin' her pet lamb in the thick of a raging snowstorm. I blow him a kiss an' say, 'I'll be back, sweetheart,' which makes Handsome cock his eyebrow. Then I follow Brownie into the hall.

Over my shoulder I see this Clancy pour a drink out for Roy, an' I think I was right the first time. Handsome is class, all right. I'm beginning to think I like class, especially when it's in the shape of this fancy Clancy who's got everything them screen heroes has besides which he ain't celluloid but has a very fetching flesh an' blood look. I think it is a matter for a little wistful thinking that we are engaged in a sordid murder affair instead of some hot blooded romance, which I have an idea he an' I could carry on very well in this den if Roy would lend it an' go to the races.

But this is not to be because, after all, old Brownie is gnashing his gums in the passage, an' there's a unknown corpse whose identity would puzzle even information please on the radio, so the sweet thoughts which have come to my mind pass away like a forgotten dream.

I see Roy take the glass Handsome has offered him, an' I leave 'em lookin' like they was club mates, an' Clancy has come to help his old college chum in his time of stress; but I tell myself, I gotta remember that, with all his class an' his romantic smudgy eyes an' accent, this fancy Clancy is a copper, an' his friendly ways are maybe a mask to lure Roy to put his trust in him, an' thus, at the same time, put his neck in a noose, which is a thing I would consider very unfortunate, because he is a nice guy, an' I can paint a picture of him giving me his arm (an' a small mink maybe), an' him takin' me places no poor copper's daughter ever set foot in before, like I suppose he has taken this Malwa dame who is absent but who he has married.

Brownie's in the corridor, an' I say, 'Listen, Brownie, I want you to come into the bedroom a minute,' an' he says, 'My time is all your own. Which bedroom?' I ignore this coarse remark, an' I lead the way back to the chamber of horrors.

The body's still there an' the fingerprint fellers and photographers are packin' their gear, and do they give me the once over? One of the photographers starts unpackin' his camera, pretendin' he thinks the inspector wants me took, but Brownie waves him away with a sour look. He's a fresh guy so he says, 'Too bad. Anytime, kid, you want me to make a exposure just give me a call-up,' an' they all laugh an' tootle off, while I pretend I'm too dumb to know it's an insinuendo.

But, I think to myself it is very hard on a young girl that the very sight of her should wake up such remarks from low heels like these photographers and why wasn't I born bandy, an' then I think of other guys who have more class, an' I think, Well, it's my cross, an' I gotta bear it.

Brownie is a bit fractious because he don't ever like no one to notice the things he's got his own eye on. He gives the impression to these photographers an' fingerprinters that he has got a high moral tone but, when we are all alone except for the corpse, he puts his arm around my waistline, an' we stand lookin' down at the murdered guy, an' Brownie says, 'Ain't life terrible, Rosie? To be took off like that! Stabbed in the midst of sin!'

He gives me a familiar squeeze, just to emphasise the moral he is pointing at. I get away from him with a very subtle squirm I have learned how, which practically looks natural an' just a commonplace physical motion. I would give it as a idea to any young modern girl who might be caught in a similar position, that it is a good thing to learn this squirm, because it leaves a guy not sure whether you did it on purpose or not and, therefore, he doesn't get too much down in the mouth like he would if you was to be less subtle.

Moreover, he is able to take it as a sop to his vanity of which, usually, he has a very great quantity, an' is not left with a idea that you have turned his attentions down flat. Therefore he will say to himself, She was just thinkin' of somethin' else, an' it was not a deliberate move to get away from me, an it was nice while it lasted, an' there is always a tomorrow.

While I make this subtle an' elusive motion I give some taffy. 'Look, Brownie, darling,' I say, 'you gotta remember there's a gentleman present,' meaning the sheik on the bed, of course, an' he likes this darlin' bit an' grins, an' is good-tempered at once. I go on. 'There's some things I want you to note down an' remember.'

He is feeling young an' skittish. He says, 'Say on, sweet child.'

'Sweet child, nothin', Brownie,' I say. 'Just forget for a moment I'm Rosie, an' try an' remember I'm Miss Bosanky of Bosanky Investigations. I want to call your attention to this boudoir bed.'

I then point out to him the things I pointed out to you two hundred thousand pages back that the bed ain't got any creases in it only where the body's parked, an' there ain't the sign of any long hair such as this Malwa might be expected to leave.

'So what?' he asks. 'It don't mean nothin', Miss Bosanky. She mighta been in the room, but she mightn't have got so far as going to bed.'

This might be right, too, but, while I can see almost any guy coming in an' killing another guy who was in bed with his wife, I can't see so plain that same guy coming in and seeing his wife all dressed up with even her furs on, perhaps, and walking over to the sheik in the bed an' killing him with a knife. For one thing I think it would be a very submissive thing for a man to wait there in a bed till another man came an' killed him.

'Just the same, Inspector, I would like you to note the point I have raised on behalf of my client,' I say. 'Moreoever, I would be obliged if you would smell this guy's hair.'

'I have,' he says. 'It nearly made me sick.'

'There you are,' I tell him. 'You're a policeman with a

good lusty stomach, too. You've hit the nail right on the head, Brownie.' I give him the old familiar title again, because I want him to feel proud of himself. 'If this hair oil gives *you* a turn, what sorta turn would it give this Roy's wife who is a sensitive dame, as you will find when you catch up with her. You have guessed it in one that she would just as soon sleep in a bed with a prize pig as have a smell like that wafted under her nose.'

'Yes, that struck me at once,' he says, the old liar, and he goes on, 'But these dames does some funny things, Rosie, like the Duchess, you remember, who had a ice-cream vendor for a co-re.'

I say I know it, an' I do, because I have myself even, after a restless night, been looking outa my flat window into the alley an' there is the garbage man collecting the cans. It is the dawn, an' a bit of early sun peeps down on to this young feller who has got his muscly arms bare up to the shoulders, and he's some sort of a foreigner, an' he's got a face you could make a Greek God out of. He picks up the can an' swings it on his shoulder, an' I think, If instead of a can it were a young nymph about five foot one inch with her red hair caught by the rising orb while he carried her shrieking to some far mountain lair, it would be a very pretty picture, only I don't know about the shriekin'.

So you can easily see, if a dago dustman could wake such romantic ideas, I think maybe Brownie has got something and Malwa may not be allergic to the oil this gink in the bed has rubbed on his head. But I give one more sniff an' I don't believe it.

There comes to me a passing horrid thought. Perhaps this dame has no sense of smell! There are some people like this, as I very well know, like the young turner and fitter with who I picked an off day to go to the zoo, an' who got into his best romantic moments at the back of the lion cage where there was such a thick aura that I had to keep on blowing my nose while this turner and fitter had no idea what was in the wind.

I think this, too, does not fit, because Malwa has practically secured Roy in the first place by the aid of a bottle of Night of Love Perfume, although even this could be a blind, an' just a lure, in the same way that some insects in natural history throw off an enterprising stink an' it attracts the male or vice versa.

It all boils down that the sooner I can see this Malwa the better for my peace of mind.

In the meantime I decide I will stick to my first ideas, which is intuition ideas, and more to be relied on when given birth to by a woman than any cold, hard formulas laid down by a man.

I say to Brownie, 'Officially speaking an' on behalf of my client, Roy, I ask you to observe the disrumpled state of the bed and take cognizance of the smell of the hair oil used.'

'I've took cognizance, Rosie,' he says grinning. 'Anything else?'

'Yes,' I say, an' pull back the bedclothes off the oily guy. I point to the big toe on his right foot. 'I'd like you to notice this toe, too.'

I stoop a bit to show him. He stands beside me an' puts his arm about me again, with his hand having a general upward trend, an' spends quite a time looking at the toe saying, 'Um,' an' 'Hah!' an' pretendin' he is very interested an' that I have raised quite a good point, but I know damn well he has got that parental feelin' again.

I think what a terrible thing it is to be a copper to who a corpse don't mean no more than a bedpost – he has become so familiar with 'em he can even start lesson one in the way to a girl's heart in such sinsister circumstances, which proves up to the hilt what I was taught in school, an old proverb saying, 'Familiarity breeds attempt'.

Brownie keeps on this 'Um' an' 'Hah', squeezing me a bit more each time, an' I say, 'I want you to notice the presence of a corn an' write it down in your little book.' Then, though it is more difficult in a stooping position, I once more take recourse to that subtle physical movement, which I have already mentioned, as if I hadn't really noticed he had a clutch-as-clutch-can on me. I pull the bedclothes up.

Brownie promises he'll remember about the corn, though what the hell it has gotta do with it he don't know. I don't either, because these are modern days when you cannot go round, like you would in the dear, dead times of long ago, with a glass slipper, asking all the men in the kingdom to have a corn plaster tried on and which anyway would be ridiculous because if ever a plaster belonged to a guy it belongs to the guy in the bed, because haven't I pulled it off his toe?

I think anyhow I have got it in my bag, an' it ain't as if it were an acid that will eat away the leather or poison my lip-stick, an' it ain't doin' no harm. I think I will keep it because, anyway, it will be a nice souvenir of my first case in which Roy Stockforth Adams was or was not hung.

We stand in a contemplative mood lookin' down on this disaster in the bed.

'There's another thing I don't think you've rumbled to,' I say.

'Oh,' he says, 'what?'

'He's wearin' Roy's pyjamas.'

'The devil he is.'

I can tell he thinks this is a bit thick, too. Men has funny notions because, up to this minute, I don't think that Brownie has had anything but hard feelings for Roy but, now, when he thinks this sheik has pinched his pyjamas, he has at last given him a kind thought an' sympathy for having such a thing done to him.

'Moreover,' I say, 'will you please note he's done the buttons up in the wrong places?'

He gives a close look. 'So he has.' He grins. 'But I guess he didn't care so long as he had the buttons undone in the right places.

I ignore this double intender and say, 'It seems very strange to me.'

'Why?' he says. 'Maybe he was a bit excited when he got into 'em.'

'True,' I give in, 'but would you like to know what I think, Inspector Browne?'

'Naturally, Miss Bosanky,' he says, kidding. 'Your years of experience make anything that falls from your lips like pearls before –' He sees his eloquence has led him on the wrong tack, an' he breaks off quickly. 'Anyway, I'd love to hear.'

'I think,' I say, 'that he didn't put those pyjamas on himself. *They was put on him.*'

———

Brownie stares at me for a moment or two as if I'm crazy. Then he says, shakin' his head, 'Oh, no, no, Rosie, my red-head. You're lettin' your imagination run away with you.'

'Yes,' I say, 'and maybe a little imagination wouldn't be wasted in this joint. If Roy Stockforth Adams had had a little more imagination, he wouldn't have told you the truth.'

'He lied about that bureau drawer,' Brownie says.

'Not on your life he didn't,' I tell him.

'Anyway,' he says, 'he didn't want to open it, an' when Clancy got to work there was the coat an' pants!'

'An' what about the shoes and collar an' tie an' boots? I suppose this guy would wear 'em.'

'I suppose he would – boots anyway,' he admits. 'Well, I think probably your pal Roy has burnt 'em, or something.'

'But he's carefully kept the coat an' pants, 'eh?' I twit. 'It don't seem sensible to me. He keeps a coat an' pants which he wouldn't be seen dead in, does he?'

'I don't say he was goin' to *wear* 'em,' Brownie says. 'He just mightn't have had time to get rid of 'em.'

'He could have got rid of 'em instead of toddling round to see his pal an' findin' me. No, Brownie. I guess he told the truth about that drawer, all right.'

Brownie is a obstinate devil. 'He lied about the money. There was no money in the drawer. Why did he say there was?' I say maybe he made a mistake. If a guy has gotta lot of money loose all the time like he has given an indication, maybe there will come a time in his life when he spends it without thinkin' and leaves the cupboard bare.'

'I don't believe it,' Brownie says. 'I don't think it is possible for a man to forget he has a hundred pounds in a drawer.'

I think it would be for me a very hard thing to forget also, but then I am a better realiser than Brownie that he and me an' old Roy are not in the same class.

He says, 'I'll go and enquire some more into this money business.' He grabs me by the arm, but I hang on to the head of the bed.

'One moment more, Brownie dear,' I say very soothing. 'I'm only a kid, an' I only been in the investigating business hardly a few hours, but I always recollect what my pappy said.'

'God res' his soul, Rosie,' the old wolf says and makes it an excuse for holding me again. 'What did he say?'

He said, I tell him, that I was never in any case to jump at conclusions like you was prone to do.

'Did he now, the old basket,' Brownie says.

I go on. 'You think little Roy has done this murder. Well, I don't. I tell you one reason why I don't, an' that is, if he hadda shot this greasy sheik in the bed I mighta believed it; if he'd stood at the door an' thrown a poisoned arrow at him I mighta believed it; but what I won't believe is that Roy came into this boudoir with his nice sharp paper knife, an' walked across the carpet from the door to the marriage bed, which is a tidy distance, and stabbed the guy. It is a bit too premeditated.'

Brownie thought a bit. 'P'raps the guy was asleep?'

He mighta been at that. But, no, I say, not Roy. Even if he's a murderer he would still have class. I can't see him creepin' on a sleepin' man, even if it's his wife's boy friend, and killing him in his sleep. It ain't just Oxford.

'Ain't you ever noticed,' I ask Brownie, 'how when I leave a room, he always stands aside an' lets me go first?'

'Why?' Brownie asks.

I don't tell him. You can see what I am up against, working

with a man who hasn't got the remotest idea of the basic laws of etiquette.

'An' there's another thing, Rosie,' Brownie says, 'and that is that this friend of yours killed him in some other place an' put him in the bed. It would be a sort of ironic gesture.'

He carries on. 'I can see him carryin' the body across the dim-lit corridor, laughing softly in a maniacal way and dropping the corpse of his wife's lover on to the snowy sheets.'

Brownie is waxing poetical but at the back of his speech is a idea though not quite the one he has got in mind for he's hell bent on pinning this crime on to Roy who is very convenient to his hand.

'I see your little inquisitive nose turned up in doubt,' he says. 'Sniffing at my idea! All right, Red, I'll give you one more poetic fancy.'

'Go on,' I say, 'I like poetry.'

He is very fond of the new form of dialogue he has hit on. He speaks with a lotta drama. 'I see this sheik in bed – *here*. He is waiting, listening. His heart beats with excitement. Will his lost love return to make up the quarrrel he has had with her? "Malwa, my darling," he breathes, "where are you?" And, then, I see a form float silently across yonder corridor. It has come from Roy's little room and, concealed in the filmy, foamy drapery it is wrapped in, it is carrying Roy's little knife. Slowly it pushes open the boudoir door. "Malwa," the sheik cries. "At last. You've come back." She floats across the carpet and bends over him. "Malwa, my love, my own." She answers him, "Yes, Harold, I have come back – for *this*."'

Brownie makes a big swish with his hand like he was striking a dagger into a body, an' I remember now my pappy taking me to a police social where this same Brownie had recited a poem about a foreign god with a green eye.

'Bravo,' I say, 'but how do you know his name is Harold?'

'I don't,' he tells me. 'It is just a poetic license.'

He is in a high good humour because, whatever he is telling me in this dramatic manner, he don't believe a word of it. In his heart he thinks it is just a simple case where a man has been fool enough to kill another man and quite likely have got rid of his wife by the same method.

When we get back to Roy's little den, there's the Prize Suspect, an' his glass is nearly empty, an' this Sergeant Clancy is having one himself, an' the way Roy looks at me an' the way Handsome looks at Brownie I know something has happened.

I can tell right off, without any word bein' said, that this long devil with the smudgy eyes has been pullin' some sort of old-school-tie, man-to-man stuff, and I reckon Roy has spilled the beans, whatever they are. Brownie pours himself a drink he would be ashamed, or too mean, to take such a lot of in his own home, and gives me a weak one, an' we are all sittin' round just as if we was all pals together, instead of which there is, according to at least two people present, a murderer in our midst. Then as the inspector puts down his glass Handsome says, 'Mr Adams has just been telling me he received an anonymous letter tending to make him suspicious of his wife's conduct.'

'Oh, no, no, Clancy,' Roy puts in quick. 'I didn't quite say that. I said I had a nasty anonymous letter and that it had made me anxious. I didn't say suspicious.'

'I'm sorry,' Clancy says, while Brownie glares at him because whoever heard of such a thing, a copper being sorry?

'Anxious was the word.'

The inspector says, 'Where is this letter?'

I stay quiet because I don't quite see where this might be leading.

Clancy says, 'Mr Adams says he has apparently mislaid it.'

'A helluva thing to mislay,' Brownie snorts, and it is too, when you come to think of it, but I can see what has happened. It is class comin' to the surface again and Roy playin' the Sir Walter Whatshisname because he's already given me the letter and he don't want to put me in wrong with the police.

I sit as quiet as Mona Lisa on a monument waiting to see what more Roy has spilled, but I feel I could pick him up and smack his tail for being so dumb as to fall for this good-lookin' Clancy's soft school-tie talk.

This anonymous letter pleases Brownie in one way but, in another, it's got him puzzled because why has Roy told about it? You'd think this is one time in life he'd keep his own confidence instead of which he has put his neck out like some old-fashioned turkey who was tired of livin' an' was glad it was Christmas.

I can see Brownie tryin' to get his grey cells workin'. He is tellin' himself it ain't as if Clancy has slapped Roy around because he can see by the nice set of Roy's tie an' the way his hair is stayin' put, an' he ain't got either a bruised eye or a cut lip, that Roy has made a voluntary declamation. And Brownie don't know whether he likes this for another reason, and that is that Clancy, by his classy manner, has persuaded my client to spit out this information. In his heart he don't think that Handsome is such a helluva fellow he could *persuade* a guy to get hisself hung.

He can't make it out, Brownie can't, and, on top of the doubts I have already sown in his mind, he don't look as happy as he did when he came back into the room. So he goes off on another track and puts Roy through a lot more about when did he see his wife last and was they on good terms when they parted and what was his movements last night and is he sure he don't know the dead guy and why did he hide the dead guy's pants in his drawer and what has he done with his boots and hat, and, half the time, he don't wait for the answers, especially the one about the pants and things, because already he is worried why Roy should keep in such an unsensible place a coupla articles which will be exhibit A when he comes to have his trial.

At last I cough an' say, 'Excuse me, but didn't I hear some mention of missin' money?'

Brownie's forgot all about it for the moment, but he says then, 'Yes, Adams. I thought you said you had some money in that drawer where we found the clothes.'

'Yes,' Roy says, 'that is correct. I have always some money there.'

'I found none when I searched,' Clancy puts in.

'I can't believe it,' Roy says and carries on quickly because he's a guy with such class he never wants to hurt no one's feelings, an' I do not think he would step on even a poisonous ant without beggin' its pardon. 'I don't mean I doubt Mr Clancy's word,' he says. 'Not for a moment, of course, but I don't understand where the money could have gone.'

'How much was there exactly?' Brownie enquires.

'Oh,' Roy says, 'I wouldn't know *exactly*, old boy. About a hundred I should say, off-hand,' and then he stops sudden and his mouth goes open and doesn't shut. I get it he has remembered something that has rocked him. 'Oh, my hat!' he says at last. 'I clean forgot. Not a hundred pounds by a long shot.'

'How much?' This from Brownie, with his jaw set like an Iron Duke.

'How much?' Roy repeats and begins to think again. 'Why, with what was there before, oh there must have been about six hundred.'

Brownie gasps, 'Six hundred *pounds*.'

'Yes, of course,' Roy tells him. 'Mind you, I'm only guessing, old boy, because I don't know how much was in the drawer before.'

'Before *what*?' Brownie is exasperated.

'Before I put the five hundred in,' Roy says. 'Y'see, I won the five hundred on the Lincoln Cup.'

Clancy says quickly, 'But the Lincoln Cup was run over a week ago.'

It's easy to tell this Handsome would know all about horses. He's got, for all his drawing-room manners, a good outdoor look about him, an' I can just imagine him in the saddle an' ridin' hard. I think it would be a sight to see this handsome beast mounted on some flash filly. But of this I will speak more anon. Just now I am more interested in Roy's present predicament which, now that six hundred pounds has disappeared, seems to be gettin' more an' more complicated.

'The Lincoln Cup was run over a week ago,' is what Clancy tells Roy, an' Roy says, 'Yes, on Saturday week. I collected on Monday, an' when I got home from the club I tossed the notes in the drawer. I forgot all about them till now.'

Handsome gives a deep sigh and Brownie's eyes are showin' signs that they will leave his head almost at once. He can't quite get the idea that there is anywhere in the world a man, a real man in a coat an' vest an' pants, who wears braces an' shaves his face, who could have five hundred pounds in notes an' toss 'em into a drawer an' forget all about 'em until there's a murder did.

But, more an' more, I am getting the psychology of this Roy Stockforth Adams. I reckon he's one of those whose family has got an escutcheon thing, which has printed on it in a foreign tongue a motto which, when you get to the bottom of it, means 'Easy come easy go'. I think it is a very nice thing to be able to toss five hundred pounds in a drawer last Monday an' forget all about 'em till today.

I think, too, it's a nice thing for Rosie Bosanky to have a client who can do such a thing, an' who has started out to be a simple cuckold, an' is now on his way to be a principal performer in a French passion crime.

Maybe havin' those Bosanky Investigations account slips for which I have paid for 200, printed so short was a penny wise an' pound foolish idea, because I can see the expense sheet in this case is likely to have a lotta items.

'D'you mean to sit there an' tell me you threw five hundred quid into that drawer where, already there was a hundred, over a week ago an' you have never even looked at it since?' Brownie cries.

'That's it, constable,' Roy says. 'It didn't jolly well dawn on me that anyone would pop in and pinch it.'

'Who do you suspect took it?' Brownie asks.

'Oh, I haven't the foggiest.'

I think I will add a note of comedy. 'Maybe, the gink in the bed in there took it in exchange for his pants.'

'Oh, I'd hardly think so,' Roy says because he is not a man who has a quick idea of a humorous saying.

'Who knew the money was there beside you, Mr Adams?' Clancy enquiries in his softest accent.

Roy tells him. 'I don't know. No one, that is, except Malwa. I think I told her. Yes, I did. I remember now. She passed the door as I was stowing the old notes away in the drawer. She stopped a moment, an' I remember she looked positively ripping. I said, "I picked up five hundred on the Lincoln Cup. I wish you'd remind me to buy you something."'

This Roy is inclined to grow on a girl. You can see he has a generous instinct in every pore an' is a guy who would share his last million with a pal. I try and reconstruct the scene of Malwa standin' at the door to the corridor in such a close vicinity to the five hundred pounds of notes Roy is putting away in his drawer.

I wonder is she thinking how much of it will he spend on her if she asks him in the right spirit at the right moment, which is how I would be. If I was her I would know right now what I would buy, even if he gave me only a fracture of the money, and this is the hat I seen in M'lle Fifine's, which I told you about, an' which I would know how to wear, if ever a girl did.

It is a hat which is of green felt and some tulle an' velvet ribbon, an' there is a wisp of a feather, an' it seems almost a blasphemy to talk about it like this because it is the way the felt an' the feather an' things are put together that makes this model a thing of rapture an' joy forever.

I am day-dreaming of this hat when Brownie's coarse voice interrupts the sweet picture I have of me steppin' out of M'lle Fifine's and hardly in my right mind because this damn lid, which is like opium to my soul, I have such a craving for it, has cost seventeen guineas and you can argue how you like it is cheap, too, for how it makes a girl like me feel.

The coarse, interrupting voice of Brownie is saying, 'I put it to you straight, Adams, that your wife pinched this dough an' has done a bunk.'

Roy blinks at him as if he can't hardly believe his ears, an' then he says, 'But that's nonsense. Why should she take it when she only had to ask? I've always given her whatever she wanted.'

I wonder has he. Maybe he's wrong, this Roy. Maybe he ain't give her what she wanted. Maybe, I think, she has got some of that exotic stuff in her veins, which comes through living in the mystic east, an' a little bit of being chased round a harem by a wild eunuch and clean into the Sultan's favourite four-poster is what she needs. Instead of which this Roy is giving her a lotta kind words an' gentlemanly behaviour and a lotta dough when, as far as I can see, the ladies in the harem don't get paid at all, except for their keep, no matter how hard they try.

In the reverse, I am considerin' that perhaps this Malwa has got away with Roy's five hundred pounds and more for another reason, which no one knows but her, because it has come to my mind that it would match up very well with her askin' Roy every now an' then for a small cheque for a secret purpose disconnected altogether with any natural things she might buy in the way of unders and overs, an' which he has confessed he can't see on her back even if he has been able to arrange a date in her boudoir which, on account of this philately complex he has got, I think is very doubtful.

Brownie is asking him about the servants and was they honest, and Roy is laughing him to scorn, because they are very old retainers, an' wouldn't stoop to such a thing as to pilfer, even if it was £500 though, I reckon, with their holidays on full pay and all, these old retainers have a very good idea how much bread is on their butter.

And then Brownie says, 'Well, Mr Adams, I shall have to request you to stay in the house, an' I shall put a man on to see that you damn well do till such time as such action as I shall decide to take will be made known.'

He has now got it into his nut that there is something a bit different about this case to what he first thought although I can tell he is bidding adieu to Roy with a thought in his heart it would be better for him to confess right away an' then he could be tried in a coupla weeks an' hung, an' the whole affair cleaned up.

I hear a rumpus in the hall an' a copper puts his head in the door to say there's a lotta press chaps downstairs so I have to borrow Roy's wall mirror and, even then, to stand on a low chair and fuss up my hair. I put a bit of powder where it is needed, an' duco the lips while Brownie goes out to get his fill of publicity. I then hitch up my suspenders to get a straight line in my stockings, an', when I am all set I look round to see Fancy Clancy quizzing me with a evil gleam in his eye, which, somehow, I find very palatable.

Poor old Roy has seemed to have got, by now, a stomach full of his troubles. His head is sunk down in depression, an' he hasn't seen a half of what Clancy has. So far as this handsome animal is concerned, he may be a very strong six foot guy very partial to outdoor sports but, from the evil gleam I have previously told you about, I bet my young life he has plenty of fun indoors, too.

When I put up my sign, 'Rosie Bosanky, Investigations,' I told myself I gotta be an impressionist, which means I have to take a good care that, when I make a contack with anyone who I consider will be an important factor to me, I must impress such personality as I may possess upon them. Up to now, though, I have found that I do not have to go to any great shakes on my own account because I would have to be blind as Balum's Ass not to know that Dame Nature has put a hallmark on me; but, just the same, I have come across a proverb which says, 'Nature unaided fails', an', when I think back less than an hour or more, it was by helping Nature in a way that I got this client Roy and his £60,000 per a.. An' I got to protect my client, ain't I?

I've got a hunch that this Clancy might be one of my

important factors, an' that he is a guy that will not be averse to a little impressing, too, so I stand up very close to him an' play with the middle button of his uniform. This is my way of helping Nature.

I say, 'Listen, Handsome, I want you to keep them press hounds away from Roy here.'

He says, Okay, he will, and gives me a look which is very contemplative. To break the monotony of the way he is getting a blue-print of my shape and all, I say, 'How comes it a fine upstanding stranger like you is cleanin' the boots of old Brownie?.

He gives a good-natured laugh. 'Well, Rosie,' he says, 'just for the moment I'm playing Boswell to his Jolson.'

I don't get this because what has Connie Boswell and Al got to do with this case? But, I have since met a man with a curious kink for going into public libraries, and he tells me this Boswell was not Connie but a yes-man to Jolson, and, whenever Jolson spoke, he would say, 'Make a note of it,' and Boswell would put down every damn word, many of which was a superfluity; but there was enough over the mediocre mark to give the critics sufficient to work on and give him the label of a great man though not so well known as his fellow namesake who gave to humanity the famous Mammy song.

Clancy has got so close to me I think I can feel his heart palpitating. He is breathing very hard, too, an' I reckon it is only his idea of class that keeps him from taking a more active interest in my affairs. This class feeling is due to the near vicinity of old Roy, though the poor thing is more dead than alive, and, so far as noticin' such conduct as human emotions, I don't think he would even pay heed if Bing Crosby himself was to drive a horde of wild bulls through the room singing give him his boots and saddle.

Clancy says in a kind of a strained voice, 'It's whatever you say, Rosie.'

I look up and it seems a terrible long way from where I am looking at this button I mentioned to where he has got his lips a little bit open so I can see his white teeth. The next thing he has got me squeezed by the two arms and he's sayin', 'I'd do anything for you, anywhere, anytime.'

An', I believe, if I'd took him at his word he would have.

---

CHAPTER 5

The pictures which the press boys took came out very good, an' there was one with my legs crossed to which a paper gave a big two column, like I was a film star. Also there was a write-up about how young I was and how, in pursuit of my chosen career, I discovered the body of the unknown corpse to who Brownie has given the working title of Harold.

There was also a lot more about how my hero father had trained me how to be a sleuth, and also a point-to-point description of the old anatomy, and even in a column for dames there was a par which says, *sub rosa*, that I have a retrousse nose, which may or may not be a compliment but which I am too busy to worry about, so it will have to wait until I can find time to have it interpreted by a good classical dictionary.

I have let the writer boys in the know about some of the things I think which has taken the sting out of Roy's case and lifted it from the sordid to a higher mystery class of murder and got it a lot more space than if it was a mere bagatelle like a French passion crime of which the papers are so sick, they are now a clot on the market.

While the lads are crowding me most anxious to be sure Rosie was spelled with a 'i.e' or a 'y' old Brownie is as mad as a hatter, an' I have to tell them that, after all, he is the Big Police Whistle and, for heaven's sake, give him a break, which they promise to do, though they said, as far as they were concerned, Brownie was a pompous old basket. I tell them, though, that he is an old and dear friend of my father and looks on me like I was his own daughter, which woulda been all right, too, but one of them printed it granddaughter, which I bet Brownie didn't like much, beside which it was a bit thick and, when I come to figure it out, he just couldn't be unless he was the Boy Wonder, or something.

Before the press boys go, I ask 'em to take a picture of what I have called God's Gift to Women. I think I will trot out Handsome as a reward for him keeping Roy from a lotta sordid publicity he would hate like a dose of arsenic. But, to my surprise, Clancy won't have his picture took, an' I don't know whether he is afraid of the inspector or has he some ulterior reason.

When the press boys have gone forth to publish the news, I try and get a quiet word with Handsome while Brownie has gone to powder his nose and old Roy is still buried in a deep depression amid his forgotten etchings. I slip into the Chamber of Horror to see what Clancy is about.

He is standin' at Malwa's dressin' table, an' he has one of her silver hairbrushes in his hand and is touching up his locks while he looks at himself in the glass. And, believe me, he has something to look at.

A bit of sun has sprung up and is shining through a window, and it is just catching the top of his head like it was a little fairy beam kissin' its mortal offspring, like in Gilbert Sullivan's opera where a member of parliament has had carnal knowledge of a girl who is found out to be immortal, and such a fuss is made I think at first I have got it wrong and it is immoral.

Anyway, this fairy beam is tickling Handsome's top-knot, and to me he has the view of a Greek god with his clothes on, and I bet if they took them away from him an' stood him in the park on a pedestal with a good-sized fig leaf instead, even this Einstein would say he was a pretty artistic piece of still life, though, if such was the case, and he really was put on that

pedestal, you wouldn't catch me in that park without my runnin' shoes, because I am of the opinion that this Clancy
wouldn't be too damn passive on his pedestal, and even the
youngest can be warned, by goin' to any good art gallery, that
these Greek gods of whom they make statchers, very seldom
take any heed about notices, such as 'Keep off the Grass',
where a dame is concerned.

Such like poetic thoughts have been running through my
mind while I watch Handsome delicately touching the tips of
his moustache. Maybe you are thinkin' it would be kinda cissy
for a big brute over six foot to be caught looking at himself in
a mirror but, somehow, I don't feel it that way, and when he
looks round and sees me peeking, he don't blush or look con-
fused because I have caught him, but says, 'Oh, hello!' an'
goes on with his toilet.

I come a little way in the room, and he puts down the
brush very quietly and smiles at me.

I say, 'I'm just movin' off, an' I thought I'd give you my
card in case there is some business we could talk over some
time.'

I give him my card, of which I have had 200 printed at 5/-
per hundred, an' he takes it and gives it the look that is called
scrutinising, which means that he reads it very carefully. He
says he is very glad to have it, because he has just remembered
that there is some business he has got in mind that he would
like to talk over in private, that very night if I can make it.

He suggests maybe it will be a good idea if we go to some
quiet place an' eat a spot of spaghetti, and then, after we have
talked over the business, we can relax, an' he will show me his
curios up in his apartment an' tell me about his experiences in
the North West Mounted Police.

I say I like the sound of this spaghetti, but I seen a lotta
curios in my time, and there's been so many fillums about the
North West Mounted Police I doubt if he could show me
anything that would interest me. He says I would be surprised, an' I guess I might, so I don't make no rash promises. I

say I will take the spaghetti, an' thank you very much, but I will leave the rest on the lap of the Gods an' I hope to myself it won't end up on the lap of a Greek God like I was gettin' poetic about a few paragraphs back.

Handsome raises my pasteboard card to his lips and kisses it, then he puts it away in a top pocket an' gives the pocket a little tap for all the world like it was an old world romance an' I am a lady fair who has passed a token on to a cavalier to go to the wars of the roses with.

It is while I am having this pleasant thought that I hear Brownie's hoarse voice from the corridor hollerin' where the devil is everybody. So I take a farewell of pleasure for business once again an' have a look round the boudoir because, after all, Roy is payin' me for my time an' is entitled to a square deal. The oily sheik has been taken out of Malwa's bed and by now, I guess, is on a cold hard slab at the morgue where I bet he looks more at home.

Brownie and Clancy are drivin' back to town, and the former gentleman offers me a lift. I say one moment, please, an' pop in to say *au revoir* to Roy. He is standing at the far end of the room. I can see his face in its profile position. It's half in a shadow and it's a very clean cut, aristocratic face, and he's not a handsome big animal like Clancy, but he's gotta look of steel springiness about him which is the difference, if you know what I mean, between a lion, which is all head and haunches, and a slinking tiger, which is all rippling sinews.

As I stand there and he does not see me, I think he has got something, this Roy, that no other guy I have seen has got. I can't imagine him even in his underpants up on a park pedestal let alone a fig leaf, and I feel a bit of a lump in my throat because it comes over me in a wave that he is in a hell of a position with a corpse found in that bed and all, an' a lot of damn policemen trying to herd him on to a scaffold.

I wish for a minute I was not only about five feet tall but was one of them hefty big-hipped and deep-bosomed wenches to who Jeffrey Farnol has given birth so I could fold him on my breast like I was a mother whose favourite son was on his way to a long vacation in a slave plantation. But I ain't, so I cross over softly, an' he don't hear me until I am quite close, an' then he looks round with those melancholy eyes, and I give him one of my cards and say, I gotta be goin', but my telephone number is on the pasteboard, an', if he wants, he can ring and, in any case, I'll be seein' him.

He says, 'Thank you. Thank you very much, Rosie.'

And I say, 'Don't you worry, Roy. I'll bet it'll be a long, long day before you're hanged.'

He says, 'I'm afraid the constable thinks I did it.'

I say, 'What the heck? *I* know you didn't.'

He looks at me and doesn't speak, an' then, all at once, he has picked up my hand an' he's bent his head down and has kissed my fingers and though if you knew my life's history unexpurgated you'd never believe it, I'm tellin' you when his lips touch my hand I get a kick of a sort I never got before no matter where I was kissed.

I gotta tear in my eye, too, which is a thing a good kiss didn't oughta start, an' I make a break for the door because Brownie has started his hollerin' again. I look back, an' Roy is standin' by the window like one of those old aristo's in the Paris revolution who said it was a far, far better thing than he had ever done.

By an' by, I am sittin' in the front seat of Brownie's car between him an' Clancy and Brownie's drivin', for which I am thankful, because it keeps his hands busy, and this Handsome has to behave hisself also, because he is in the presence of his superior officer who isn't very superior at all, if you ask me but, just the same, we're a bit crowded, an' Brownie keeps pushin' his leg against mine, playin' he's tending the brakes and gadgets, and on the other side Handsome is crowding my other leg, making out there's not enough room, and so, by the time they drop me at my office, I'm feeling pretty crumpled, an' I'm damned if there isn't a ladder started in my stocking, which makes me as mad as hell, because I've only had them less than two days, and it would never have happened if I'd taken a taxi.

I have to put this ruined stocking as a expense against poor old Roy, too, because, though it don't seem hardly fair, it would never have happened if I hadn't been out on this case trying to stop him being hung, would it? All the same I can't see Brownie, or even a fancy Clancy, passing a item like that on an expense sheet, an' yet I know as sure as, at this moment, I have my leg curled under me and I am sitting on my suspender button and it is hurting like the devil, this Roy is not goin' to quibble over a mere pair of stockings when he has got his mind full of a possible scaffold and he don't even know where his wife is, or is he a cuckold or not.

Which just shows once again that it is best to have clients who have class.

I have hardly had time to switch the radio on in its quieter volume, because I always like to have my ears peeled for any special piece of police news which might come across, and got out my pencil an' pad to figure out the debits an' credits for the expense account in this Roy Adams case, when over it comes.

Brownie has got to work with all speed, and there's a nice example of vocal culture expressing the hope that anyone knowing the whereabouts of Mrs Roy Stockforth Adams of So and So will they please inform her that she should get in touch with Such-an'-such, an' I can see that old Brownie is playin' the game careful for all his insinuendos to Roy about him having did her in along with her paramour and hid her body.

Well, for his own sake, if this is so, I hope Roy hid the body more carefully than he hid the oily sheik's striped pants. I figure that Brownie will have the radio boys being nice an' polite in their messages for a few hours, or maybe till morning, an' then will burst out with 'A description of the missing woman is as follows'.

The announcer follows up his request by saying he will

play a tune from Beethoven, which I find, with the volume turned low, is very good music to work out the case to on my pad, because I can't do it if swing is on, even if it is Arty Shaw's arrangement of a classic master, which would interrupt my thoughts because it would tend to make me wonder what would be the classic master's arrangement for Arty Shaw.

I am a silent worker for a good hour, an' then the phone rings and this is its first effort since I paid the deposit.

It is Brownie saying he thought it might cheer me up to know that they found some of Roy's fingerprints on the dagger handle, all right.

'Oh, yeah,' I say, 'I guess they was a nice set, which makes the case all open and closed.'

'As a matter of fact, Rosie,' he says, 'they weren't. They was right low down on the handle and there was even some on on the side of the blade that didn't get into the dead guy.'

I let that settle in and then I enquire, 'An' whose was on the handle where the killer musta held the weapon?'

'The killer musta wore gloves,' he tells me, 'because there's only bits and pieces that might be this Adams's.'

'I get you, Brownie,' I say. 'The Roy prints is there quite natural because he has a habit of using that knife to open his letters with instead of his thumb. This killer musta had gloves on and picked up the knife and blurred Roy's.'

'Ain't you the little red-headed wonder?' Brownie purrs, an' I can picture him grinnin' into the phone. 'But,' he goes on, smooth as silk, 'you can't have moved in society much, Rosie, or you'd know that gentlemen like this Roy Adams has been known to wear gloves theirselves.'

I ignore this. I bet if it comes to knowing anything about etiquette there is not much this head copper could show me, because he is a type of man who, when the soup is on, is very liable to be a strong opposition to a radio.

I ask him, 'And who was the deceased guy? Did his prints match up with any in your well-known collection?'

I can tell this has wiped the grin off his face because he uses a very different tone when he speaks next. 'That's the hell of it, Rosie. The dead guy never left a single print in the whole damn joint, as far as we know. We have already gotta set of all the servants that we have rounded up. Now what do you make of that?'

I say, 'I suppose you've thought of this, Brownie. Roy goin' round with a damp duster an' wipin' them off, bein' careful to leave all the prints of his ancient retainers. After he's stuck his favourite knife into the visitin' sheik, I mean. An' then, of course, he had to take all them tags and marks off the striped clothes he had so foolishly planted in his philately drawer, an' burn the guy's boots and socks and what-have-yous, an' find a nice restin' place for his hat, supposin' he wore one. Oh, an' I forgot, he also had to murder his wife an' hide her body. Some job, Brownie,' I say. 'No wonder the poor boy was lookin' a bit peeked.'

'I can recognise you are bein' sarcastic, Rosie,' the inspector says, 'but you gotta always remember that this Adams feller is a well-educated chap who could perhaps use his nut in doin' a murder. Perhaps he is puttin' us to a helluva lotta bother. I have an idea myself that he is a bit of a Macky Avelli.'

I do not know this dago crook he has mentioned, but I am not going to let him get away with a slur like that. I tell him that so far as I am concerned Roy is as white a man as he is himself an', if ever I see true British stock, he has got it up to the neck.

'Now,' Brownie says, 'don't fly off the handle, Rosie. What's the matter? Are you fallin' in love with this Adams or something? Because if you are, you better be careful. You gotta remember that he's still gotta wife – or he's got a wife still.'

He gives a big laugh. I don't get it. He explains. 'He's still gotta wife or he's gotta wife *still*. *Still*, d'you see? Meanin' she's dead. It's a joke.'

You can see what I have gotta put up with because a man

who can make a joke of this type to my mind has a very poor sense of the ridiculous. I am just about to tell him I will ring him up on Tuesday week, by which time I will have seen his point, when suddenly he goes all official. He speaks in a very prim voice.

'That will be all, Miss Bosanky. Good afternoon.' He rings off, and I know someone musta come into his office who he don't want to overhear him calling me Rosie, because he will usually bring a telephone chat to a finality by saying, 'Here's one to go on with,' and make a kissing noise which, if it gives him a satisfaction, I bet isn't half as much a satisfaction as it is to the girls in the telephone exchange who are probably wasting their time listening in an' saying, 'Did you hear him, the old goat?'

I think, though, after all it will pay a young girl to be in with this Brownie, old goat or not, because he can be quite a good guy if he would just be a head copper an' not think so much of the time he used to nurse you on his lap an' you didn't have no say in it. I think I will practise a new motto which is to keep my temper outa my tongue and never do or say anything which will stop this Brownie from keepin' on hopin'.

---

CHAPTER 6

Over the gilded spires of the great mosque the sun has rose to cast its golden glow upon the sleeping city, only this ain't Russia, an' there's no sun, but it's raining like hell, an' it's just next day.

I'm down at the office early because there's one or two things I wanta fix before I tootle off to see Roy, an' I gotta do one or two other chores, too, in connection with this misplaced corpse case. One thing I wish to give attention to is that railway ticket. You will recollect I have found a return half of a fare to Brighton. All night I have been thinkin' about this an' other things which have built up a wall of sorrows for old Roy.

In the end I have decided to give the ticket to Brownie, as a good-natured gesture, because it is my candid opinion it isn't worth a damn, an' that it was placed in Roy's corridor as a fresh herring across the path of justice. I think it is a clue which is too damn obvious because I cannot for the life of me think there would be a crook capable of doing a murder and wipin' away all fingerprints who would leave a railway ticket in a tidy hall where no one could miss it. I think it is just an idea to link up with the anonymous letter Roy has thought so odious.

I ring up Brownie to ask him what news an' tell him I musta been a dimwit yesterday because it only came to me as I was lying in bed early this morning what the joke was about Roy having a wife *still*, and I have been laughing like hell ever since. He then tells me that they have been down to Brighton and checked up about the Adams couple at the hotel there and nobody could swear the woman was the one in a photo which they had with them an' which depicts this Malwa.

But they have got it quite clear that the man Adams which stayed there with her isn't the least little bit like the sheik we found in her bed.

He says that this news has given the case a new complication, and, furthermore, there is no news at all of Roy's wife although the message for her to report has been going over the air all night. He thinks perhaps Malwa has got away with Roy's money from the philately drawer an' run off with an unknown guy, an' the guy who we found dead has got no more to do with the case at all from a divorce point of view than the flowers that bloom in the spring, ha ha, but has perhaps, come to the house for some other reason and been murdered by Roy.

I thank him kindly and tell him about the railway ticket, an' he says he oughta give me a good slap in the pants for withholding evidence. I have to plead that in the excitement I clean forget it. He says, knowing what they know about the Brighton pub couple and, apparently, the man at the pub having no connection with the corpse so-called Harold, this railway ticket makes everything more complicated still.

I think he is right about this, but I don't tell him I have an intuition that the ticket is a plant. He tells me he will let me know if Malwa or her body turns up, an' I think it is a wise thing to say in a sweet tone, 'Good bye-ee' and make a very gentle kissing sound on the phone which, after all, is a very small concession for a girl to make but which will keep Brownie up to his promise to tell me what's cookin'.

I've hardly had much time to look at my write-ups and pictures in the papers about which I have already related, but I now cut them out an' think I must buy a book to paste them up in to show my gran'children. I dismiss from my mind the idea that this paste-up book is an expense item that could very well be set down against the Body in the Boudoir Case but has got to be put against what is called by Big Business 'Overhead', and includes such expenses as entertaining blondes which the auditors cannot see their way clear to put down in the books under its real identity, though once I knew a businessman who was spending so much on my dinner I told him I did not want him to run himself bankrupt on my account. He said not to worry because he had a special arrangement with his firm by which his expenses went down under a heading which was called, 'Man is Not Made of Iron'. He said his directors were not fussy because he is a man who is very good in his line, and, when a man like him brings in a lotta contracts, the directors can afford to shut their eyes to a great many things which would be considered very deleterious in a man who could not bring home the bacon.

I have found out that he is certainly a very good man in his line, but it is not the same line as he is in for his directors. I think, too, that he has a cheek to think that I won't mind going down on this Man is Not Made of Iron expense sheet, so I say I will now go and powder my nose, an' I give the cloak-room dame a tip to show me how I can emerge the back way. And, in case any auditors are wondering whoever it is that is down on this Man is Not Made of Iron account for that night, it is not little Rosie Bosanky.

While I am recalling to mind the picture of this alert young business man standin' with the cafe bill in his hand, and I am wonderin' how long he waited before he knew it was a blue duck, the postman has brought me a letter and it is from Roy Stockforth Adams.

When I open this letter I say, 'Rosaleen Bosanquet, you oughta be ashamed of yourself. You're so damn anxious about makin' yourself a success in your profession you're gettin' to be a Queen Midas wantin' everything to turn to gold, an' even a expense item like a rotten old press book to paste up publicity money couldn't buy, you want to write down on a gentleman's account where it don't belong. You give me a pain.'

Because, outa this envelope Roy has addressed to me, there falls like a manor from heaven, a cheque, and this cheque is for a hundred, an' it is signed 'Roy S. Adams', and it has gotta be paid to Rosie Bosanky and no one else. I can't hardly believe it, but there's a note, too.

Dear Miss Bosanky

In the stress of today's happenings I quite forgot that you would, of course, need some money to carry on whatever investigations you are planning on my behalf. I am afraid I am appallingly ignorant of these matters so I am sending you a cheque on account which will put the matter on a business footing, as it were, and you can let we know if the amount should be inadequate for your present requirements.

Yours very truly

Roy S. Adams

Now this is something that shows real class and I get the feeling that I gotta earn this dough. I make up my mind I'll prove this Roy is no murderer, which is something perhaps he knows already, but I'll also prove that he ain't a cuckold either, which is, I think, the way he would like it to be, because I got a dame's intuition that, though this £60,000 p.a. client I have wangled is not so damn prim and proper he has gotta pass by a pair of female legs like they was the seven deadly plagues, so far as Malwa is concerned, it is a case of night an' day you are the one. And that is how I like it.

I am putting the cheque in my bag and thinking I will potter round to the bank to make sure it isn't all a sub-conscious dream an' Roy isn't just some friendly maniac who has a delusion he is the rich Count of Monte Carlo and all I have been seeing isn't a actual fact but, like in a play by amateurs which is called the 'Seven Keys to Baldpate', where there is a heck of a lot of excitement, and then, at the end, it all turns out to be a playactor's dream.

But Brownie ain't a dream, though you could class him as a bit of a nightmare, and Harold the corpse was no hollow mockery so I have a great deal of confidence in this cheque although, already, I know damn well the cheeky devil in the bank will give a clandestine look at me out of the corner of his eye an' wonder how I got it.

I am putting the cheque in my bag, I say, when there is a rap on the door and I sit down an' I grab the phone an' put it to my ear though no one has rung it.

I shout out to 'Come in' and then I talk into the phone in my best voice. 'Thank you, Don Luiz. At the Spanish embassy? Okay. I will be delighted.'

There is no Don Luiz, an' it is only a name that has come to me haphazard from a conversation with a girlfriend who had also gone to a play by Gilbert Sullivan and there is a Don Luiz in it, and although she says there is a lotta good tunes (but a bit old) she cannot make head or tail why it is called 'The Gonorreers'.

I say 'Good bye-ee' into the phone to this phantom of the opera and by this time the knocker has come in.

He is a middle-sized feller with his hair plastered down on each side of a parting you could ride a bike along. His clothes give me the idea that he is wearing them for the first time and they are not accustomed to him. He has little pig eyes and a large smile which I do not like, and he has gold in his teeth which I do not like also. I tell myself that if he has come round to be a client of Rosie Bosanky Investigations he will have to produce evidence that it is worth Rosie Bosanky's time because I cannot fancy myself working in harness with a guy who looks like this, even if he turns out to be Lord Muck.

He puts his stick and gloves and his hat on my desk. His hat is upside down, and he drops his gloves in it an' sits down in a chair I have offered him with my eye while talking to this Spanish spectre, Don Luiz.

When I have put the phone down an' pretended to make a memo on my pad he says, 'You are Mees Bosanky, of course?'

I take it that he is some sort of a foreigner. He smiles and shows all his gold teeth at once an' although I am saying, 'Yes, what can I do for you?' I am thinking how could a girl ever be a wife to a guy like this one who has blown in.

'Mees Bosanky,' he is saying, 'my name is Rudolf Berenski, and I have been reading about you in the papers in connection weeth this so sad affair of the man who has killed his wife.'

This don't make me like the guy any better, and I got some trouble in holding my tongue from making a very strong protest, but I bottle it down to saying, 'You didn't come here to talk about the Adams case, Mr Barenski. I gotta lotta work an' –'

'Oh,' he says, 'but that ees precisely why I have come to see you, Mees Bosanky. That ees, if we can talk confidentially.'

'That all depends,' I say, 'if you come as a client –' I give him the idea that I have got my ears back, which is true.

'Oh, but I do,' he says. 'I am – we, our family, are most anxious.' He takes out his pocket book and unpeels a ten pound note and puts it in front of me. 'Thees ees just a little guarantee of good faith. Yes? To ensure everything ees strictly confidential.'

It has never ever been any trouble to me to make my eyes glitter at the sight of money. I say, 'Well, money talks.' I pick up the tenner and put it in my drawer, and I think I have given a very good facsimile of a girl who would go to a very great length for a ten pound note.

'That ees good,' he says. 'Now we understand each other, Yes?' He looks me over with his little pig eyes and says, 'Eef you will permit me to say so, Mees Bosanky, I am not surprised that Inspector Browne ees so very much your good friend.' Into this title 'good friend' he gets a leer, and he waits to see how I take it.

I take it very well so far as this pig-eyes is concerned. I do a bit of a smirk because I can see he's been readin' between the lines in the papers, or maybe he's been hearin' something that Brownie has boasted about which is not more true than that there was really six Dionne quintuplets. This smirk registers. 'Eet ees a very useful thing to be such a nice-looking girl who ees an investigator and have such close friends in the police.'

I say I agree with him, but sometimes I have ideas above policemen even if they're head coppers. I say I have found this, Mr – er Barenski, that when you boil it all down, a young girl with a good appearance has only one friend in the world an' that is her bank account, because so many evil men are always trying to get the better of her. I have therefore decided to make it my motto in life to sock away for a rainy day because a girl will not always be young and have a surplus of allure.

I pull open the drawer an' take out the ten pound note he has give me and give a little start of surprise. 'Why,' I say, 'I woulda swore you gave me a twenty pound note an' this is only a tenner!'

He likes the way this conversation is going and I am interested right up to my ear-rings wonderin' what this piece of plastered hair has got to do with the affairs of a classy line of goods like my client, Roy.

He takes out his pocket book and releases another ten pounder, but he doesn't pass it over. Instead he tears it in half and he gives me one half and he puts the other half back in his book.

I give him a very savoury smile. 'Fair enough, Rudolf,' I say. 'After all I gotta do something for my money.'

'Eet ees not that I do not trust you, Mees Bosanky,' he says, 'but I am only, shall we say, an agent for my family. I shall be most happy sometime to give you the other half of the note.'

'That suits me,' I say, like I was now greedy for anything he would care to throw me. 'Tell me what you want I should do.'

He shifts his chair closer and looks around over his shoulder. I write on the back of an envelope 'Back in One Hour' and I show it to him. I then stick it on the outside of my office door and lock the door on the inside. He gives a sigh, an' I have the idea that this new client is plenty worried.

He says, 'Mees Bosanky. My family ees a very old, proud family. Eet ees very anxious that eet should not be touched by scandal. And now there ees very great danger that eet may be, shall we say, besmirched.'

'Say it how you like,' I tell him, 'but come to the point.'

'Very well,' he says. 'My family ees connected in a distant way weeth the lady this Mr Adams has killed –'

I interrupt him. 'Just a minute, Rudolf. I don't like the way you keep on sayin' Mr Adams has wiped out that dame. You have to remember that Mr Adams is a client of mine an', even if things do look very black against him, I am not going to admit that everything is the way the police think it.'

I can see he likes this because I have a hunch he is very keen to know just what the police are thinkin' about the little affray at Roy's mansion.

He shrugs his shoulders. 'But, surely, from what I have heard eet ees quite a plain case. A gentleman ees deceived by his wife. He keels her lover, ees eet not? What else could the police think?'

I let out a big sigh. 'You might be right at that, Rudolf,' I tell him, 'but Adams ain't confessed – not yet, anyhow.'

He shrugs again. 'Well, what matter? I do not wish to waste your time, Miss Bosanky. Eet ees nothing to me – to my family – who has killed this nasty man.'

'No?' I say.

'No,' he goes on. 'But we are much concerned to know if this Adams man or whoever eet ees killed the person the police have found dead has not also killed his wife.'

'Malwa?'

'That ees her name – Malwa.'

'But she is not dead?'

'You do not think so?'

'No – at least –'

'You see,' he says with a grin, 'you are not sure. The

police, they are not sure, either. Last night they are asking for information on the air. This morning there ees a message on the radio giving her description. Eet ees plain the police think she has been murdered.'

'Well, Mr Rudolf,' I say, 'suppose she has?'

'I am supposing nothing,' he says. 'My family, however, think eet ees most important to know what steps the police are taking to find her – or her body.'

I don't care for this 'or her body' stuff. The way he says it, too, it has a very Dracula-like tone. I can't help saying, 'I gotta idea which might be wrong an' that is that your family is not so keen on this Malwa.'

He says, 'You are a very shrewd young woman. I may tell you, in confidence, that Malwa ees, shall we call it, the black sheep. The little ewe who has taken the wrong turning. When she was quite a girl she was a constant source of worry to my family. Always they were in fear of some scandal.'

I say, 'You told me she was just a distant connection of your family. Why didn't her more near relations keep her in hand?'

'Unhappily,' he says, 'her parents were engulfed in an earthquake when she was quite a child.'

This matches up with Roy's story of what Malwa has told him.

'Too bad,' I say, 'an' your family looked after her?'

'In a way,' he says. 'They had her placed in charge of some nuns, but, of course, she couldn't stay there forever.'

This also matches up because Roy has told me about these kindly nuns.

Plaster Hair goes on. 'Eet was after she left school that our troubles began – our anxiety started, shall we say? Not that there was anything serious, just girlish peccadilloes and escapades but sufficient to give us unceasing worry. You know what old families are, Mees Bosanky?'

I look at him, an' I find it very hard to find a castle in his background. I can look at Roy, and with my eyes shut, I can see an escutcheon and a family tree. But this new client's

family tree, I bet, wouldn't amount to a aspidastra in a board-
ing-house bathroom. I ain't got much class myself, and well I
know it, but I gotta scent for values, and, if I have to make a
valuation of this Rudolf Barenski, I would only put him on the
lowest rung because there was none under it.

I have read in a volume where, if you took a man, even if
he was a fillum star at a thousand a week, when he was dead
you wouldn't get more than 3/11 for his remains which are
nearly all composed of match heads and water. When I look at
this Rudolf guy, I think you would be lucky if they offered you
two bob the lot, take it or leave it.

But I only think this. I say, 'I quite understand, Mr
Barenski. Go on, *if* you please.'

He goes on. 'There came a time,' he says, 'in Bombay, eet
was, when one of these escapades almost landed her into the
hands of the police. Eet was a most distressing time for the
family. But I was able to use my influence and she was saved.
Just after that she met this Mr Adams and was married very
suddenly and went away with him. We – the family – were
greatly relieved. It was a wonderful thing to know there was
no more responsibility, no more fear of scandal. And, now,
alas, eet looks as if all the old life might be raked up again and
my family involved in more dreadful publicity.'

I say, 'But how will it help the family to know what the
police think an' what they are doing?'

He tells me, 'If she ees not found they will do nothing
because what can they do that the police cannot? If she ees
found they fear she will talk and they will become involved in
all the nasty scandal which ees so much to be deplored. Their
names will be smudged over all the dirty newspaper stories.
They could not face such a thing. No, they will go away somewhere where she cannot reach them.'

The more he talks, the more I don't like this guy. To me
he smells. He has handed me a story I think would be an insult
to my intelligence, even if I was the oldest inhabitant in a
lunacy asylum, and he has laid out a tenner and a half, which

shows he has got something on his mind that is making him damn anxious.

I pick up the half of the ten pound note and look at it, and I put it in the drawer with the full ten pounder. I give a fac-simile of a girl trying to come to a serious conclusion an' at last, I say, 'Listen, Rudolf, I am a girl who likes to talk plain an' to the point. I can understand how anxious an antique fam-ily like yours would be over this unhappy affair. I found the body of this gink in Malwa's bedroom when I was acting for this Adams mug so he could get more evidence for a divorce. But if they hang him, which is a likely event, he won't be any more good as a client for a divorce. He won't care is he a cuckold or ain't he. It won't make no difference. Now, I figure you been readin' them papers today, an' you got it in your bean that I am the head constable's pet girl. You gotta idea that I can lay my head on his manly bosom any time I like and he will tell me all his life's secrets. Well you're goddam right, Rudolf. This is how I see it when I think of the one and a half ten pounds you've give me and the promise you've made. You want I should keep you wise as to what's cookin'.'

I lower my voice a bit. 'Well, why not? What has the damn police ever did for me? Got my father killed off in a gun duel an' give me a testimonial in money, which wouldn't keep me in brassieres let alone a Mae West. And now I gotta work. And I gotta eat, ain't I?

'I don't know why you wanta know what's goin' on an' I don't care. This family stuff may be on the level or it may not. What the heck? I don't care. All I'm interested in is the dough an', if I like to pass on to you what I hear, they can't hang me, can they?'

I can see he's lapping it up. 'No, no,' he says, 'of course not. They would never know in any case – not from me – or the family. I think you are a very wise young lady.' He blinks his little pig's eyes. 'Eet ees understood then. You will keep me advised. Remember eet ees not what the papers print we wish to know. Eet ees what ees *going* to happen.'

I say, 'I get you, Rudolf. But, get this. If it turns out important to you – the things I spill – I trust you to see I get a deal.'

He has got up and is reachin' for his hat an' I think I would
just as soon trust a coupla rattlesnakes with my pet white
mouse; and, again, I think, This guy don't only smell, he
stinks. All at once I find I am going a bit goo-ey.

I shut my mouth an' draw in my breath, but not so he will
notice it, and I know I am right what I am thinking, an' it
may be nothin', or it may be a helluva lot, but this Plaster
Hair, who claims he is a distant relation of Malwa Nawadi, is
throwing off the same nasty odour as was on the head of that
greasy sheik that I came on in a murdered condition at old
Roy's mansion.

---

CHAPTER 7

I don't know whether it is this stink from his hair or it is the idea that he might have a close relationship with the dead sheik, but I feel kinda swooney, so I lug out a bottle, an' he says he don't mind if he do, which gives me time to pull myself together.

While I am pouring he pulls on his right glove in a careless fashion as if he ain't thinking what he is doing, an' this is the hand he takes the glass with. I realise that, whether he has an old family tree or not, he isn't making me a present of his prints.

He says it is nice to have met up with someone he can trust in this matter, which his family has so much next to its bosom. If he gets all the dope about what Brownie has found out an' is going to do, an' what they have brought to the surface about this Malwa and the terrible man who has been murdered, the family will not be unmindful and, in the meantime, he wants to impress upon me that secrecy is the watchword.

He says he will ring up that night about eleven, and I say that will do very well because I have a date that evening with a policeman pal for a private chat and I hope to God my sugar-daddy (which I leave him to guess is old Brownie, the poor dear) will never hear of it.

He laughs at that and says a girl must have some fun, must she not, and, at the same time, has got to be wise in her generation and recognise what side her bread is buttered upon. He goes out with a fixed idea in his mind that I am a dirty little pimp who would sell her gran'ma for a mass of potage.

After he has left I open the window to let the stink out and look at my wristlet watch, an' it is nearly 11.30 o'clock, and then Jeanette Mackie, who I have been expecting, bursts in the door and says, 'Hello, Rosie.'

I don't wait a minute. Before she has time even to ask where's the hoosis I have a one pound note stuck in her fist and some small change and I am saying, 'There's a guy just left here with pig's eyes and a new flash suit. He's got plastered down hair under a bowler hat an' has lavender gloves and a nobbed stick that looks like he ain't used to it. He's imitatin' a gentleman. Tail him up. Tail him all night.'

Jeanette is already being pushed outa the door. She raises her eyebrows. 'All night?'

'Well,' I say, 'nearly all night. Go like hell an' ring me up. If you've lost him when you get down stairs come back.'

She is a girl who is quick on the uptake, is this Mackie wench. Almost while I am talking she is grabbing herself a lift. I think I am a very lucky girl to have such a cobber who can get a idea so fast an' ask only one question. I think, too, I am getting in the money with Roy Stockforth Adams's £100 cheque in my bag an' this Plaster Hair's notes in my drawer.

I put the whisky away where it won't be a temptation to celebrate, though I do not think whisky is a good tonic for young girls taken in unmeasured terms. I put my legs up on my desk and relax. I close my eyes and let myself dream, and, in my fancy, as plain as a parson's nose, I see that seventeen guinea hat in M'lle Fifine's, floating through the air towards me, nearer and nearer.

Work it out for yourself, any of you dames. Yesterday I was just a poor working girl with a name on an office door; today I am a picture in the papers an' with a lotta hooey publicity, which, if you took it to any good editor with a mass of gold in your hands and asked him to put it in his columns, he would kick your backside out of the place; an' this has cost me not a damn penny! Also I have a bank cheque for a hundred, an' a ten pound note beside half a ten-pound note, which is as good as complete. Forget about this half a tenner, an', if you are good at sums, it adds up to one hundred and ten pounds. An' I didn't have it yesterday, did I?

So what? I ring up this Fifine an' I buy the hat, an' wouldn't you?

I ask Mamselle, who I can tell by her parley voo has read about me in the papers, and seen my pictures, to send round the lid by a fast office boy. She giggles in a French fashion and says, 'Oh, Mamselle Rosee, all office boys in these days is fast,' an' I think she is right, an' this goes for their papas, too. She says she will do it, an' I can hear her singing out, '*Ally, ally,*' which is the Paris habit of saying get a move on.

There is a knock at the door and I think perhaps it is Jeanette come back, but it is only the agent for the building. I can see, by the grin on his fat mug he has been reading the papers, too. He says the little office next to mine is vacant on account of a bankrupture, and, after what he has heard, he is sure I will need more space an' a waiting room for my clients.

He says maybe he is bringing coals to Newcastle, but it is simply amazing the number of people nowadays who want some one else watched, and what with the war an' all, he gives his opinion that they will increase an' multiply. For an instance he gives his cousin Ethel who has her husband watched for weeks an' then finds out her old man is having her watched, too. He thinks maybe he will soon have to charge me for a new oilcloth outside in the passage because so many clients will be wearing the old one out.

He is what the medical men would call an incurable optimist, but I think he has said a mouthful whether he believes it or not, because I have made up my mind that I gotta have an assistant. The agent says, 'Yes, Miss Bosanky,' 'No, Miss Bosanky,' 'As you say, Miss Bosanky,' though, when I first see him, he is giving me a cold stare and asking was I sure I could pay the rent.

This assistant I have in mind is Jeanette Mackie, who, by the way she has not come back, I know has got on to Plaster Hair's tail, and, if I know anything, she won't let off till she knows where he eats an' beds an' who his friends is, if he has any, which seems to me it could hardly be.

I want to tell you that this Jeanette is a nice piece of home produce. She is three inches taller and three years older than yours truly, which makes her a possible twenty-two and she is a very refined dame who would always go to the ladies' toilet to hitch her suspenders if there was gentlemen present. Not because she has got nothing to show neither for she is a filly who is very well turned out in a slim way an' has a very change-daily air.

Also she has a refined face which is very pensive, with dark eyes, and her blue-black hair is drawn in a bun on her neck, which is an old fashioned hair-do, you might say, but is very suitable to her. She is also refined in her face make-up and dress because she is one of those dames who can't afford to go hay-wire adorning the old frame but buys everything good so it lasts a long time an' always looks swell an' ladylike.

Besides this she has been to a school where they use only the best English, an' she can spell but not add up too well. I can add up but not spell, so I reckon we should be a good team for a office; besides which we are two hot numbers in our line because I have told her a lot about the dramatic history of life in the raw as learned me by my dad, and, though you would think to look at her she is too much of a lady to take on a job with a rough-house Rosie like me, you got another think comin' because, though she has gotta face like a saint, she has nerves like a steel tractor an' just when you think butter wouldn't melt in her mouth she is just as likely to be spittin' bullets.

This Jeanette also has a very reliable nature as you can see by the way she went tally-ho an' away in pursuit of Rudolf

Whatshisname as soon as I gave her the scent. She has just lost another job because she has got no interest in kissing the boss an' it has given him a inferiority complex to know he is a washout as a Don June.

He says he thinks for both their sakes she'd better go, but, as far as I can see, it is better for his sake than for hers because he will be linin' up as usual for his pay envelope while she will be tryin' to work it out whether she will live longer on a cuppa tea an' one good dinner per day or just eat three spare meals.

As far as I can learn this Jeanette don't kiss any guys at all, and she is not one with an open mind like me whose motto is come one come all if you know what I mean, which is safer than having the torture of finding out that, like the poet says, you have give your heart for a man to tear.

No man is going to tear my heart if I know it, not even this Handsome Clancy who, I bet my high heels, at this very moment, can't keep his eyes on his work for thinkin' what might be going to happen to me at 10.22 p.m. or about.

I am wonderin' how much I ought to pay this Jeanette to be my offsider. I decide I will start her at three pounds ten a week an' give her more any time she is broke and, if Roy Stockforth Adams eludes getting hung, I'm hoping he'll have a lotta friends who will want their wives watched or vice versa, and so I will build up a high class clientelle and, by an' by, Jeanette an' me will take a little visit to New York, U.S.A. This I would like to do because this is the burg, you will remember, where that snake Stalozzi knocked off my pappy, an' I am always hoping one day I will meet this person an' maybe manoeuvre him into a position where it will be a very easy thing to stab him in the back one night, which I bet I could very well do.

I don't think anyone in New York would go into mournin' for him either, because he is such a skunk he would sell his own sister to be a white slave. I think it is more likely they would say, 'Well done, Rosie,' and have one of those processions down Wall Street in which millions of confetti are showered by the population from sixty-storey windows.

I have finished this triumphant march down Wall Street in my mind and am turning to greet the crowd in old Broadway when a kid comes in with the hat from Mamselle Fifine's. I give him a tip an' I can see he is starin' an' starin' at me and then he says, 'I don't suppose, Miss Bosanky, you want an office boy?'

Now this is a thing I think I will have to take on. I like the look of this kid because he is a very earnest kid who has large, round spectacles an' very fair hair an' a hat which is too small for him. He also has a lotta freckles.

I say to him, 'Are you wanting to leave the hat and underclothes business?'

He says, 'Yes, Miss Bosanky. Gee, I think it would be great to work with you. I don't think there's any higher career in life than for a boy to educate himself to find dead bodies and bring the fiends who caused them to the bars of Justice.'

This is a very good speech because it has a strong moral tone, besides which it shows this kid has a lotta enthusiasm. I give him the once over again, an' he don't look like anyone the fillums will steal from me in a few years' time to take the place of Robert Taylor. This is okay by me because with this Jeanette Mackie who, as I told you, is a swell piece, and me with my what-have-yous, there will be quite enough glamour about the place already.

However, I don't say nothing, but I think I will try this kid out a bit more, so I take the lid I have bought out of the box, an' I stand in front of the mirror, and I put it on, an' then I turn round an' look at him and say, 'And what do you think of *that*, Ronald?'

He puts his two hands together like he was in a kind of an ecstasy and shuts his eyes a moment, but at last he says, 'Oh, Miss Bosanky, it's *wonderful*,' the damn little liar, because he don't think it at all. He's wonderin' how any dame outside a madhouse could be seen dead in it. Just the same his remark shows he has tack.

'Think so, Ronald?' I say. 'It's wonderful, is it? And it's also seventeen guineas.'

'Pooh,' he says. 'What's seventeen guineas for a hat if it makes a girl feel like a million dollars?'

I engage this Ronald. I tell him he can start as soon as Mamselle Fifine can let him go and this, I find, is at once because he now lets the cat outa the bag he has been sacked.

I have now got my staff all okay. I leave young Ronald in charge and tell him what to do if Miss Mackie comes back, an' then I tootle off home. I have a bath and a powder-up, and I put on my best sheer silks an' a pair of French panties, which have cost me their weight in gold, and I get into my best shoes and my cutest outfit and, all the time, I haven't looked into the mirror once but done it all by the sense of touch.

Why? Because at last I put on this dream of a hat. I shut my eyes and fix the wardrobe mirror, an' then I open my eyes an' walk right at it just to have the pleasure of meeting me. If I was my worst enemy, I could only say I am a sight for sore eyes.

I cock the seventeen-guinea lid the slinkiest bit, an' I think it is a good thing perhaps for his peace of mind that Handsome Clancy hasn't got a television set, because it is still a long time yet till he has promised he will show me his curios.

I lock up and go downstairs and take a taxi. I think I will go out and cheer up poor old Roy an' see has he talked hisself any nearer the scaffold.

I now put in as evidence a fragment from the diary of Ronald Gaylord. I have given it a good once over before I let it go before the eyes of the printer because this Ronald is a whale for intimate details and, in his boyish delight, he has given a most verbatim description of me which makes it sound I was like one of those so-called Persian gazelles who were whisked out of warm beds on their bridal nights by visiting Jinnies just to please the whims of some Arabian Knight who had lit on a magic lamp an' it had gone to his head if you can call it a head.

November 9

12.10   Engaged by Miss Rosie Bosanky the famous woman

sleuth. [After this comes the part I have knocked back. – R.B.]

12.25   Left in full charge of office.

1.00   Lunch.

1.10   Do a practice shadow of suspicious looking old gentleman who has a look of anxiety. Trail him to lift of new building. Ascend with him to 9th floor. He goes into Men Only. I wait about. He comes out and goes into nearby office. I call in. There is a blonde at a desk. I ask her can she tell me the name of the man who has just come in, because I think it is my Uncle Alick. She says it is Mr Witherspoon, and he is her boss, and his first name is Ferdinand but she calls him 'Spoony'. I make excuse and duck. Still, it was good practice.

2.00   Back from lunch. Read all the newspapers about the Roy Adams case. I think it looks black for this Mr Adams. We will have a very hard job to prove his innocence.

3.00   No one has come in.

4.00   No one has come in. It is not exciting like I expected; not as many people as in the hat shop. Miss Bosanky has left a ten pound note and a half a ten pound note in an unlocked drawer. Have taken their numbers. There is also a sheet headed 'Expense Account for Misplaced Corpse Case' but there is only one item, 'One pair of silk stockings ruined in police car', and even this is crossed out. In the other drawers there are a lot of miscellaneous items I do not think have any bearing on our case. Found a swell collection of pictures of victims in various murder cases in packet marked 'Private'.

4.30   Miss Bosanky has rung up to ask has Miss Mackie called. I say, 'No, she hasn't.' She says, 'Okay Ronnie, you can scram. Put a note on the door to inquire at Home Address.' I say, 'What about the ten pound note in the top right hand drawer?' 'Oh,' she says, 'have you found *them*? You can hide them somewhere safe. What else did you find?'

I tell her I have found the collection of murdered victims which I admired very much. She says, 'You haven't wasted much time, have you? I suppose you are referring to the ones in a packet marked 'Private'.'

I tell her yes, but I have put the photos back and you would never know they have been interfered with.

She says, 'Do you know something, Ronnie? I think you are a

type of marvel I have never till to-day set eyes on. Did you find anything else?'

I tell her nothing important. In the bottom left-hand drawer I have noted one pair of woman's imitation silk bloomers with small hole in left rear; one pair lady's slippers, size 3, with left heel well worn; one box of Glowgirl face powder; also two –'

She interrupts me to say, 'Oh, my God, Ronald, don't go into any more details. Do you know what I think? You are going to be one of the world's A.1 detectives if you can learn to keep your mouth shut.'

I tell her that all I have seen is sacred, and wild horses couldn't make me divulge anything I have come across in the course of my investigation.

She says, 'Atta, boy, Ronald. Now, you scram.'

I ask her isn't there someone she wants me to shadow tonight, but she says no. 'You behave, Ronald,' she tells me, 'an' one day if you are a good boy I'll take you to see the morgue.'

My new boss is a very nice woman.

5.00   I am just leaving the office when a post-office messenger brings a special delivery letter for Miss Bosanky. I sign for same. By holding it up to the light I can see contents are about two pages in length and written in pencil in what I think is a female hand. I decide I will not go home as Miss Bosanky told me but will await any developments which may be revealed by this special letter.

———

CHAPTER 8

While I am tootlin' out to see Roy in the taxi I am feeling pretty good because I have now got not only a new business with a rich client and one bum one, but I have also got a staff and a new hat. I think it is a funny world an' all the people in it are play actors, and none of us know what lines we are going to speak because yesterday this Mamselle Fifine woulda wanted cash on the nail for the lid I am now wearing, but today she don't even send a bill an' says she will be delighted to have me in the shop at any moment.

And if, yesterday, I hadn't put my two legs up on my desk in a mood of despondency and desperate hope, this Roy Stockforth Adams would not have come in, an' I wouldn't have got his cheque; an' I wouldn't have had this Ronald Gaylord for a office boy an' old Plaster Hair wouldn't have emerged from whatever stone he has been lying under, an' I wouldn't have sooled Jeanette on to him, but she would be still looking for a job where the boss wouldn't want to kiss her. Which all goes to show that Shakespeare's plays are right, and, if you could only understand them, they would give you a great moral uplift.

The police wolves are prowling about Roy Adams's mansion, an' they are a bit chary about letting me nose round, but they allow me to ring up Brownie. I purr a bit in a way that sounds it might be promisin' a lot but, when it came to a court of law and he had to answer on oath if the counsel said, 'Tell me the *exact* words the woman used', they would prove to be of a type which is called innocuous, and he would be laughed outa court.

Brownie makes me promise I won't do nothin' I don't tell him about, an' then he gives orders to the coppers they can turn me loose.

First I go an' see poor old Roy who is very well-dressed again with a different suit and a silk tie. When he sees my hat, he can't hardly believe his eyes. He keeps on sayin', 'My hat! My hat!' which it is, too, in a way, when you come to think of it, because it will come out of his cheque.

I go right up to him an' reach my arms up an' pull his old head down, an' I pout my lips, which is a hint anyone could take that he had been granted a lease-lend to go almost to a limit. But I know by the way he kisses me he has got his brain full of this Malwa and wherever can she be.

He has fished up two of his old retainers and got them back at the mansion, an' one is what is called his Man, who is a sort of Dog Friday and looks after his clothes and things and makes sure that he would never commit such a *foe par* as to go out without having a flower in his coat.

The other is a good wholesome old soul who has been a cook for his father before him an' has charge of all the recipes which have been handed down to the third and fourth generation. She is now in the kitchen preparing his midday fodder.

There is a maid coming back soon who is Malwa's offsider, and Roy thinks she might know something and be able to give a private hint where Her Ladyship has gone.

The poor boy is very anxious about his wife because surely, he says, she would have heard it on the radio or someone would have told her, which you would think they would rush to do, too, because I do not know hardly one dame who would have enough repression to stop her saying, 'Oh, my dear, what do you think? A strange man has been found dead in your bed. Your husband wants you to go *straight* home.'

Roy says very serious, 'Do you think Malwa has been

murdered, Rosie?' and he looks so haggard I tell him not on his life, though, between you an' me, I am rattled, too.

He asks me to have a chop with him, and it is served in the upstairs den because the coppers have requested him to be confined in his room till such time as old Brownie can make up his mind will he put the handcuffs on Roy an' have the whole thing finished and done with, or will he think up some other guy to arrest.

I tell Roy that I have got a staff of two good workers already on his case besides me. I ask him does he know a guy called Rudolf Barenski.

He says no, he don't. I tell him he ought to because he is a distant relative of Malwa's.

'Indeed,' he says, just like that. I tell you this Roy would believe anything.

I say, 'Did she ever mention him or any of her relations?'

'No,' he says, 'I rather gathered she had none.'

I look at Malwa's photo on his desk with its quiet, strange expression and eyes like a Mona Lisa, and I think of the blob with the plastered hair an' the walking stick an' the gold teeth, which I hope young Jeanette has, by now, chased to his lair.

If I had been this Roy and someone had said this guy was a relation of this Malwa's, I wouldn't have said, 'Indeed!' No, I would have made a sound which no one, even a college professor, could write down, an' which is a good rich fruity sound I can do very well, but which Jeanette is too much of a lady for, an' if she tries it, it is like a nun who has made a slight mistake.

I give Roy a ball to ball description of this Rudolf. I give it to him so exact that he says he wishes I coulda waited till after lunch, because he didn't have much appetite anyway, and now it has practically dwindled to nil.

I say, 'Now, come, come, you must be a good boy an' eat up your dinner.' I ask him to tell me all he can remember about Malwa that is not purely of a personal and intimate character, but only those bits just before and about the time he married her in this Eastern port. He says again about the kind nuns, and I say, What about the time between when she left the kind nuns and the night you see her on the boat deck?

What has she been doin' an' where has she been, because even in these eastern climes a girl has to eat even if it is only curry and rice or a Bombay duck?

He says, 'Malwa made it plain to me that it was painful for her to talk of her past, an' so, naturally, I didn't.'

Naturally, he didn't! Can you beat it? He has £60,000 p.a., and naturally he didn't!

'You see, Rosie,' he relates, 'I was in love with her like I am still. When you see a lovely rose in your garden, you don't ask it about its past. You know it was a little bud and it blossomed into this beautiful thing and you want to take it and wear it next your heart, always and forever.'

I like this Roy for this speech, an' I wish one day someone will come along an' take Rosie Bosanky the same way an' not be too damn particular about the interval between when she was a little bud an' when she was a full blown flower in the garden of life.

It is a speech, too, with a very romantic sound, which is like one I was made on a dark night by an insurance broker. 'Look at the stars, Rosie. They are like the windows of angels' bedrooms. If you watch you see them popping into bed and switchin' off the light.'

I suppose I have a trained mind, and I always want to analyse things, and that is inclined to take the romance out of life, because I watched these little heavenly bedrooms for a while, an' I got the idea if the angels were switchin' off the lights, they were every now an' again switchin' them on again for one thing or another.

To get back to Roy. I ask him, 'You married her and didn't know anything but her name was Malwa Nawadi and her parents has been associated with an earthquake?'

'Yes,' he says.

'And I suppose,' I say, 'she didn't know anything about you

either? She wouldn't know by any chance you had £60,000 p.a.? I suppose you didn't tell her?'

'No,' he says, 'of course not. Why should I?'

He looks a little hurt. Now, he is a nice guy but, I tell you, this boy is a museum piece. I can tell now it is a good thing I have got Jeanette Mackie for an offsider because she is the sort of dame who would understand this class business to the bitter dregs, an' miles better than me, who has a very dirty mind about wenches who have been blossoming unseen an' then spring up from behind earthquakes an' marry a man with £60,000 p.a..

I think perhaps this Malwa has class in the same blood test as Roy and wouldn't bother her beautiful head whether he was a millionaire or a bank clerk who has won a prize for a boat cruise; and then I remember those amounts of money he has told me about that his wife asks him for but which she don't use to dress herself up with and which is not to send to any aged parents because they will not require same on account of their calamity.

Roy can't remember the amounts – not all of 'em, anyway, but he has been payin' 'em for a coupla years, and it was about the time he begins this payout that something has come between him and his wife.

He calls it by a word 'indefinable', but he means it is something like something is wrong only you can't find out what the hell it is an' who, if any, is to blame. This is a kind of thing which is most likely to occur between people who has class while, if they are like me, they would say things out loud and have a damn good row an' it would be all over in a cuddle an' squeeze an' don't you think it's time we should go to bed.

I ask Roy not to say anything about this Rudolf the Smelly, and he promises he won't, not even to Handsome Clancy if he comes in. I warn him against this Clancy devil, but I don't tell him I have a date for a *tate-a-tate* of a personal nature with this same snake I have told him I wouldn't touch with a forty-foot pole, because it would be what is termed a anomaly, and I can't even pretend, when I think of that Clancy bird's smudgy eyes, that I am going to meet him and just discuss whether you should nationalise the coalminers or hand the whole thing over to the government.

Roy's Dog Friday emerges and says that the maid Malwa had is now in the mansion, an' I go out an' see her. The name of this maid is Felicity, an' she is a trim piece. I ask her to show me Malwa's wardrobe and will she know which clothes she has took with her and how many, an' she says she will be delighted.

Well, we take a peek, an' I will say this for Roy, it is like I expected and then some. He has bought this Malwa with his unbounded cheque book an assortment of uppers an' lowers an' over alls that is like a dream from the Arabian Nights only it would have to be set in a very up-to-date and chic salon of a Paris fashion.

There is so many of this and that it might be the modern home of an up-to-date King Solomon who wanted his wives to do him proud, an' hang the expense. Outa the corner of my eye I get a load of this Felicity who is modelled on a chic style, and I bet, on her nights off, she has taken many a little loan of some of these knick-knacks, because even if Malwa was a chancellor in an exchequer she could never remember all she has in this wardrobe.

But Felicity has got 'em all off pat and her furs and things beside, and she tells me that the only things missing is the suit Malwa wore when she left, an' which the police have already got a description of, an' a coupla other simple frocks. I ask her about the underthings Malwa has took, an' she gives a sniff an' says, considering all she had to pick from, she would consider them to err on the side of a plain an' unvarnished respectability. Malwa has told this Felicity that she just wants to get away from things, but where she is going to get away from them she hasn't said.

I get from this information the idea that the odious letter Roy has received from an unknown friend is more phoney than ever, because, put yourself in the place of a dame who was about to run footloose with some wayward sheik – a dame, mind you, who has a warehouse full of lingerie like is now piled before me in Malwa's boudoir – would you dash off with just a few of those things you could aptly describe as serviceable?

I further learn from Felicity that Brownie's hounds has shown her and all the old retainers a photo of the gent who has been murdered, an' none of them has ever seen him before. I leave her to carry on the flirtation she has begun with a young copper on the lower floor.

I go back to Roy, and I inform him I cannot prove it, but I bet all I know an' more he is not a cuckold, which cheers him up no end to see what a faith I have in Malwa although, if you ask me, it is a very funny thing for me to be telling him this because, when I first took up his case, that was the thing I expected I was going to prove up to the neck.

Brownie has been at Roy with a small toothcomb, rakin' him for information, tryin' to make him admit he knows this oily deceased sheik, but Roy says how can he admit such a claim when he don't know him from Mickey Mouse. I gather old Brownie has gone off in such a state of mind he don't know whether he oughta keep on waiting till the radio finds Malwa or start digging in Roy's garden for the body.

I get Brownie on the phone, an', like I promise, I tell him what I have deducted since I came into Roy's mansion. I tell him about the almost dowdy things Malwa has gone off with, and he says, 'So what?' So I have to be very patient because, after all, he is just a man and has a very queer outlook, which you might say is almost blind when it comes to things which any dame would see at a glance. I explain in words he can understand.

I say, 'Now, supposin' you an' me was goin' to have a meeting – you know, Brownie, clandestine, and you had a pair of long underpants with a darn in the seat, and you had still another pair which had a little bit of blue edging and was fitted snug into the figure like an advertisement for Men Only in *Esquire* which would you choose?'

He says, 'I get you, Rosie, and it's a point well taken, and someday soon I would like to go into the details more close.'

He's in the mood now to agree to what I want, and I ask him will he do a little favour for me? There is a young Greek I have met in a personal way who is staying at a hotel not too far away. I kid to Brownie this Greek has been playin' up with a lady who is the wife of a new client I have got. My client, I say, has found out he is a very hot member and thinks he has a record longer than your arm but it is only second-hand information, an' it may not be true.

I ask Brownie will he send two men along to see this Greek at eleven next morning prompt an' find is he anyone they have on their books, because, if he really is a guy with a record, he can give it to me, an' I will give it to this client of mine, an' he will give it to his wife, an' she will get such a shock to find she has been standin' on the very brink of a moral precipice that she will go back to her husband an' be forever thankful to him that she has been saved from taking a false step.

He says he can do it because he always likes anything with a moral tone, and the men will be there at eleven o'clock on the dot.

I am very sorry for this young Greek in a way because apart from an Eastern nature which is prone to hot-bloodedness he has really made no more advances to me than to tell me a limerick about a Turk in a harem who was opening a fresh tin of women, an' one of the dames says she supposes it would mean a 'new Bosphorus'. It is a joke, he tells me, about a river in Turkey but, if you ask me, it seems more like a joke on the women this Turk has employed to be bandied about from harem to harem.

I think, though, it will not do this Greek any harm really to have two coppers call on him and ask him has he been a good boy. Maybe it will be a warning to him to go straight, and I will have killed two birds with one stone, because my only idea is to provide something which I can pass on to old Rudolf, the Plaster Hair, when he rings up, to show I am *aw fay* with the movements of the police in advance an' know every little thing they are hoping to find out about this Misplaced Corpse case.

After all, Rudolf has been good enough to pay me a ten-pound note, and I reckon it is up to me to give him a run for his money and, perhaps, put him in a mood to send me the other half of the second tenner.

I go back to the office, and Ronald Gaylord has not scrammed because there is a special delivery letter come in, an' he has been tearin' his conscience whether he should open it or not. I think he may be a stickybeak, but that is what good little detectives are made out of, and, when you boil it down, it is a good *tray*. But I will tell him the bottom left-hand drawer is sacred to me only an' never to be opened until my eyes are closed in final death.

This special delivery note is from Jeanette Mackie. It says:

Dear Rosie

The gentleman dodged about a great deal. Obviously, he had no desire to advertise his address. I did not lose him, however, till an hour and a half ago when he went into a tobacconist's at 181 Walgrove Street.

I took a window seat in a cafe opposite and waited for the best part of an hour. When he did not come out I walked across the road and went into the shop. It seemed the only thing to do because he certainly had not left it. I thought he must either know the people in the shop very well or it was his business. And he wouldn't know me!

There was a girl behind the counter but no one else was in the shop. It looked like one of those lock up shops because there was no stairway leading to any upper floor. There was, however, a back door at the top of a few steps and I realised that our man must have gone that way.

I asked for some cigarettes and had a word or two with the girl. After a while I asked her would she mind allowing me to use the lavatory.

I thought for a moment she was going to make some excuse, but she said, 'All right, up the steps. It's not classy. Don't be long, because men come in sometimes – customers – and want to go there.' I thanked her and hopped up the steps and went through the back door.

If you knew this Jeanette you would know that she is not telling you this inside story of her life for nothin'. She goes on:

Outside there was the lavatory which stood by itself, two of its walls adjoining the walls of the buildings alongside. They were all of stone and brick and there were no windows. In a corner next to the lavatory was a water tap. I went into the lavatory and, so that you will understand, I have drawn a little plan.

It is the first plan of a hoojakapippy I have seen, an' it won't draw any first prize at an architects' convention, but it tells me all I want to know. You gotta imagine yourself opening the door and going in an' the first thing you notice is that the door opens from right to left and the old sit-me-down is on your right, which is a hell of a idea and would drive a W.C.T.U. crazy because anyone might forget to lock a door and then anyone else might barge in an' there you are for the public gaze.

In her ladylike way Jeanette gets on to this queer architecture right away and stickybeaks till she finds that the door of this joint has been took off its hinges at some time an' altered round so you can't blame the first architect, who had a good moral outlook, but have to pin this social crime on some other heel who, for his own dark purpose, has had the door shifted round. Jeanette says there is no doubt about it because she can see the marks where the old hinges has been moved from.

This is how she goes on:

I thought this rather strange and sat down to think. The man never came out of the front door of the tobacconist's. If he went out the back door he would be in this cul-de-sac surrounded by high walls. If he came into this lavatory where did he go then?

I coulda told her one place he coulda gone so far as I was

concerned, but Jeanette doesn't know this guy to talk to, and she wouldn't have such morbid ideas anyway.

She carries on:

Right in front of me – that is, on the wall that would be behind the door when it was wide open, is a big calendar – the biggest I have ever seen, like the ones they use in shipping offices sometimes; and it is mounted on a piece of wood that has been plugged into the wall. It made me curious.

I can picture this prim Jane sitting there feeling curious. And wouldn't you in this Katzenjammer hoosis with the door the wrong way round and a calendar fit for a giant stuck on the wall like it was to remind you that time marches on an' you can't stay put for ever and a day?

And mind you, she has got in her head, too, the fact that Plaster Hair has made a get away through this joint *somehow*, but how?

I give you Jeanette Mackie again.

I thought it very strange to have such a large calendar and have it mounted like that, and I took a close look at the plugs. I am almost sure they are dummies and that the mounted calendar is really a door that opens in some way and is hiding an opening at the back.

I was just about to try a quick experiment when I heard the door outside – the one leading to the shop – open. The girl who served me cigarettes called, 'Everything all right?' So I had to come out.

I thanked her and said something about being glad the rain had eased off and worked the conversation round till she told me she didn't go off duty till five. Then I told her I didn't know this part of the city very well and asked her how I would get to Crowborough Street.

She gave me the number of the bus and told me where to wait and I walked down the street. I saw her standing at the door and she watched me get on the bus, but I am sure she did not suspect anything.

I feel sure, too, because you have gotta know this Jeanette Mackie to appreciate how much a lady she looks. I can see her putting on this act and getting away with it very well an' no questions asked an' no suspicions aroused. I tell myself I am very lucky to have an offsider who can be so refined in such a delicate situation because I know that, if I was to carry on like Jeanette, this tom in the tobacconist's woulda took one peek at me an' told me there wasn't one an' she had always to time it or dash into some friendly neighbour's in an emergency.

Jeanette writes:

I am writing this from a post-office. I telephoned you but got a shock because a man spoke. He sounded screwy as if he was putting on a deep voice and he said he was Mr Gaylord and took charge in your absence. I knew you had no man working for you so I played dumb and sent this instead.

I bet she will get a shock when she finds that this Mr Gaylord, who has been doing a facsimile of Paul Robeson, is Ronnie the office boy; but it shows this lad has got the initiative spirit, and I shoulda told her he was on the staff. But, no, I shouldn't, because, when I sent her to chase Rudolf the Smelly, Ronald Gaylord was not yet on the horizon with my new hat.

I start thinkin' I will not reveal the price of this hat to Jeanette because she has got a Scotch flavour in her make up that is prone to think, if you paid seventeen guineas for a mere hat, you are on a moral slippery dip.

Jeanette finishes up:

A little after five o'clock I shall return and look round again. I'll have tea in the cafe opposite, and, if the gentleman in the bowler appears, I will follow on. If the girl is not in the shop and there's another one in her place I'll try and get into that little outside place once more and try and find out about the door behind the calendar because I am sure as eggs, Rosie, your man went clean through that wall.

I think things are beginning to move. This Plaster Hair has definitely got something to hide, and I have an intuition that he has got something to do with poor old Roy's tragedy, and, in any case, look at it as you will, even Ripley would say, there is something fishy about a man who goes into a hoosis an' never emerges.

But, if he has got something to do with the corpse Harold (so-called) I wonder why he has taken such a chance on coming to see me with his dirty bribery an' corruption. Well, maybe, there is some reason he just *has* to. I don't know; but I got Jeanette's word that he has been very careful to see that no one follows him to his home address, an' now he has walked into a tobacconist's an' gone out into a cul-de-sac and done a vanishing act in a lavatory which is a kinda conduct I bet you would never find in a thousand years among real classy old families.

Therefore, now more than ever before, I do not believe this family story he has given me. At the same time I do not think that Rudolf would have enough guts to stick a knife into another guy unless he was asleep. I think he is a guy with a mean streak who would sell you for tuppence if it was to save his own skin.

'Unless he was asleep!' Ain't that just what Brownie said with reference to my client Roy? He mighta killed this oily sheik when he was in the arms of Morphia!

Ronald Gaylord's eyes are nearly jumping through his specs because I haven't noticed that when I put the first sheet of Jeanette's letter down, he picked it up and read it as a matter of course, and he has now finished the second. He sees that I got something to think about, and he is dyin' to be in on it.

I ask him does he mind doing a job instead of scranning home, and he says would I lead him to it?

'Is it about the murder, Miss Bosanky?' he asks.

I tell him it is and it is pretty important but, on account that it is not generally known he is workin' on the case, there is no immediate need for a false beard. He says he can see that, too.

I tell him I'm going to trust him not to do anything silly or talk his head off.

'Gee, Miss Bosanky,' he says, he's so enthusiastic, 'you could trust me with me britches off.'

It is not a nice way for a young lad to talk in front of a lady, but he says it quite impersonal and, after all, it is only what is called a colloquilism which means it don't mean a damn thing, an' it is only his way of saying he is with me a hundred per cent. cross his heart an' may he be blistered in hell before wild horses could drag one word outa him. He would also be as secret as the grave.

I tell him he better be because, at this moment, a man's life may depend on his silence. He gets that and likes it. He is very keen, this freckled kid with a too-small hat. I think he is an ugly duckling replica of Rosie Bosanky when she was his age, and I bet my old pappy woulda showed him the ropes like I made up my mind I am going to do.

I tell him I will henceforth call him Operator No. 2.

He says it is okay with him.

'No,' I say, 'I will call you Operator 2X.'

He likes this even better. I tell him to scran round to 181 Walgrove Street an', if he doesn't know where it is, don't ask no one. Just find out. He says he has got a map an' it has got pin-pricks on it showing locations he thinks are suitable for crimes. He hopes, I bet, this Walgrove Street has got a pin prick.

'When you get there,' I say, 'it will be a tobacconist's, as you have already read in my letter; but you don't go in. You don't look as if you were even thinkin' of going in. You must wear an air as if this 181 Walgrove St don't mean a thing in your young life which, at the moment, it don't.'

I tell him this because he is so damn keen I think he might try something on his own account which would make the girl, or whoever was in the shop, a wake-up.

He says, 'Oh!' and he is a bit disappointed.

'But,' I go on, 'I wanta know what is the building along-side it and both sides of it and at the back of it and also on top of it and at the back of the buildings which is alongside it. Get me?'

It sounds like one of them questions you put to the Quiz Kids an' you got ten seconds to find a result, but he gets what I mean practically instantaneous. I tell you the more I think about this Ronald Gaylord the more I know why he has so small a lid, and the more proud I am of Rosie Bosanky for bein' such a sensible Jane as to buy a seventeen-guinea hat which will pay a dividend like finding this young youth.

Operator 2X has got his hand on the doorknob, and I say, 'I want all the dope an' list of all the tenants an' what they are, but I gotta have them by half past seven. If you can't get 'em all bring what you can by then, but no later.'

He says, 'Where shall I report, chief?' an' I tell him at my flat address an' be sure it is not after seven thirty. I have to tie him down because this is half an hour before I am to meet this Clancy devil for a *tate-a-tate* about his memoirs.

Suddenly Ronald finds he has got to make a phone call, and he grabs it up, and, while he is dialling, he tells me that it is to his home because on account of not taking much interest in the hat business it has been his custom to get home even before knock-off time.

I jot the number I have seen him dial on to my pad, because it will be useful in case this Operator 2X gets hisself bumped off in some affray with dope runners or ambitious young men who want to get an uninvited entry into a bank, and I have to break the news.

Ronald gets his home an' he says all in a rush, 'That you, mum? I gotta new job. It's a honey, mum. I gotta work late. Don't worry, mum,' and before they have got their breath at the other end he has rung off which is a very good way to put a stop to any arguments for or against. He makes a dash for the door. He sings out to me, 'I'll be seein' ya. Seven thirty. Good bye-ee,' an' he's gone.

It is the fastest thing I seen since the long-ago day I took up the phone an' someone had rung dad to tell him a nephew had pushed an uncle off a high building three streets away an' the mangled body is lying in the gutter. I beat the old man to X marks the spot by fifty seconds.

When Ronnie has gone I think I will ring up Roy and tell him his prospects of bein' hung are not so good. Then I think I won't because I don't want him to have any false hopes, and I think he is so damn sure he didn't do it, even in a dream, that he has never thought it might come to such a pass that, one mornin' early, he would have to have his hair cut and not even give a tip an' walk out on to a scaffold an' be turned off.

This picture which comes into my mind of poor Roy with a rope on instead of the nice cravat he has on this afternoon, and which musta cost a pound if it cost a penny, makes me feel sad, and, like the travellin' fillum star Kilpatrick, I bid a reluctant farewell to my office with this thought in my heart that never more will scaffolds be filled by innocent guys but only by such vermin as that snake Stalozzi who shot my pappy over in New York.

I tootle off home, and the rain looks like it might pay a return any minute. There is a thundery feel in the air, and I peel off an' put on a warm wrap and have a lay down on my little bed. I am very well satisfied I can come home like this and rest the old frame while I have two good an' faithful operators hot on the job, an' I think, too, as I lie on my back, I have never in my life seen such God-awful wallpaper as is in this flat, and, now I have got a business and a staff and a double office an' a new hat an' it looks like there is a fair chance Roy is not going to be hung, I ought to take time off and look round for a apartment that has got more class.

I have dozed off a bit while I am picturin' in my mind something with a good thick carpet an' figurin' what sort of wallpaper would go with a girl with red hair, when there is a knock at the door, and I think it is the lady caretaker or maybe Jeanette. I sing out, 'Come in,' an' Ronald Gaylord emerges.

If he notices I am doin' a startled faun act he doesn't show it. I tell you this Ronald is as impervious as a plaster saint, an' while I am busy pulling my negligee into a more modest arrangement he has plonked himself down on my bed and fished out a notebook from his pocket.

I lean over his shoulder, an' I can see he has got the dope which I put him on to collect. It is all set out under a general heading:

OPERATOR 2X

CASE OF THE M.T.B.

I know what this M.T.B. stands for because I have been a kid myself an' have had all the symptoms which this Ronald is now revealing in such quantities. I know it stands for Mysterious Tobacconist Shop.

We sit on the bed together and go through this dope he has brought, and a lot of it is the deadly routine stuff that my pappy used to moan about – the stuff you gotta weed out till you come to the core. When I have weeded with this bright Gaylord kid, and he has told me what he has seen while pre-tendin' he has a message to deliver to some guy in the buildin' by a name no one has ever heard of, I can see he has a very good head on him for this kind of investigating.

He discovers there are some good-natured guys who think it is a bit hot for the poor little basket to be sent lookin' for someone at this hour of the evening when all good unionists are at home or at the pictures an' they help him try an' find this unknown feller to who he has to deliver his phantom message.

There is one joint he knocks at the door of, and, when no one answers, he tries the door, and it opens an' he puts his head in, and he says it looks like a sorta anteroom like it might be for a dentist, only it would have to be a dentist with swell ideas who would give his patients red plush to wait on before he said he was ready to drill the life out of 'em.

There is no one in this room, which is on a second floor of a building next to the tobacconist shop I told you about, an' there is no lift coming up to it so Ronald has had to walk the distance. He says you couldn't get into any other part of this floor unless you went through the red plush ante-room.

I have an intuition about this room, and I ask him to tell me some more. This boy has his head screwed on correct because he tells it to me so I can see it like I was looking into the mirror of life. I think this boy, if he doesn't grow up and get hisself shot in the course of business, is very likely to become a author and maybe write fillums and have his name up just after the lion roars along with the artist who made Joan Crawford's frocks.

This room has some pictures on the walls, and, though they are not exactly in the class of the little boy feeding a swan, there is one of a swan who is with a piece called Lida, an' it has a title, 'Lida and the Swan', but Ronnie, bless him, says this Lida is not suitably dressed for a visit even by a swan with a long neck.

There is a door in the room besides the one Ronald Gayford is stickybeaking through, and this door has a picture on it which is of a dame sitting on some green grass, and it is called 'Innocence', and it is a thing Operator 2X has never before seen because he has a old fashioned idea that a picture is a thing you hang on a wall to hide a dirty mark an', if you gotta have something on a door, it is a hook you can hitch your hat to or a wet overcoat.

I tell you this boy has gotta nerve. He says he goes over to the other door, pretendin' he is goin' to knock, if someone should pop out sudden an', while he is there, he lifts up this Innocence picture an', behind it, is a little opening like they have in the cells in all good gaols, only, Ronald says, this opening is shut.

He is tryin' to make up his mind whether he will knock when the door opens suddenly an' a man comes out. I want to get this all in the right order because it is eating into my mind that this room with the posh plush furniture and the picture on the door has got a link up with what Jeanette Mackie has reported.

There is a technique used in both cases which is similar, an' that is that in the ante-room discovered by Ronald the little opening in the door is covered by a picture, an' the door in the old hoosis made famous by Jeanette, at the back of the tobacconist's, is covered by a calendar.

I ask Ronald what sort of a man this is, an' he says he is this sort of a man. He has a hat with a wide band which is dipped over his forehead and it is a pearl grey colour. He has also a pearl grey suit on with a striped soft collar and a magenta tie in which he has got a pin which is like a horseshoe and it has got in it three small diamonds.

He has got a breast-pocket handkerchief which is the same colour as his tie, and his trousers has a good crease an' wrinkles at the top of each leg, like those some guys wear an' don't have to use braces which I would say was a very good convenience.

He has tan boots that have a fresh polish, and he has hands which have very long fingers, and, on the middle one of the left hand is a gold ring with a ruby, and on this hand at least, because Ronald says he didn't have time to see everything, this guy has little bristles of black hairs on the knuckles.

He also has a face the colour of which, Ronald says, is like dough, and he has a longish upper lip, which has a black moustache parted in the middle, an' his eyes have pupils which are like black shoe buttons only twice as hard.

I have a very clear picture of this guy. While Ronald tells it not exactly plain in the way I have put it down, but with a lotta boyish adjectives an' excitement in between, I can see he has a very poor opinion of this man he has met in the plush room. I think he can already see, in the eye of his mind, the prisoner being walked with slow music from a death-cell, while His Majesty the King himself is waiting in an ante-room, ready to pin a medal on him, Ronald Gaylord, the minute the doctor has pronounced life extink.

_____

CHAPTER 9

Something gets me while the boy is spilling this life-like portrait. It is a funny feeling, and I don't know at first whether it is indigestion or intuition. I make him tell the description over again and then I know it is not indigestion.

I say, 'Go on, Ronnie, boy,' and he goes on. He relates how the guy asks him in a hard voice what he wants and how he got there. He says he walked up the stairs because a man somewhere down below told him he might find up there the guy he is lookin' for. The man asks him what's the name of the guy for who he has got the message, an' he says it is Mr Alfred Thomson, and then the man asks him his own name an' where he works an' he says it's Robinson and he works at a joint where there is about three thousand employees and I wouldn't be surprised a coupla dozen Robinsons. The man then tells him to get to hell out of here which he does.

I sit thinkin,' and, by and by, when I keep on sayin' nothin', Ronnie asks in a sorta voice he might be goin' to cry, 'Ain't I done a good job, Miss Bosanky?'

I turn my gaze on the poor kid an' he has gotta lot of anxiety in his eyes, so I put my arm round him an' I give him a kiss on his freckles an' I say, 'You betcha life, Sherlock. You know somethin'?' I ask him, 'I reckon I'm goin' to remember this job you've done, Operator 2X, all my born days. I reckon there was a Divine Faith watching down on me when Mamselle Fifine sent you round to deliver my new hat.'

An' that brings me to the point of rememberin' I have gotta date with Handsome Clancy to eat spaghetti an' hear his north-west mounted memoirs, so I tell Ronnie he's gotta raise already an' he scrans with a grin over his chops like a mother cat which has done a encore with quintuplets.

I begin to dress myself from the skin out in a way I think will make me worthy to wear a hat like I now got for the first time in my life, an' to get ready for this *rondezvoo* with Handsome of the Smudgy Eyes.

This Handsome has got such a fillum actor expression he would give any girl something to live up to, because I am betting, when I take his arm tonight, he will not be in his uniform but will be dolled up like he was Robert Taylor in an evening dress with tails an' all like he was off to some weddin' but not his own, because I can read his mind like a book, an' he is a resemblance to a untamed stallion frisking out on the wild open spaces playing with fire in a bold haphazard way, tossing his head and laughing, laughing careless like, defying the laws of gravity with his sunny smile, unwilling to bend the knee and submit to the altar.

But, somehow, as I am dressin', I find there is a funny feelin' got possession of me, an' I think of all the things I been eatin' an' all the things I been doin' an' what date it is to see if I can find a reason why, all at once, even this new hat I got don't seem to have such a kick after all; an' why, when I oughta be feeling like I am a young an' innocent girl faring forth with flowers in her hair to meet a lover I am suddenly not thinkin' about faring forth, or waiting swains, or keepin' a tryst but I gotta feeling which I can't tell is it my stomach or my heart, or is it only my head.

I sit down on the bed an' in the silence of my room I think over what these old and faithful servants, Jeanette an' Ronald, have found out, an' I know then what is the matter with me. I have given birth to a mission in life.

I know now that, from this moment on, Rosie Bosanky has gotta purpose which cannot be delayed, and for tonight anyway, she is a changed woman which is bad luck for this Handsome Clancy, an' I bet, if he knew, he'd be saying Hell an' Damnation.

I keep on sittin' on the bed with Ronnie's notebook which he has left, an' I concentrate all I know on this building in which he has seen the guy in the grey suit with a ruby ring an' hair on his knuckles. I take out from my bag the note which Jeanette Mackie has sent me concernin' what is at the back of the tobacconist's.

When I have got through concentratin', I have a plan in my mind which, it seems to me, will get this Handsome Clancy more upset still because I gotta ring him up an' tell him it's a blue duck. But I am a good-natured dame when it comes to birds who have set their minds on a thing, because I do not have to throw boquets at myself to know that I have the look of a *femme* who a man sets his mind on very easy an' from who he has great hopes. I know it must be lika blow in the face to get a message that all his optimism has been shattered because it is all off for tonight an' I can't meet him.

I ring up Clancy an' tell him, an' just like I expected, I can hear him say Hell an' Damnation, but I tell him the night is but a pup an' there must be a whole string of good telephone numbers he could ring up, an' what the heck? A girl who is blonde or brunette or a red head like me, they is all the same under the skin, an', besides which I bet there are plenty who do not know life in the raw like it has been taught me by my pappy an' who would have a more intense desire to improve their minds an' listen to his memoirs and have him show them his curios.

I bet this is true, too, an' I think it is a bit wistful that I have to give up *la moor* all because of some dirty crook. I think it woulda been a night which a girl could write down on the tablets of memory, an' it would do her a bit of good in her old age, like this Nina Lenclose who was a French bit and was chased all through the palaces of Europe even after she was fifty and then sat down an' wrote a Decameron about the gay life of her times as related by a number of young gentlemen under a tree while a plague was blazing.

I allow myself a little dream about what mighta been with this Fancy Clancy I have laid on one side. I think, even if he has learned his experience in the cold wastes of the frozen north with those mounties, you only got to look at his smudgy eyes to know if he kissed a dame it would be a sell out an' like it was the whole French foreign legion back from some hot desert on weekend leave.

I give a big sigh an' then I step outa my bit of French fluff an' I climb into a pair of bloomers which woulda won a word of praise from the matron of a Temperance Hotel. I strap my favourite pistol to my right leg in a very cute way my dad has taught me so I can walk like there was nothing there any more than a garter.

I then put on an old skirt which is long in the hem an' a knockabout blouse. I smother up my hair with a scarf that is not too flagrant in the way of colour. It is now coming on to thunder an' there is a pretty show of lightnin' with some quick follow-ups of loud cracks, an' it looks like it is going to be a good night for Handsome Clancy if he has got on to any of them telephone dates, because it is not a state of weather when a dame can keep on walking indefinitely, an' I have found out from my experience that a flash of lightnin' an' a loud clap of thunder comin' close together is as good an excuse almost as even a Big Dipper or a Tumble Bug in a Luna Park for a girl to grab hold of a sheik and then what.

My window has a nice view of the blank wall of the next door building. I take a peek an' I know it is rainin' because I can hear the water dripping down from above where the gutter leaks. It is now near quarter past eight o'clock an' there is no word from Jeanette Mackie.

I remember what she has said about takin' another shot at that old hoosis with the phoney door an' I don't like it at all. I don't like it because this Jeanette is a dame who has got the pluck of a bull-terrier dog who, once it has got hold of something, will not let go until you have unlocked its jaws.

I think this tobacconist's backyard is not a nice place for a ladylike piece, such as Jeanette is, to be in, because, even for a young girl to be within a hundred miles of a lousy heel like the one I think young Ronald Gaylord has met up with, not to speak of my old friend Plaster Hair, is like walking in your bare toes in a den of deadly rattlesnakes only six times worse. And no Jane is going on the road to Bonus Airs if Rosa Bosanky can hold up the traffic.

I put on a raincoat, and, in the pocket of this, I slip a very handy little revolver which is one with which I fired a competition with my dad as to who could hit a ace of diamonds most times at twenty paces. I then write a little note, an' all it has got on it is the name of a street and a coupla numbers. I put it in a envelope and address it to old Brownie and leave it on my dressing table, because I know, if tomorrow anything has happened to me of a adverse character, he will be the first one to call round with flowers for my funeral and asking a helluva lotta questions as to how I come to pass out so abruptly.

So once more like the Kilpatrick travelogue, I say a reluctant farewell to my seventeen guinea hat an' my special perfume and I step out into the bleak street, an' I wonder what poor Roy would say if he could see me now.

I think he would sit down an' write me another expense cheque, an' I wish he could have television in his home-made prison.

I walk a bit then take a taxi and tell the driver to go to a cinema which is in the district to where Jeanette has tailed Rudolf the Smelly. The grand duke, who is a commissionaire there, opens the taxi door, but I do not try any Betty Grable way of getting out, but ease out nice an' respectable like I was a girl who would only take a taxi on a wet night and would balance the expense even then by going in the cheap seats at the pictures.

The commissionaire is a good lookin' six footer with a nice fair moustache, an' I think it is a far cry from the Russian steppes to the steps of a movie house. He has a big pull by havin' a lotta blue uniform decorated with gold braid which gives an imposing effect, but I gotta be careful to remember he may not even be a Grand Duke let alone a Russian, and, also, when he is not in this gay uniform, he may have an appearance in the vicinity of a dope. And, then I think, What the heck? He isn't lookin' at me anyhow!

You see, I got so used to guys makin' a quick approach I'm always on the *Quay Vive* but, tonight, I have forgot that I am not my usual self but a drab Jane in a bandana wrap-round for a headpiece an' a mackintosh with a gun in the pocket, which I suppose is enough to give any guy the idea that a dame is not worth a second look.

I wait a while in the cinema lobby like I had a date but it is a blue duck, an' then I scran. It is drizzling with rain an' the thunder is still rattling round but not so bad.

I have a good idea where this tobacconist's place might be, an' I make tracks, but on the way I put in a call from a public phone to the place where Jeanette boards.

I get the news, 'No, she ain't in an' she ain't been in since before lunch and she ain't left no messages for nobody.' I then ring back to the apartment where I live, and it is the same there too. I spend a bit more an' I get old Brownie an' I ask him does he know a gambling joint or what have you in Walgrove Street an' I think the number is about 180 or so.

He says yes he does. It is run by a chap named Sidoli, but it is on the level an' they have never had any complaints but they are keepin' an eye on him. I say thanks and ring off before he can ask any questions, an' I bet he's mad.

I then carry on towards this tobacconist's an' it is starting to rain harder. When I get near the joint there is a big crack of thunder an' the rain starts coming down in buckets. Everybody has gone for shelter, I guess, because I don't see anybody. The tobacconist's is closed and there is no light.

I stand in the doorway like I was sheltering from the rain and take a squiz up an' down the street. There is no one. It is pretty dark in this doorway, but I have a small torch. I see there is no padlock like you'd think would be put on a lock-up shop an' the lock that *is* there I make short work of. It is a job that woulda made old Roy open his eyes, I bet, because I get it open an' leave it in such good order that it is like the old saying love laughs at locksmiths, because, if you told a locksmith this lock had been tampered with, he would laugh in your face, but he would be the goat because you would be doing the most laughing. Hence the saying.

I close the door behind me and listen. All is as silent as the morgue on an off day. I flick the pencil torch about an' I see a cash register showing 'No Sale' and everything is nice an' neat like a respectable shop closed for the day. I take a peek behind the counter and there is nothing there that is unexpected.

I think I will now take a look at this back door Jeanette had told me about. There is no key in it and it is not even locked, which makes me suspicious of movin' too fast because, if there's really a door behind the calendar in the old hoosis, anyone at this minute might be coming my way.

I put my torch away an' take out my gun from my pocket an' stand quite still in the dark, listenin'; then I softly turn the handle of the door and pull it open ever so little so, if anyone is outside and comin' back, he could think it hadn't been closed properly an' maybe it was something to do with the storm that has caused a current of air and blown it open.

It is dark outside the door an' the thunder begins another session an' I don't take any chances going out. But, after a while, the noise eases off, and I stand listening again. Then, when nothing happens but the sound of rain drips, I step out into this cul-de-sac Jeanette has related an' flash the torch about.

Everything is just like she says. There is the old hoojah-kapippy with the door a bit open and in the corner is the wash tap, and all round, high walls that a Dracula could hardly climb on a calm night.

I push open the door of the hoosis, and it is just as my offsider said. If the architect who built it saw that door he would break his heart because, as soon as you give the littlest push, you can see the old sit-me-down with the naked eye.

I go inside and I close the door nearly an' flash my torch. It is a stone floor and stone walls and there is the calendar. I am staring at the plugs that hold the board on which it is mounted to the wall when the torch beam falls on something on the floor.

It is a little imitation posy Jeanette wears sewn on her bosom. I pick it up, an' now I have a pretty good idea that this Jeanette has been to this hoosis for a second helping, because the first time she went she had a good excuse an' I don't think anyone with her Scotch instink would have lost a posy like that on such an occasion.

I have an idea that what has happened is this: she has come back and been caught an' she has yanked off this posy an' dropped it as a guide that someone might happen to follow. I reckon this is right because, when I bring the torch to bear on this little bit of decoration, it has the look as if it had been torn off. I don't like this a little bit.

I put the posy into my pocket and, just then, I fancy I hear a noise somewhere that is not in the shop or in this cul-de-sac blind alley, so it must be on the other side of the calendar on the wall of the hoosis.

I flick out the torch quick and step out into the alley affair and I scran round the corner and flatten up against the wall. I hope whoever is coming he is only coming through the phoney wall into the hoosis for what a hoosis is for. But I think it will be a false hope because I have a intuition that this is a pretty sinister joint as Jeanette musta found out.

I am quite right a hundred per cent because I hear a little click and then I hear a footstep like someone was stepping out on to the stone floor in the little house. There's another little click an' next thing, this person has emerged out into the fresh air.

With a torch this person throws a beam on to the door to the shop, and I note that he stops dead an' gives a little grunt like he was surprised. I know he has seen the door is a bit open.

He begins to turn slowly round and I stick my gun in his back. I keep my voice down an' speak just loud enough so he can hear me tell him the pleasant news, and this news is, if he makes any move that is not a move I have mapped out and planned for him, I will pump a bullet into his guts.

This is a thing he does not like to hear, an' he stands very quiet and obedient. I do a quick frisk, and he has a gun which I take an' place in my mack pocket. I am keepin' the collar of my coat turned up high around my neck but he can tell by my voice that I am a dame.

He says, 'Can't we talk this over, lady?'

I say, 'If you talk here it will be your last words.'

I request him to march into the shop. When he is there I tell him to go to the cash register. I tell him I want all that is there. I want him to think that this is a stick up for dough. There is quite a bit in the machine, and he hands over a wad of notes. I got the gun well in his waistline because I think any minute he might try an' slam me with his torch.

I can't see this guy very well, but I know it ain't the one Ronald had his little chat with because he has a thick figure and Ronald has described the bird in the plush ante-room as on the slimmer side. I am keeping behind him so he won't see me neither, because the only clue he might get as to who has got him at the end of a gun is my height.

He says quiet like, 'If this a stick up what were you doing in the alley?'

I say, innocent, 'Why not, mug? It happens to all of us.'

He says, 'Oh, I see. It's like that!'

I think I have registered so I go on, 'I didn't know it was a gentleman only,' an' give a coarse laugh as if I was a bit on the common side. He's thinkin', It's all right; she is just a punk who has blown in to pinch the petty cash and got herself taken unawares. Maybe she ain't even been in the hoosis with the magic door.

We are both standin' behind the counter, an' he says, 'Well, for God's sake, I never ever thought I would be robbed by a dame.'

'You live and learn, mug,' I say an' make him take out what money he has got on him an' put it on the counter, but I have a lapse of memory and forget about the half of my ten-ner which he has got in his wallet.

While he was doin' this, still with his back to me, I ask him don't he ever read the papers where he will find, day by day an' hour by hour, women are getting to be the equal of men, and in some cases, twice as good. I tell him, for all this mod-ern trend, I don't like the idea of him bein' in the same room with a lady and with his hat on. I tell him to take it off an' dig him in the ribs with the gun to learn him it is no idle request.

He takes off his hat and puts it on the counter, too, and, straight off, I get a whiff of that same damn stink that the greasy sheik in Malwa's bed had on his hair. I can tell now by his shape an' his voice an' this malignant odour that what I have suspected is right, and this guy at the end of my gun is no other than my client, Rudolf the Smelly.

I think I will ask him where is Jeanette, but the man is such a damn liar his word wouldn't be worth the paper it was printed on, so I get another plan.

I say a Jane might as well have some smokes, too, since she has a tobacco joint under her control. I tell him to get me some from under the counter where I can see some boxes. He says okay an' stoops down to get some.

And now is where a little trick my dad has taught me comes in very handy. I give my gun a flip an' it spins round an' the barrel is in my hand, an' I belt the butt down on Rudolf's head. I am very glad this parlour trick has acted so well because, while it is dead easy to learn the art of twisting the gun, an' I can do it in the dark, it is not so easy to get guys to practise on.

Rudolf makes a sound like a sick toad and flops. It is the first an' I hope the last time I have ever done such a deed to a client.

———

CHAPTER 10

I have to step on Rudolf to get out from behind the counter, but he don't even groan. I throw my torch on him an' lift his eyelid an' I know, from what my pappy has taught me, I musta hit him in the right spot with the proper weight behind it because the object of this trick is not to concoct a corpse but to make the guy (who could be termed the receiver) as good as dead for half an hour.

I think I will allow myself twenty-five minutes to have a nose round an' see whatever type of joint it is that has such an unusual entrance as through a hoojah-kapippy.

In half a tick I am back in this cul-de-sac blind alley and gettin' an eyeful of the big calendar which Janet thinks is hidin' a door, an' that it is through this door that our friend, old Rudolf, who has collapsed behind the shop counter, has been doin' the vanishin' lady act.

To look at it you would think that this big piece of three-ply wood with the calendar mounted on it was plugged into the stone wall. It is a very cunning idea and very unsuspicious, unless you have a mind like me an' Janet who are always on the track of what Janet calls the *bazaar* things in life. I play my torch on these plugs and begin to feel them, beginnin' at the top.

Nothin' happens so I bend down and try the bottom ones. I give the right hand one a hard press with my thumb just for luck, and I hear a click an' the damn calendar swings out like it was the march of time, an', behind it, let into the wall, is a door. It is a door which comes nearly to the floor, but not too far upwards, an' you have to stoop to go through.

It is not locked, though it could be, and I reckon perhaps old Rudolf, who I hope is now having some horrid dream about his past life coming home to roost, figured he would be going back soon.

I open the door and I am in a narrow passage, but it is not a stone floor but some rubber stuff so you don't make any noise when you walk. I think this is a good idea, and when I get my office fixed up in a first rate style, I will use this idea instead of a carpet, and then I think, No, I won't, because someone like Brownie would always be sneaking up and catch you when you was bending.

I stand an' listen in the dark, but all I hear is a lotta silence so I nose along with the old torch an' soon there is some steps, an' these have got this rubber stuff on, too, an' I reckon anyone movin' in this narrow passage it would be like the hush-hush of death in its most silent form.

I go up to a landing where the steps take a turn an' I climb these. I go about twenty-five and there is a door.

I turn the handle an' outside all is dark as Hades an' I can't see or hear a thing. Then I notice something, an' that is that this door at the top of the rubber steps has got no handle on the outside. I reckon if you stood in the hall, or whatever it is I have emerged on which is at the top of these steps, an' you closed the door you wouldn't know there was such a thing as stairs there because, when I give it the once over with my torch, I can see it is just like the panels of the wood all about it, and you never could tell it was a door at all. If you was to lean against it, an' it wasn't properly closed, it would swing back an' you would fall down the stairs an' break your ruddy neck.

If I shut this door I don't see how I am going to open it again in a hurry if I want to make a quick getaway, so I pull it to when I get through, but I don't pull it tight.

My torch shows me I am now the only inhabitant, as far as I can see, of a very innocent-looking hall. A bit off is what I take to be a widish stairway goin' down to a darkish floor below. On both sides of the hall is the panelling I told you about, like is outside the stairs I have just come up, and there is no door at all except one about half way to the stairs going down to the dark next floor.

I moose along the carpet to this room an' I try the door. It opens, too, but inside is like a fillum palace when the day show has started an' you have just come in from the street. I can't see a thing. I stand an' listen before I switch the torch on again.

I am not much surprised that the old beam shows me I am in this posh ante-room with the plush furniture my Operator 2X has told me about.

As plain as my nose is on my face I know when I see this room, that the tobacconist's shop an' this joint an' Rudolf the Unconscious an' that lousy lizard with the hair on his knuckles Ronald Gaylord has met up with, are all mixed up together, an', somehow, they has all got to do with poor old Roy's tragedy.

I also have a pretty good idea that Jeanette Mackie is somewhere in this joint beyond the door which I can see with a picture on it of Innocence like Ronald has described, only it is a very vague description he has given me because it is a art-study of a dame in no clothes sittin' on a grass plot with a gay little butterfly playin' hy-dee-hy with Stella an' Ruby.

When I think of that pale grey snake, who I think might very posssibly be behind this frolicsome picture entitled Innocence, and young Jeanette bein' in the same vicinity, this is a thing I do not like at all. I think of my own gun an' old Rudolf's, which I am carryin', an' I feel to see that my little weapon is nestlin' safe and familiar against my leg, an' I reckon I am like some armoured train goin' forth to take a chance with the enemy, an' I decide I will do a commando raid by stealth to see if Jeanette is in the neighbourhood.

I think I will have time before Rudolf is once more his old bright an' cheery self to take a peek-a-boo beyond this work of art which is on the door. I am about to try if it will open, when I hear a sound. Someone on the other side is goin' to open the door on which this innocent dame is being tickled by a butterfly.

I got no time to scran, an' I don't know where I would scran, anyway, because anyone who was comin' would be on my tail in two ups. I sink behind a high-back chair in a corner an' wait. I got my gun in my hand, an' I am very pleased at the moment I am only a pocket Venus an' that this plush chair can swallow me up from the public gaze because the guy who comes in switches on the light.

He walks straight through the room I am hidin' in an' goes out the door. I hear him walk down the passage outside. He is a heavy guy, an' that's all I could say about him because the one peek I give shows me he is wearin' leggings, an' that's as much as I can see.

In a few moments he comes back an' starts for the inner door of the room I am in. He says, 'I tell ya, chief, that Rudy is a careless bastard. He's left the stairs door open. Or was he comin' back?'

An' then I hear another guy. He musta come to the door an' been standin' there an' little Rosie is very thankful that when she peek-a-boo'ed round the chair at the heavy guy's leggings it weren't on the side where this other bird was standin'.

If you was ever in the unhappy position you was being tortured and there was a head-torturer sitting in a nice armchair drinkin' a glass of pricey champagne, and he was to say between sips, 'Would you mind twistin' the thumb-screw a little tighter?' or 'Kindly oblige me by crankin' up the rack again,' an' you could get a good picture in your mind of this Head Torturist's voice, then you would have a nice idea of the class of elocution this guy, who is standin' near me at the door, has got.

He says, 'He's not coming back,' an' he pauses a bit and then he adds, 'One night he won't come back at all.'

The heavy guy laughs. He says, 'Now you're talkin'. I tell ya, chief, sometimes that guy gives me nightmares, he's such a dope.'

The man with the oily voice, who I guess is this lousy heel that Ronnie has had a dialogue with, says, a little impatient, 'All set?'

'Everything's okay,' the other comes back. 'I got the car in the lane.'

The oily voice says, 'Let's go.' But that only means they got some business in the inner part of this joint an' I gotta stay put. But it ain't for long. They come back an', this time, I got the idea that the big feller is carryin' something, an' then I know because he gives a coarse laugh. He says, 'Some baby!'

The way he says it with a kinda leer I get a cold feeling in my heart even before the oily voiced guy says, 'Keep the rug well round her,' that this bundle he is lumping towards some unknown destination is Jeanette.

I bet my bottom dollar they has her nicely tied up in some sweet way only such dingoes would know how with a dirty gag wipin' off her lipstick. Either that or they been pumpin' some dope into the poor kid an' she don't know no more what's happenin' than that lousy client of mine, Rudolf, who is still, I hope, having a tormented sleep in the shop downstairs.

Now, I bet you gotta notion that this is the time when I pop up from behind the upholstery an' give a good facsimile of a gallant policeman's daughter bailin' up two tough guys with a revolver she can shoot the eye of a needle out with. But you would be wrong, because I ain't actin' in no radio serial play where you can get yourself all balled up in the hands of assassins every night an' week after week and maintain your health an' strength until the sponsor for the programme says he has had more than enough.

No, in the first place I can't swear an oath that this bundle the guy in the leggings is carryin' is Jeanette, an' it might even be a pet St. Bernard bitch, because this oily voiced louse has said, 'Cover *her* up with the rug.' This 'bitch' is a word I do not enjoy to hear at any time an', even in my thoughts now, I do not like to use it when Jeanette is around, even if she is unconscious. An' what sort of a goat am I goin' to be if I pop up an' say, 'Not so fast old cocky,' an' it turns out to be a lady dog after all?

In the second place I gotta stay put because what the hell am I doin' here anyway? I ain't the police, an' even bein' a friend of such a policeman as Brownie don't make it right that I should act on my intuition and break into a premises an' hit even a smelly louse like old Rudolf on the head and hold up two gentlemen I have never yet cast eyes at.

I gotta remember that this little posh ante-room I am hidin' in is an ante-room to a joint I ain't never seen. I think whatever Brownie says about no complaints there'd be plenty of complaints if those who had 'em was in a position to make 'em. I think Jeanette Mackie is one who would make a very loud complaint.

I figure I am in the ante-room of a very low high-class gambling joint where, if you was a mug, you would spend many a happy hour winnin' a bit here an' there, till one night, in some strange fashion, Dame Fortune has turned her back on you and you have lost a helluva lot more than you have ever won. I bet, too, that if you could get the entry to this joint at about two in the morning you would find some classy lookin' dames draped over the furniture and a very pricey liquor bar which would start a temperance reformer foamin' in his sleep.

An' back of all this coarse revelry would be something about as sinister as Boris Karloff in a old dark house. Something about which old Brownie has had no complaints because he has his mind only on the single-track purpose of gambling, an' I have always found that high-toned gentlemen who lose their money at such joints are always very modest about makin' too much of a yelp about it, but are inclined to let sleepin' dogs lie.

But I only got intuition about these matters, and I have seen enough of what goes on in court to know intuition ain't evidence, such as, even if you could see by the light in some sheik's eye, that in one split second, he was goin' to throw all his gentlemanly instinks to the wind an', before you could get clear, he would be tramplin' over you and all would be lost, an' you had such an intuition about it that before it could happen, you donged him with a mallet, you would not get away with it in a law court if you was unlucky enough for some snoopy policeman to have witnessed you.

Because, as I get it, you could talk about intuition till you was black an' blue and the magistrate would only say back, 'But what did he *do*? What did he *do* that you should dong him?' And it would perhaps all end that you would have to go to gaol or get a suspended sentence when you know damn well, if you had left it a minute later an' not used your intuition, you mighta passed the rest of your life in a vain regret. If I was in parliament I think I would get this law altered.

These deep thoughts are passin' through the old grey matter at a rate like I was an entry for the Schneider Cup while I am gettin' the cramps behind the plush chair and the big guy in the leggings is carryin' out the bundle I think is Jeanette.

The oily guy is saying, 'Get this, Pete. You take her straight out to the dump, see. You put her upstairs in the end room. Lock her in an' scram back here for me. She'll be out to it for a coupla hours. But you better be sure. Get me?'

This Pete says, 'I get you, chief. I'll dress her mug up pretty.'

It is now as plain as a pie-staff to me that the bundle, if not Jeanette, is some dame who is doped, an' Leggings is lugging her off to some two-storeyed joint an' is going to gag her in case she should come to in his absence. It is good information an' straight from the louse's mouth, but how the hell is it goin' to do me any good, because these guys are already outa the room, and I don't know whether one of them, or both of them, is goin' downstairs with their human luggage.

I gotta take a chance. I stand up an' cross to the outer door an' listen. I hear the guys' voices and, in the light that is comin' from this ante-room I am in, I can see they musta already started down the rubber stair I come up. I go to the door of this stairs an' it is still open, so I figure the oily-voiced guy will be comin' back.

What has got me puzzled is the geography of this joint. If I heard right, Leggings said he had the car in the lane. What lane? It can't be a lane which he has to reach by goin' through that phoney hoosis an' then by way of the tobacconist's shop Rudolf is now occupyin' as a temporary tomb. Because, if so, he would have to lug Jeanette out through the shop and into the street, and even if she is wrapped up in a rug and doped an' all, it is not a fashionable thing for a thug to do to carry an unconscious dame in such a condition through a main thoroughfare.

I feel I just *gotta* take a peek down the stairs. I can hear the guys talkin' an', from the flash of a torch one has got, I see they are standin' on the landing, where the stairs take a turn to the magic hoosis below. The light flicks upward a moment an' I jump back because I think the oily guy is now comin' back, but all I hear is a click an' then nothin' more.

I take another peek and both guys have gone so damn sudden I have to rub my eyes. An' they ain't gone down to where Rudolf is dreaming oh my darling love of thee. I think I must be slick an' do one of these things I think of:

Number One: I can nip into the joint on the other side of the Innocence dame's picture which would be a mug's game because I am putting a lotta faith in the intuition I got that this is a gambling joint of the first water but rather dirty water an' a lot else besides an' I won't have time to give it a close up because the slimmer guy who has haled Jeanette off is likely to return up those rubber stairs any moment.

Number Two: I can scram down the main stairs which is

the way I guess the mugs who visit this joint to gamble will come up later when the night life gets into its stride. I would be a mug to do this because what does it learn me except I might get into the street quicker an' find this lane they have been chatting about.

Number Three: If these two guys ain't gone down the stairs to the restin' place of Rudolf, who I have got into my mind is no more popular with his friends than he is with me, they have gone somewhere else which is not far away. In which case I have gotta look slippery an' go their way as far as the landin'. I make up my mind to do this and take a peek at this landin' where they have vanished, an' then continue en route to the street via the shop an' have a quiz round to see can I find a car in a lane which looks like it is waitin' for some unconscious passenger.

I decide I will take on Number Three. I go down the rubber stairs like Hamlet's ghost, only a female one with red hair an' a gun in its hand, because I know if that snake Leggings is calling Chief, an' who, if I remember, Brownie has called Sidoli, should suddenly become an apparition on the stairs he will put a bullet into me if I don't get it into him first, which I don't want to – not yet, anyway, because I think he is a guy who the public taxpayers is entitled to see in a dock with a judge wearing a little black toque wishing him *bong voyage*.

When I come to the hoosis I go through the phoney wall and, even if I stop to close the door with the calendar on it, it is, just the same, the record time in which I have been in and outa such a place.

I flash my torch on the door of the shop, an' it is just like I left it, so I step inside an' take a peek behind the counter, and there is old Rudolf! They have forgot to use the carpet sweeper an' there is a lot of cast-off papers and cigarette butts on the floor and, lying there, with a big bump on the back of his head, he looks very sordid. He is still good and out, and, if he comes up on the dot, he has still got seven minutes in the realm of the subconscious.

I think I will take another peep into the cash register to see has he played fair with me. It wouldn't look so good if I was a real burglar an' only pinched half the doings, because that is what I would like the world to think – that I am just some common or garbage breaker and enterer and not a Robin Hood who would only take half a poor man's dough an' leave the rest to feed his starvin' wife an' children.

There is another thing, too, which I am thinkin', an' that is I am not sure whether this Hair Plaster on the floor is goin' to tell anyone about this hold up if he can get out of it. I get this idea from what I have heard the guys upstairs talkin' about, the grand total of which is that this Rudolf is too damn careless already an' is to be took care of in a way they know how, an' in a very little while. About this I am not weeping any tears.

I step on Rudolf Barenski once again to get to the cash register, which I open, an' there is no more money except some chicken feed for small change. There is a packet of cigarettes there, however, which is a new brand to me an' I think why not. I may never be this way again.

All this that takes so long to tell happens in an eyeblink because, when there is a guy like this snake Brownie calls Sidoli and who Ronnie has described verbatim, within a radius of me, I do not care to linger. Besides, I still have an anxious feeling about Jeanette.

I ease out of the shop an' I have just got the door closed again when a copper looms up from nowhere.

'What's the game?' he says.

I stoops down like I was lookin' for something. 'I dropped my cigarettes,' I says. 'It's all right. I got 'em.'

'Okay,' he says. 'Well, take my tip. Don't hang about doorways.'

I know what he's thinkin', but I kinda like his manner. He's not tough and he ain't no bully. I say, 'Thanks. I won't.'

I'm movin' off while he's watchin' me, an' then I stop. He's a decent guy and he's gotta voice I woulda liked to have heard a lot more of, but this ain't the time. I toss him the packet of smokes I have taken from the cash register.

'Take 'em for a keepsake,' I say. 'Goodnight.'

'Thanks,' he says in a sorta surprise. 'Goodnight.'

I suppose this is not a good thing to do because I have forgot that the brand of this cigarette packet is not a everyday kind and if there should be a stink about this breakin' and enterin', this packet of cigarettes might be a clue, an' there will be a hue an' cry for a girl in an old mackintosh and a scarf wrapped round her head.

This does not give me a pain because it is a far cry from Rosie Bosanky with hair which no dame in her right senses would hide under a bushel and who is very prone to be chic in her way of dressing, even if it is a wet night. I think perhaps old Brownie is the only one who would have a sneaking suspicion about me, but I do not worry about this either because the more I see of Brownie the more easy I see it is to twirl him round my finger.

As I go past I see that the building next door to the tobacco shop where Rudolf is passing his time and which is the one on the top floor of which is this alleged gambling joint is closed up. I scran round the block till I get to what I reckon is the lane where Leggings says he has a car waiting.

But there is no car, and I am afraid that Jeanette Mackie is now on her way to some place an' that place is not a place where she would go for the good of her health.

I am sorry for Jeanette because it is not a nice thing to have to stay in some lonely two-storey house especially with some dope in your tummy, or wherever it goes, an' a gag in your mouth. But you can't have your cake an' eat it, too, so I hope Jeanette will grin an' bear it till about 2 a.m. when I reckon I will get Brownie outa his downy bed an' take him to see this oily snake in his posh gambling den an' have some of the boys beat the hell outa him an' Leggings until they tell where they have got my offsider hid.

I think it will be a good idea if I get home. The rain has now stopped, but there is still no pedestrians about. I walk a block an' there is practically no traffic on the road, but at last

I get a taxi, an' I give him an address which is not my home but is near enough.

In my room I strip off and begin to get into something with more self-respect, although I do not change the bloomers which make the gun I have attached to my leg easier to wear. I have an idea that, if I can find an escort, I might even go back to this gambling hell when it is open an' see can I get an *entree*.

Yesterday mornin', when I opened up my office for the first time to make my debut as an investigator, seems a helluva long way off. It also seems a far distant past since I see poor old Roy Stockforth who, I suppose, is now passing his lonely hours with his British Colonial stamps. I think about that handsome devil, Clancy, and I wonder where he is spendin' *his* lonely hours, an' I bet they will not be with any stamps.

I also give a thought to that young copper to whom I have given the cigarettes and who has a kind voice. I picture him leanin' against a post in the quiet silent street smokin' one of the fags, sighin' over a poor lost soul who is like a ship who has passed in the night leaving only a touching gesture. I think that a guy who has such nice thoughts would be a nice guy to know and could be very poetic under any circumstances an', maybe, I will be able, in some subtle way, to find out from Brownie what his name might be.

It is a far cry, from when I set out so blithe an' gay to prove to Roy he was a cuckold through this Malwa who can't be found, to the scene of desolation where Hair Plaster Rudolf is stretched out on his tobacconist's floor, and to the phoney hoosis through which I have went to find Jeanette Mackie being bundled into a car which has taken her to God-knows-where. All these things has got to do with each other, an' I know it.

I finish dressing an' I breeze round to my office an' I sit down an' wait because it is now getting near the time when Rudolf has promised to ring me up to see what I have found out from my so-called sugar daddy, Brownie, the head constable.

CHAPTER 11

Once more I swipe a few pages from the private diary of young Ronald Gaylord, alias Operator 2X:

November 9

9.00  Read all the police court news. Started on *Famous Trials* (by A. Dumas) but cannot concentrate so will write my diary. Out of the pages of M. Dumas's book a face kept popping.

It is the face of the man I saw in the Room of the Plush Furniture. It makes me very uneasy because it is a face that needs watching every minute of the day or night. It is the face of a man who would commit every crime in the calendar and perhaps invent some new ones.

I do not think I will sleep very well tonight. Miss B. is a real lady. I am very glad about my raise because I will now soon be able to buy a gun. But I do not think I deserve my raise yet. I have only done my duty.

I wonder – if I am Operator 2X, who is Operator 1X? I bet he is a chap about six feet tall who is as gentle as a lamb with children but would pack a big punch in a fight. I hope Miss B. will trust me to know who he is and that I will be his off-sider.

I have just remembered that Miss B. told me to find out about those places alongside the tobacconist's shop and at the back of it and I did not go to the back because I did not have time to go and be back at her flat by seven thirty like she ordered me. This is a bad break because the first duty of a young detective should be to carry out instructions to the very letter.

I know by the sounds that mum and dad have gone to bed so I

will pin a note to my pillow saying not to worry and I will pop out and take a look at the back of that building next to the tobacconist's.

November 10

1.00  Gee! I am tired. I thought I would be home in bed last night by half past ten and now look at the clock! No one has heard me come in and my note to mum is still pinned to the pillow.

I went out as set out in my diary yesterday and proceeded to the tobacco shop. It was a wet, dark night, a fitting night for crime of any description. I measured the number of steps from the shop to the corner of the street and then I walked round to the street at the back of that building where I saw the man I do not like. It was a warehouse street with very few shops and those only small and all closed up.

There were very few people about and I hid while a policeman passed. I counted my steps from the corner and when they were the same number as I had counted in the parallel street I knew I must be right behind the tobacconist's. A little to the left was a lane for lorries to go up and unload and on each side of the lane the buildings look like old out of date storehouses.

I went up the lane in the dark because I did not wish to call attention by using my torch. I felt along the left wall but there was no doorway, and at last I came to the end of the lane and kicked against a garbage tin. It seemed to make a lot of noise, but no one came. At the end of the lane there was a loading platform and I knew, of course, it would have a door.

I began to feel my way down the other side wall. I walked very quietly and, after a while, I bumped into a car and dropped my torch. I was scared that someone would be in the car because the torch made the dickens of a clatter. I waited but there was no sound. I felt round for my torch and found it and flashed it carefully.

The car was a big one. I played the torch on the number plate and can remember it. I then saw something that made me curious, and I began to feel glad I had come. The number plate was in the usual slot arrangement, but I twigged that the frame of the slot at one end folded back. You could slide out the plate with the number. I slipped it out far enough to see there was another plate underneath but, just then, I thought I heard a sound. I slipped the top plate back quickly and got behind the garbage tin.

A door must have opened almost alongside the car because a ray of light lit up the lane near the car. A man stepped out. He went to the top of the lane and then returned. When he got into the ray of light I saw that it was the man I had met up with in the ante-room I told Miss B. about.

He said, 'It's okay,' and opened the back door of the car. Another man, a big fellow, wearing leggings, came out of the door carrying something in his arms.

It was wrapped in a rug, but the rug was pulled back a bit and, as he edged sideways to get through the door with his bundle, I could see he was carrying a woman. I did not get a good look at her because I only saw her for a flash.

The big man said, 'She makes a nice little handful. Oh, boy, do you know how to pick 'em?'

The other man said, 'Shut up and there's to be no funny business. Get me? Keep her covered with the rug like I told you.'

They put the woman into the back of the car, and the man who I had spoken to earlier in the day said, 'I better get back. I don't like that door being open. On your way.'

He went inside and the door shut and all was in darkness. The big man shut the back door of the car, and I could hear him climbing into the driver's seat. He started the engine without putting on the headlights. She began to roar a bit, and I decided what I would do. I thought it would be what Miss B. would like me to do.

I know from that number plate it was phoney and might never be checked and that would make Miss B. wild. While the engine was warming up, I crept round and tried the back door of the car. It opened easily. I slipped inside and pulled it to very softly and had it nicely closed by the time the engine noise died down and the car began to move. The woman they had put in was lying on the seat very still, covered with a rug. I crouched down on the floor and hoped for the best.

I bet there isn't anywhere in the world a famous sleuth who sometime or other hasn't been scared.

Too tired to finish my diary tonight.

I'm not back in the office more than half an hour when Rudolf the Smelly comes on the line. I am glad of this because it proves to me that I have not underestimated my strength, and I have tapped him just the right way I was taught and he is not dead. Just the same he sounds a bit tired.

He says, 'You know who thees is?' an' I can almost smell him through the phone. He asks me have I got news for his family.

I got plenty, I tell him. I give him the name and address of the Greek I was telling you about who told me the limerick. I say, 'The dicks has got on to this bird. They have picked up in the Adams house a return ticket to Brighton which they think this guy may know something about. They are goin' tomorrow to put him through the hoops. I even know what time they will pick him up. It's eleven o'clock. How's that for detail. If you like you or your family can have someone watchin' them go in.'

He is pleased with this information because he thinks the police have fallen for the phoney clue someone has left at Roy's mansion to link the murder up with the alleged gentleman who has been at Brighton with Malwa, according, anyhow, to the odious anonymous letter Roy has received but which he doesn't believe, poor dear.

Rudolf says thanks very much. I say my special friend thinks it's a hot tip because he thinks this Greek and the fellow that was found dead went to the mansion together to pinch some dough an' had a quarrel and one killed the other.

This, I guess, is much nearer the truth than Brownie's idea that it is a French passion crime. Anyhow, I gain the impression that Rudolf is not pleased at what I am telling him. I gotta notion that this idea might be near enough to the truth to upset his peace of mind, and I hope it will upset it enough for him to send me that other half of the ten pound note which I should have took off him while he was unconscious though it mighta put the show away about who it was who had paid him such attention; so it is just as well perhaps if I earn it honestly.

I ask him where he's talking from so I can ring him an' give him more information, but he says the family don't want to be rung up in case the servants should hear. He says he will ring me. Which hands me a silent laugh.

I can't help sayin', 'I hope you are well, Mr Barenski. You sound kinda tired.'

He says he has got one whale of a headache, which I can well believe. I tell him if I was he I would take a coupla asperin and a hot lemon drink, and he says he thinks he will. He promises he will not be forgetful to post along something to show the family's appreciation.

The poor sap thinks I've fallen for his line of talk. I can easy understand how his pals are so sick of him they are already planning a nice premature funeral. If I was in their shoes, I think I would be doin' the same, only I would take time by the fetlock.

I come to the conclusion that Rudolf is working on his own so far as I am concerned. I think he's so scared about something that he has taken a chance that I will be a sucker an' fall for his family story about Malwa.

It all goes to prove, like my pappy has told me a thousand times, and that is never to underestimate what these crooks will do in a lousy way, because they will sell out their friends every time; and never get in your head they are so damn clever because it is only in books where they are like a Raffles an' get away with it every time and, for the most part, they are a lotta saps who ain't even got brains enough to find out that crime doesn't pay even if they have seen it described on the movies a thousand times.

I think that if ever I wise my client Rudolf that Brownie and his merry men are on to him an' suspect he has got something to do with the non-appearance of Malwa Nawadi an' the murder of the sheik who has been found in her bed, he won't be able to get into his runnin' shoes quick enough.

I don't think that a snake like the one who has despatched Leggings out to some two-storeyed dump with poor Jeanette parcelled up in a rug an' doped would be the sort who would take a chance and send a mutt like this Plaster Hair to see me with one an' a half measley ten-pound notes.

I feel glad now I have hit Rudolf too hard with my gun because I can see, if the cards are played right, he will be the sort of guy who would do a double-cross on his bosom pal even if he had just been a best man at his wedding. This may be a very handy thing because I think we would be able to throw such a scare into him he would squeal on that snake Sidoli in the gambling hell an' all his works, an' if we play our cards right, we would then get delivery of Jeanette again.

If the cards are played right, I say, but I gotta admit Jeanette is in no condition to wait for a card game.

I am wonderin' whether, by this time, Handsome Clancy mighta got through with any of those blondes' telephone numbers he has picked up, and whether I would have the gall to ring him up and ask if he would be an escort for little Rosie while she tried a job of gettin' into Sidoli's gambling hell to see what sort of a joint it really is.

I think this Clancy would look swell in his evenin' clothes an', if he has been playin' round like I gave him the office to, a girl could now take a chance, because, if I have read this Clancy aright, I reckon by now he will not be so hell bent to show any girl his curios, but will be a very keen policeman who would take a great delight in a chase after a thug who has pumped dope into a good-looking dame like Jeanette and abducted her to some old dark domain.

I will paint him such a rosy picture of Jeanette as will divert his attention from blondes an' redheads and will set his thoughts on a new angle, which will be a brunette angle, and I bet in the morning he will wake up with his brain on fire an' he will lie in bed makin' a nice build-up in his mind for a bright future occasion, though, if that occasion should ever arise, I will wise up Jeanette that this is not the type of guy who will sit down opposite a girl for a night and admire her hand crotcheting.

I think, if I take this Clancy along to Sidoli's gambling

joint, we have a nice chance of gettin' in, because he is a new one in this district an' I bet in his evenin' clobber you would never in your born days believe he is a copper, nor even a mounted Canadian. He will be more like a fugitive from a Hollywood film gang spendin' his last week's dough.

These are my pleasant thoughts when they are broke in on by old Brownie who comes through on the phone.

'I got something for you, Rosie,' he says. 'I rung you up home but you weren't there so I took a chance at your office. It ain't official yet, but I'm tippin' you off.'

'Is it about poor old Roy?' I ask.

'No, it ain't about poor old Roy,' he says, a bit sarcastic. 'It's got nothin' to do with that case. It's just something for you to show I got your interest at heart. I'll see you in the mornin', Rosie, an' by then I think I'll have it all fixed for you.'

He is just going to say goodbye but the old basket knows I will be curious an' I can almost hear him grin when I say, 'Why can't you tell me now, Brownie? Secrets always keep me awake.'

'I'll tell you this much then,' he says. 'I reckon I can fix it you can do a nice little job for us on the side. Just a clean job, Rosie. No pimping. You'll be tickled pink. It's something that needs the feminine touch. Here's the layout. One of our young chaps has got a hot tip. He's just come off his beat. It seems he met a dame in Walgrove Street and told her to beat it out of a doorway. She musta thought he was goin' to turn her in. Anyway she was so scared or flustered or maybe she just did it by accident, but she tossed him a packet of cigarettes as a love token. He says he thought nothing more about it till he signed off.'

'Wait a minute,' I say, 'before you spill the finale. What sorta dame was this?'

'Oh,' he says, 'just a cheap doll.' He goes on, 'When this boy opened the packet what do you think was in it?'

'It's full of smokes,' I say, but already I gotta hunch.

'You're dead wrong, Rosie,' Brownie says. 'It were full of dope.'

I ring through to Roy Stockforth Adams, an' before I can say anything, he is asking me have we got our hands on any news about Malwa, and I know he is plenty anxious and this anxiety is a hundred carat, though Brownie with his suspicious mind would say if a guy has killed his wife an' hid her away somewhere nice an' quiet where no one can find the remains, he would behave just like Roy is doin' an' pretend he is up to his collar stud in grief and woe.

I tell Roy there is no sign of Malwa, but no news is good news, an' I just phoned him to tell him to go to bed an' have a good night's rest, an' he says he is in bed already an' was fast asleep when the telephone woke him.

I think this don't make a picture of a lover goin' through a reign of terror for a missing wife, and then I think it does, too. Because I have found that there is nothing can keep you out of the arms of Morphia if he is ready for you, as in the case of a young foreign soldier who in history was found fast asleep with cannon balls going off in his ear when Napoleon was doing his night rounds an' the young man should have been watching for the foe.

I tell Roy, 'Gee, it must be nice to be in bed,' an' then I crack. 'Gee, I wish I was there, too.'

But he don't even notice the double intender. He says, 'I don't like you to be up at all hours just because of my affairs, Rosie. I think you should call it a day.'

I say I think I will in an hour or so. I tell him I will see him tomorrow, and I ring off because I can hear a lift door bang and there is a noise in the passage like a iron horse is being pursued by mounted redskins and who should bust in the door but Ronnie Gaylord, an' you can tell from the look of him he ain't come direct from Sunday School.

He's got no hat an' he's lost his glasses an' he's cut his chin an' there's a lotta mud adhering to him besides which he is pretty damp, too. He comes tumbling across the office an' all he can say is, 'Miss B. *Oh, oh*, Miss B.'

I hold him tight to me with a little motherly comfort till he gets calm and then I ease him into a chair. I get some water in a glass an' I pour into it just a dash of alcohol an' I give it to him. He makes a helluva face, but it does the trick. After a bit he can spill what he knows.

He has gone to have another look round the building where the gambling joint is only he is nosing round to find a back entrance. He sees the guy who spoke to him a few hours before in the plush room an' there's another guy carryin' a dame who they dump into a car.

I get it. He was so damn conscientious, this Operator 2X, he's workin' overtime and he has stumbled on to Part Two of what I was witnessin' when I lost the trail.

He relates to me how he got into the back of the car. The dame is wrapped in a rug an' lying on the seat and Ronnie is scared she is dead. But then, from something these thugs have said, he doesn't think so. He manages to get hold of her hand. She is very cold and clammy, but she has gotta pulse.

He is hiding under a car rug on the floor, but it wouldn't have mattered because the guy who is driving don't stop. This guy keeps on for a few miles through streets and then Ronnie knows, from the way he can hear no cars passing that they are gettin' into more open spaces. The road gets bumpier, an' then, from the crunch an' a slowin' down, the lad figures the car is travellin' over gravel.

By an' by they stop, an' Ronnie thinks now he is for it. He's gotta plan. He's made up his mind to make a dive the minute the car door opens and butt the guy in the bingy. He will then run like hell. He figures if he butts hard enough an' hits the spot he will wind the guy in the leggings long enough to make a getaway.

But it works out easier. The mug who is driving has switched off the headlights. He gets outa the car an' Ronnie hears his footsteps crunching off along the gravel. He hears him walking on what sounds like a board verandah.

He thinks this is as good a time as any to have no vain

regrets about leavin' the car. He opens the door on the far side and nips out and closes the door softly. It's drizzling wet an' pretty dark. The boy thinks he's in some sort of driveway an' the dark splodge where the guy has gone is a high house. Behind him is some grass an' shrubs an' he takes up a stance behind a bush an' waits.

In a minute he sees a light go on an' for a second he gets a glimpse of a open door. He knows now the guy has gone to open the house up before he takes in the luggage he has got wrapped up in the rug in his car.

Ronnie watches him pull the door to a bit; then he hears him crunching across the gravel, returning to the car. He takes the dame outa the car, rug an' all, and tootles back to the house. He shoves the door open an' he carries the dame in, kickin' the door behind him with his foot. Ronnie hears it slam.

The boy waits, an', although it is on the cold side, I bet he has gotta wet shirt with perspiration. He sees a light go up in a top floor an' a bit later another light shows at a window he reckons is a few rooms away toward the back of the house.

Ronnie waits a bit an' then begins the grand tour. I tell you this lad I have discovered through buying a pricey hat is a modern equal to the boy who stood on a burning deck. He is doing this because I am his boss an' he thinks this is the sorta stuff I want. He goes right round the house which is standin' in what he takes for a old untidy garden. There are no lights except those he has seen an' all the doors are locked. He comes back to where he started from an' the car is still there.

There are no sounds from the house. There is a tree which he finds very convenient. He nips up into the branches an' begins to climb because he figures he will be able to get a peek into the window where the first light went up. He goes slow at first because it is wet an' slippery an' he can't see, but has to feel his way. He has to be careful because, if he falls, he will probably hurt hisself and make a noise which would bring Leggings hurtling into the gloom who would hurt him more.

He's afraid the light might go off before he climbs to where he can get a preview.

The branches are gettin' thinner an' he's wet through an' swingin' about like Tarzan in search of his lost love an' its begun to rain like hell an' the sound of it falling on the roof drowns any noise he is makin'.

He also gets a unsatisfactory notion there might be live electric light wires touching the wet branches, an' if he makes a contak, it will be just a case of a dead boy hung up in the fork of a tree if he is ever found at all, which is a hell of a thought. You can see that this freckle face has got the guts of which heroes are made because, like the 600th Light Brigade, he still goes on.

He hangs on to a branch and stretches hisself full length an' his eyes are then on a level with the window, but the damn branch thinks it is playin' nursery rhymes and keeps hush-a-byin' him on the tree top. The branch is bendin' an' dippin', bendin' an' dippin', an' he knows, whatever it believes itself, it can't take it for long. He gets a hold on a branch a little higher up and heaves himself up a bit more an' then at last he gets an eyeful.

Leggings is in the room. He is standin' by a bed. He has got his hand at the back of a dame an' is proppin' her up while he gives her a drink from a cup. Ronnie has just got time to see that her wrists are tied an' her ankles, too, an' then the damn bough he is holdin' to snaps an' throws all his weight on to the one he is sprawled on an' this snaps, too, an' he goes tumblin' downward, grabbin' as he goes.

He's nearly all the way down before he gets the brakes on, an' he lies doggo, an' I bet the poor little blighter has got plenty of bruises where it don't show at the moment, as well as having his chin cut.

He hears the window above open, an' he guesses Leggings is standin' there listenin', but all that guy can hear now is the rain splashing on the roof and, by an' by, he closes the window again an' Ronnie makes his painful way from the lower branches to old Mother Earth.

He gives a thought to pinching the car but is scared the

guy inside will come out an' might start shootin' an', anyway, the pinched car would put him wise that someone was on to him. So Ronnie decides that he'll beat it under his own steam and starts off up the drive.

He's lost his glasses an' hopes they've stuck in the tree somewhere an' he will be able to get them later because they cost him 10/6. I tell him such an expense goes down to the case account an' I bet Roy wouldn't mind a item like a 10/6 pair of spectacles, even if it was twice as much, when he hears what Ronnie has done while workin' on his very first assignment. This boy has also lost his hat, too, which, if you coulda seen it, you would not allude to as a great disaster.

When he comes out at the end of the drive, he's on a rough road that goes for about a mile till it comes to a highway. An old chap comes along in a cart, but it is goin' the wrong way. Ronnie asks the driver where some place is which he has just made up in his mind an' the old boy has never heard of it, but the conversation then gets led to local geography, an' Ronnie is able to find out exactly where he is an' will know where to bring a rescue party.

'I think I will ring the police,' Ronnie tells me, 'and then I say to myself my first duty is to my chief.'

And here he is!

My first thought is that I will give this Ronnie a raise in his salary, and then I remember I have already give him one and, in addition, I will have to give young Jeanette a bonus on account of her bein' doped and maltreated. I think, if I keep on this way, I might as well give my operators the damn business. So I give Ronnie a kiss instead.

I ask him how he got back, and he says a car come along and it is bein' driven very slow an' reluctant, an' there's a young guy at the wheel an' a girl sittin' beside him straight up like she has corsets boned with ramrods. The car is movin' so slow Ronnie can easily jump on the runnin' board.

He asks the young couple are they goin' back to town, an' the girl says yes. He asks for a lift an' the girl says, very prim, to the young fellow, who has gotta scowl as if he has just lost the opportunity of a life time. 'Have you any objection, Mr Whittaker?' Mr Whittaker says, 'Oh, no, by all means, Miss Pendlebury. Make it a party. This young gentleman may be better company than *some* I could mention.'

The girl sniffs at that, an' Ronnie gets in the back, an' the chap drivin' puts his foot on the accelerator like he was drivin' his spurs into a horse, an' begins to eat up the miles, which suits Ronnie very well. But the girl says, 'Don't you think you're behavin' a little reckless, Mr Whittaker?' The young guy gives a cold ironic laugh. 'What the hell?' he says, 'Who cares whether I live or die?'

'I don't know what was the matter, Miss Bosanky,' Ronnie tells me, but to me it is stickin' out a mile it is just one of those cases that is common in the life of young dames who are taken out for motor rides by young men who are prone to run out of oil. The conversation reaches a climax and the young girl demands her rights to be taken home on the instant, where-upon the young man thinks life is not worth livin' and has a firm belief that, if he had a sharp razor, he would at that very moment commit a deed upon himself he would regret all his born days.

I do not explain this to Ronnie because it is only one of those things that can be learned in the hard school of modern life, an', besides, there is no time; an' another thing is I am thinkin' hard. There is something queer in what he has been tellin' me.

I get it at last, an' it is why is this Leggings holding Jeanette up an givin' her a drink? Because, didn't I hear that snake Sidoli who was present when she was carried off from the gambling hell say she would be out to it for a long time?

An' if she was doped how could she be sittin' up an' takin' refreshments, an' why was her limbs tied up? I get an idea that gives me a slap in the face like a cold bath.

'Listen, Ronnie,' I say. 'This dame that was takin' a drink? She was a swell piece?'

'I'll say.'

I give him a nice picture of Jeanette like I saw her last. I think he hasn't had much time on the top of that tree to notice too many damn details, so I make it as clear a picture as I can, but he can only say it might be. I say at last, 'Well, did you notice her hair?'

'Only,' he says, 'that it was all untied.' He thinks it might be brunette hair, but he is not sure, which doesn't help such a helluva lot.

I say, 'Did you notice her fingers? Did she have a ring on or anything?' and he says he didn't notice.

'Well,' I ask, 'how about ear-rings?' but he can't remember. It's the same with her clothes as far as I can see, too. The poor kid's wet through up there in the hush-a-bye tree, swaying about in the wind, an' no wonder he can't act like a society reporter at a garden party. He can see I got something worryin' me, an' he's that upset he can't give me a description like I want he is almost cryin'.

'Think, Ronnie,' I say. 'Just relax and try an' *think*. Ain't there *something* you noticed! Some little thing that would be a clue about this dame so I would get a line on who she was?'

He thinks a long time an' at last he looks up, an' I know he's thought of something.

I say, 'No matter how little it was, tell me. Even a trifle might be important.'

He then says, 'It was only a little thing, Miss Bosanky. This dame who was sitting up had her skirts all ups-a-daisy. She had sheer gun metal stockings we sold at Fifine's for 23/6 a crack. The tops had been rolled back to about one and a half to two inches under the knee. I got no evidence, but I deduct she was wearin' very abbreviated lingerie because the way her dress was mussed there was a lot of bare skin. The stockings were secured to either limb by a black garter about a quarter to a half inch wide and decorated with small posies of pink rosebuds.'

The little blighter! No wonder he fell off the bough!

But I coulda hugged him. I know damn well now that this sheila he has had such an intimate view of is not Jeanette Mackie who is the sort of dame who would think you had a one-way ticket to hell if you wore your stockings done up with anything so expensive as rose buds.

No, this sheila they have got stowed away in the old dark house ain't Jeanette at all. She's none other than the missing link – Mrs R.S. Adams, Malwa Nawadi that was, poor old Roy's wife.

CHAPTER 12

While we have been talkin', Ronnie has been dryin' himself off by the radiator an' now he looks like the hot springs and geysers they got in New Zealand for the tourists to throw soap into.

I tell him he better scran home and get hisself a nice lemon drink an' a coupla asperins, and if he don't feel well in the mornin' he can take the day off in bed on full pay.

He gets up stage. 'What do you think I am, Miss Bosanky? A cissy?'

Just for a moment I have an idea I will ask him to step along with me to where I have decided I will go. An' then I think, No. No honest, God-fearin' parent is goin' to thank me for takin' the apple of their eye to watch what I hope I'm going' to do. So I tell him again to scran, an' he beats it.

As soon as he has left and it's all clear I make sure the little weapon is alongside my right knee and in good workin' order, an' I think to myself, I shoulda let Ronnie see this because he woulda gotta thrill of a life time an' I bet in one swift glance he would know the make an' the number of the gun an' that I gotta small mole from five to six inches from my patella in a northwesterly direction.

I slip on my coat in which there is also my other gat which I carry for more immediate requirements, and I take out the gun I took off old Rudolf an' leave it in a drawer after I have unloaded it. I take the ammunition with me because I ain't goin' to have Ronnie takin' any chances if he gets to the office before me. I go downstairs an' ease along to a taxi stand, an' I locate the guy I want.

He's a decent youngster about twenty-three, and he has a wobbly leg which don't seem to make no difference to his personality because he has eyes which look like he musta been born smilin'. He has a set of white teeth which I bet, if he felt like he had to, he could kiss a girl with a lotta fervour. I can imagine, if you had a moonlight night an' a lonely beach an' the languorous waves rollin' in from some far foreign clime, a girl could kiss this lad so hard she would emerge with his ears in her hands.

But I got no time for personalities. I get in this cab and give him an address just to keep him movin'. When we have gone a little way I tell him to pull up.

'Listen, Buck,' I say. 'I gotta proposition. I wanta engage you all night.'

He kids he gets me wrong.

'Oh, boy! oh, boy!' he says.

'Can it, Buck,' I say an' I let him see this is one time, any-how, when I am serious. 'I mean, I want this cab all night, maybe, and some of the time it mightn't be so healthy to be in it or near it. I don't know. I don't know how this thing I got in my mind is goin' to turn out.'

'Whatever it is,' he inquires, 'is it on the level?'

'Sure it's on the level, Buck,' I tell him. 'It's so much on the level that it might mean the difference between a young dame who could be your sister from going home to her lily white bed or taking a one way passage to Bonus Airs.'

He gets me. His eyes go wide open an' even the smile goes out of 'em. I think it is one of the ironic things of modern life how you can appeal to a man on the grounds of his own sister, an' the very next night he is actin' the wolf to some other innocent girl who also has a brother.

Buck says it is okay by him whatever I say. I give him a five-pound note. It is one of the notes which Rudolf the

Smelly has been so kind as to give me outa his cash register, so it don't cost me nothin'. I am so damn generous I tell Buck he can have another five pounds when we finish for the night.

I think this kid likes the idea of a night drive with yours truly, besides which there is something about five-pound notes which has a lotta attraction for some people. I get out an' climb in beside him an' I give him the location of this old dark house Ronald Gaylord has laid his hands on.

It is easy to find when you know how. When we come to the turn off from the highway we move along the track for a while an' then ease off into the bushes at the side. I tell Buck to put the lights out. He puts the lights out and just because he is a nice kid I give him my friend's special in the dark so he will have something to think about in the lonely hours while I am away on business.

When he has got over his daze, I tell him he can now sleep in his car till mornin' light is here but, if the said mornin' light comes an' there is no Rosie Bosanky on the horizon, he must go like hell to the nearest phone an' ring up Inspector Browne and get him an' his armoured column to tear out to the old dark house like all hell was let loose.

He says couldn't he go with me where I'm headed, but I tell him he'll be more use where he is in case I need a quick getaway. He promises he will go to sleep.

'Okay,' I say. 'I bet, too, I know what you'll dream.'

He's a nice kid and I hope he does.

I walk carefully along the road keepin' my ears peeled an' thinkin' that, after all, I've ditched Handsome Clancy again, because now I may not be goin' to the gamblin' joint. The idea of Roy's Malwa bein' in this two-storey mansion in an old untidy garden with her legs an' arms tied, an' bein' given a drink by the thug in the leggings, has altered all that.

Besides which I am plannin' not only to get this Malwa into such a free position she can pull her dress down an' tell me how come an' why she has left Roy's mansion an' not stayed where she said she was, but when I got her untied I'm goin' to sit down and wait for that snake with the shoe button eyes an' the long lip an' the moustache he has parted in the middle an' the hair on his knuckles, who is comin' out to this joint later on and who I gotta hunch can tell me just where to light on Jeanette Mackie.

After a bit I find the gravel drive and locate the house. There are no lights. There is no car in front an' the place looks like the last tenants died in their sleep fifty years ago an' nobody has found out. I nose round and I find a garage. It looks a bit lonely standing there in about two square acres. It is empty.

I can't hear a sound. I tip-toe to the rear of the house and there is a door with a lock which is pie. When I'm inside my torch shows me I'm in a kitchen. I move through into a back hall an' everything's pitch dark.

The front room is a sorta living room with a settee an' a small table an' some old furniture includin' a sideboard with some glasses an' some liquor in a decanter. One of the glasses has been used lately and I guess it was by Leggings pouring himself a stiff one after his arduous toil.

There is a bedroom. I give it the once over, and it is not very interestin'. It looks to me like a man's room which is not used very often. There are a coupla empty rooms, then a smaller bedroom with two beds in it and a rough dressin' table an' a washstand.

I nose around them, and on the table there is a small round box which has writ on it 'Carew's Corn Plasters'. On the washstand I find what I expect – a bottle of some damn liquid which hasn't got any label on but which stinks so to my refined nostrils that for a moment I imagine that Rudolf is in the room, or I am sniffin' the head of that dead sheik who passed out in the bed of this Malwa of the Rose Garters who is upstairs, patiently waitin' for something to relieve the monotony.

I put the hair-wash bottle an' the cornplasters in my pocket an' this is how I see it. This Hair Plaster who is my client, and the Sheik called by Brownie 'Harold the Corpse', has been formerly livin' in this room as old college chums, sleepin' in these two beds. It don't require a great intelligence to know they have been usin' the same hair tonic.

It also don't need much savvy to know that that oily dead sheik who has been stuck by Roy's Eastern paper knife would look more *au fay* in a rough an' tumble bed like the one in this room than in a dainty little love nest like Malwa has got for herself outa Roy's unbounded cheque book.

I think I will now pay a call on Malwa, and I start upstairs.

There is no carpet on the stairs so I slip off my shoes an' put 'em in my pocket along with the evidence I have collected. There is no carpet upstairs either and I move along to the room I guess will be the one where Ronald Gaylord got such a intimate glimpse of the missing woman.

There is a room next to it the door of which is open. It is a small room that the owners of the house musta once used for linen or something but now it has got nothin' but a lotta emptiness an' a coil of rope an' some old disused bottles.

I am flashin' the torch round when I hear the sound of a door unlocking downstairs. I hear this door open and close again an' someone with a torch starts comin' up the stairs. I partly close the linen room door and with my gun in my hand, I wait in the dark tryin' to figure out from the weight of the steps is it Leggings or this snake Sidoli from the gambling joint, though all the evidence I got is that they will not be here for at least a coupla hours.

I think who else it could be that I know, and of course old Rudolf flashes to my mind. I think I will step out on him sudden an' stick a gun in his abdomen again an' make him tell what's it all about, and then I reckon I won't because he is coming towards the room where Malwa is tied up. I think it will be a good idea to act the part of an eavesdropper because I think the conversation between this guy an' Roy's dame to who he is related should be a very interesting dialogue.

I hear him cross the room and then he switches on the

electric light. There is a silence an' I reckon he's over by the bed lookin' down at the Malwa dame. After a bit I get it she has opened her eyes.

She says, 'What do *you* want?'

It is no kind of a gracious welcome, but just the same this Jane has gotta voice that on a suitable occasion could make a strong man swoon. It is velvet an' honey mixed; it is all husky sweetness, an' if it was sayin' the right words I bet all those renowned hermits who renounced their tabbies in olden days and retired to a desert fastness would rise up an' come rushin' Malwa's way, tearin' up their vows *ong root.*

Just now, however, this voice is not sayin' the right words. 'What do *you* want?' she has queried, from which I take it more than one has seen her in her present predicament.

She goes on. 'Why don't you leave me alone?' Even when she is so ungracious to this mug Rudolf her voice is still lovely, only, when you come to analyse it, it is more like honeycomb because it has gotta bit of an edge on it.

Rudolf now speaks. 'I have come to make a proposition, Malwa.'

She is wary. A few seconds go before she says, 'Yes?'

The poor mug is eager now, only he's pretendin' he don't care much which way it goes. I reckon that tap on the nut I give him has done him no good. It has lost him his nerve. If he was frightened before he cames to see me he is scared stiff now, and, as for bein' *nonshallong* about his proposition, he is about as *nonshallong* as a hippopotamus twittering from bough to bough.

He says, 'Listen, Malwa. I gotta help you for the sake of the old days.'

'*You* help me for the sake of the old days?' she says. 'You wouldn't pull your mother off a burning ghat.'

This is not a gat like I got strapped to my little pink knee but, I found out since, a Eastern expression for a kinda fiery cemetery.

'You oughtn't to talk like that, Malwa,' the punk says.

'No?' she says. 'Why, if you meant only a quarter of what you say, you'd untie me an' let me sit up and at least look like a lady.'

Rudolf says, 'I'll untie you like winkin' once I got your promise you'll co-operate. I know you, Malwa. If you say you'll do a thing you'll do it.'

She says in that bitter-honey voice, 'You ought to know. I went through enough for you in Bombay, didn't I? And what happened? You've held it over me ever since.'

'Yes, yes,' he says quickly, 'but that's all over and done with, Malwa. Anyway you've got plenty. What you paid out you never missed.'

She laughs a bit scornful. 'No,' she says, 'It smashed up my marriage, that's all.'

'Oh, now, come come, Malwa,' he says. 'That's nonsense. Why I bet that guy's head over heels in love with you.'

'And what if he is?' she says. 'What sort of a heel do you think I am that would let him go on loving me when a snake like you might have me gaoled any minute – and for something I didn't do.'

He begins walkin' up an' down an' I can tell he is a bit agitated. He's hopin' she will calm down before he puts whatever proposition he's got in his dirty mind.

After a time he says, 'Let's be friends, Malwa. I admit I've been a bit of a heel, letting you take the rap as it were. I wouldn't have turned you over, Malwa. You ought to know that. Even if you'd refused to help me.'

'I don't know it,' she says. 'I know you're a dirty blackmailer. I bet it's through you I'm in this mess now. If it isn't, why don't you unloose me?'

He says, 'I can't untie you, Malwa. I can't take a chance. Sidoli would kill me or he'd have Pete bump me off. I'd be dead as mutton if he even *knew* I was here now. You gotta listen. You gotta play it my way, Malwa. Now, listen, you gotta be patient. I'm goin' to wise your husband up where you are.'

'When?'

'Tomorrow morning.'

'Tomorrow morning?' She laughs. 'And this snake Sidoli coming here *tonight*.' She laughs again. I tell you it is strange hearing a dame with a honey voice letting this punk Rudolf see she don't believe a word he's sayin'.

He says, 'You'll be all right. He's got another Jane.'

She says, 'I thought so. I had a hunch that disgusting Pete carried someone in. Is that another kidnapping?'

I told you this dialogue was goin' to be interestin' and make it worth while for me to play the low character of an eavesdropper because I now got it straight my pal Jeanette is here somewhere, too. And, another thing, this Sidoli snake has kidnapped Malwa. But why? I dunno, but I hope to hear.

Rudolf is sayin', 'No, it weren't a snatch. This dame was stickybeaking.' He goes on. 'I got no time to stay talking, Malwa. I'll tell you what. All you gotta do is swear to what I want and when you are free get me a few hundred – say five – so I can scran. Then in the mornin' you'll be as free as a bird.'

She says, 'Yes? Well, I trusted that other one, didn't I?'

He says, 'You mean Wessex?'

'Yes,' she says. 'He was to have five hundred. I told him where he could get it, but I'm still tied up like a prize pig, and I suppose Wessex has got the five hundred and has gone.'

'Wessex's gone, all right,' Rudolf tells her. 'You shouldn't have trusted a man like that, Malwa.'

She says, wearily, 'What else could I do?'

Rudolf says, 'Anyway he won't come back.' He is silent a moment an' I guess he's thinkin' of his late room-mate who has gone off to collect the five hundred from Roy's philately drawer an' found Fate waitin' for him in the shape of a sharp, eastern paper knife.

Rudolf continues. 'Besides, this is different. All you gotta do is promise.'

'Promise *what*?' she says, an' I feel she is gettin' impatient, an' if she was in a fit position woulda concluded the conversation with this bird hours ago.

'Swear,' he says, 'whatever happens you'll always swear that the night before last – *all* the night before last I was in an' outa this room, givin' you sips of water an' things. You gotta swear it, remember, *anywhere*. You can say you heard Sidoli give orders that I had to stay here and look in on you every ten minutes an' he said he'd blow my lights out if I didn't. Say you'll swear this Malwa, an' you'll get me five hundred to scran with an' you'll never hear from me again – ever.'

He's gettin' hisself worked up by now an' goes on, 'Think, Malwa. This Sidoli's a bad guy. You got no idea what he'll do. I tell you he's so low you'll wish you was dead. An', anyway, what's five hundred? Sidoli would make your husband pay ten times that to get you back – *intack*.'

Somehow the way he gives her this intack stuff makes my flesh creep. The lousy swine is tryin' to get the wind up her, but I reckon he's not far off the truth. But there's one thing I gotta be grateful for an' that is he's give me a testimonial for this Malwa. All he wants is her promise to swear. He knows her so damn well that he's sure, if she swears, she will do a thing, she'll go through with it. It gets me, but there you are! But then I ain't been brought up by no kindly nuns whose word is their bond, but only by a policeman pappy who has a motto that it is okay to make and break a promise to any crook if he is so goddam rotten that he oughta be hung on a scaffold with a slow motion drop.

This Rudolf punk wants her to alibi him outa the murder of his boy friend with whom he has shared his hair wash an' who, I reckon, was pinchin' the £500 petty cash from old Roy's bureau when he got interrupted. Malwa has made it plain as day she was told this Wessex about the five hundred an' he has promised when he has got it he will tell her husband where she is.

Maybe he was goin' to double cross her. I dunno, but I'm always ready to believe the worst of these punks. Anyway this Wessex goes off to Roy's mansion, which is all shut up, and somebody murders him there. Maybe it was this Rudolf who is so damn anxious that someone with a good reputation will swear he was nowhere near the scene of the crime. But I don't think so.

I think Rudolf was there but a nit-wit like that couldn't think up the idea of takin' the guy's clothes off an' fixin' the corpse in Roy's pyjamas an' puttin' him in Malwa's bed.

An', while doin' it, do the pyjama buttons in the wrong buttonholes like I have pointed out to Brownie who has laughed me to scorn!

Rudolf, even without bein' hit on the head, would never think of writin' old Roy that odious anonymous letter about his wife having gone over the rails knowing she wouldn't have a chance to answer the radio S.O.S. an', by her disappearance it would look like Roy had murdered her, too, or at least that she had run away with some dope who had stayed with her at Brighton in the pub after pinchin' the £500 from the stamp album drawer which only she knew about.

I think this slimy layout has got all the hallmarks of the Sidoli snake who, through Rudolf, has planned a kidnapping which has turned out to be a murder an' now he has gotta protect himself by throwing the blame on old Roy. I am very glad to think this, too, because I want all I can get on that bird. I dismiss this Pete with the leggings from my mind because my idea is he is just a heavyweight thug who is no good for anything but bumping off guys the chief has come to hate the sight of.

I would make a bet that Rudolf has got wind of what his pal Wessex was up to an' wised up Sidoli an' they have both gone along to Roy's mansion and caught his Wessex red-handed. I would also make a bet that Sidoli is only letting Rudolf live to tell the tale because he has helped him get hold of Malwa an' may be a bit more use in this respect but not much.

By now I guess you know I got a quick mind for thinking things out because all this has passed through the upper dome while I'm steppin' out into the hall in my stockinged feet. I hear Malwa give another bitter laugh.

She says, 'Oh, no Rudolf. I wouldn't do it, not even for

you. I don't know what you've been up to. But I'll not swear any false alibi. I'll take my chance. I believe there's a hue and cry out now and you and your measley Sidoli and that great ape that yesses him haven't got a hope. You're double-crossing your pals, aren't you? But the police will get you, Rudolf, and I hope you hang.'

This is a speech which Rudolf does not like to hear. His voice turns nasty. He says, 'You forget what I know. You forget I could get you back to Bombay.'

She says, 'No, I don't forget, but I'm tired of it all. I've made up my mind anyway to tell my husband everything and take a chance. You can do your worst and now, for God's sake, clear out and switch off the light. I want to go to sleep.'

I gotta hand it to this dame I ain't never even seen except in a picture. I think old Roy has got something Bombay or no Bombay. He's got a honey who could make his life a bed of roses if he only knew how to iron the sheets. She's got guts, this Malwa, lying there, tied up an' all, talkin' back to this louse Rudolf, tellin' him to go fry his face.

He can't take it. He loses his head. He begins to tell her the things Sidoli will do to her. He tells her a few things he will do to her himself, an' they are not pretty. And when he tires of that he sneers, 'An' there's that gorilla, Pete. He has a nice way with refined dames. They ain't so refined when he's had his little play round. By God, there'll come a time –'

By this time, though, I am in the room. He is so chockful of cold fury he wouldn't have heard me if I'd walked in on the shoes which I have in my pocket. Malwa's head is turned away from him toward the window like she's be sick if she kept on lookin' at him, an' he's talking' to her back, bendin' over, spittin' out his poison.

I think it is time to get tough.

I use a simple term. I say, 'Boo, louse!'

Rudolf whips round an' I smack him across the chops with my gun. His head wobbles like it was comin' off, but he's got enough sense left to feel for his gun. He gets it out, but I beat him over the knuckles an' he drops it an' lets out a yelp. The gun falls on the bed an' I smack him on the other side of his face. I enjoy doin' this.

When his head is a bit cleared, he looks up and his eyes nearly pop outa his head as he recognises who has been payin' him these slight attentions.

'Why, Mees Bosanky –' he begins.

I tell him to hold it. I tell him to cut the dame on the bed loose, an' I stick the gun into his guts to let him see I'm impatient. While he's doin' it I tell her, 'You don't know me, Malwa. I'm actin' for Roy. They think he's murdered you an' hid your body.'

Her eyes open wide, an' she's too astonished to speak, I guess.

When her arms are free, the first thing she does is sit up and pull her skirt down over her legs. I told you this dame has class.

In a minute she is sittin' on the side of the bed. Then she suddenly comes over queer. I reckon it's the gettin' up so quick after being Houdini'd so long. She begins to topple sideways on the bed. Rudolf starts to say something, but I just can't be bothered. I smack him over the kisser again an' take a peek at Malwa.

But she's game. She's hung on to herself. 'I'll be all right in a moment,' she tells me. I pick up this rat Rudolf's gun an' put it in my coat pocket, an' then something happens I am not keen about. I hear the front door slam and footsteps start comin' up the uncarpeted stairs. I count 'em an' I know there's two guys on their way.

There's a sort of corner wardrobe made by running a curtain across a stick. It ain't much, but it's the best thing offering for a hide out. I dig Rudolf in the ribs. He's a bit dizzy, but he ain't so dizzy he can't get every word I say. I tell him I'm goin' behind the curtain an' I make him stand in front of it but facing the door. I tell him I'll be just behind him, an', if he spills one word that I been here, he'll get it behind the ear the moment he squeaks.

I ask him does he understand. He says he does. I say will I plug him now an' take a chance with these mugs or will he do as I say? He says he will do it.

I am behind the curtain but, through a chink, I can see the door. The snake, Sidoli, and the ape, Pete, comes in. They stand in the doorway. Sidoli has a face like a bad cheese, but the ape is grinnin' an' looks at Rudolf and Malwa who is tryin' to make her hair tidy.

'Well, now!' he says. 'Ain't that nice?'

Apart from Malwa sittin' up, they've seen she is quite untied in all particulars. Sidoli is still not sayin' anything but his eyes are glittering.

The ape says, 'What did I tell ya, chief? He's too damn careless. He's lit up the joint.' He crosses the room an' pulls down the blind then he goes back an' like a good yes-man, he takes his stance just behind Sidoli.

Sidoli looks at Rudolf with his cold eyes an' he says, 'Why did you untie her?'

'I – I,' Rudolf begins and stops. I guess he has remembered what is behind him. He's in one helluva mess.

'What are you doing here, anyway?' Sidoli asks still in his refrigerator voice.

Rudolf don't answer, an' I can picture his mouth gaping. I think he has gotta very good idea that these newcomers have been plannin' somethin' for him.

The ape says, 'I tell ya, chief, there's sumpun funny goin' on here. He tells us he's goin' somewheres else an' breezes out here. What's he doin' here? I'll tell ya. He's let the dame loose, ain't he? He was goin' to rat, the lousy bum.'

'No – *no*,' Rudolf shouts.

'Shut up,' Sidoli says in his quiet voice.

There is a little pause. I can hear Rudolf sweatin' blood. I am almost sorry I hit him more than once. Sidoli's eyes shift the littlest bit as if he could look over his shoulder an' at the same time keep 'em on the poor mug in front of him.

He says, 'Listen, Pete. You ain't had much exercise lately. You oughta do some digging.'

'Diggin'?' the ape says, astonished. Then he slaps his thigh an' gives a great belly laugh. 'I get ya, chief. Diggin', huh?' He stops laughin'. 'When?' he says.

'Soon enough,' Sidoli says in a low voice an' takes another quiet step toward Rudolf. He don't say another word but puts his hand under his coat. He is so quick on the draw I hardly see it.

All I hear is this poor basket Rudolf's voice. It begins with what is supposed to be some words but goes off into a little squeak. Then he gives a great sigh as if all the wind has gone outa him, and crumples.

Sidoli looks down on him without movin', an' says, 'Stick him in the linen room for now,' and, when the ape picks him up, he says, 'Take his gun first.'

Pete begins to frisk the corpse. He looks up, grinnin'. 'He ain't got one,' he says. 'I always told you he was a careless bastard.'

He lifts up all that's left of Rudolf as if he was the carcase of some small cow, an', when he's passin' Sidoli on the way out, the snake puts out a hand an' rests it on the big mug's sleeve though he's not lookin' at him. If ever I see hell let loose on a man's face, it is in this Sidoli's at this moment. He was an evil louse before, but this shootin' has done something to him. He has tasted blood an' got his appetite wetted. I got all I can do to stop myself lettin' him have it between the eyes because I see the muscles of his face move for the first time since he has come into the room an' I know he is leerin' at Malwa.

I see his tongue pass over his lips, and I get a glimpse of his teeth under that parted black mo he is wearin'.

He says to the ape, 'When you've dumped him, get our little friend from the other room.'

The gorilla gives one of his hoarse laughs.

'Now, you're talkin', chief. What's cookin'?'

Sidoli says, smooth, 'Why, Pete, how can you ask? We've got company. We're goin' to take the ladies down to our nice, quiet lounge room an' play games.'

The ape laughs again. 'Suits me, chief,' he says. 'I always was a ladies' man.'

A minute later I hear a thud as he dumps the body in the linen room next door. His footsteps echo over the boards while he walks toward the room where I guess they got the other sheila tied up.

Sidoli keeps on starin' at Malwa; then he goes over to her walkin' like a cat an' lifts up her chin with his hand. She gets up suddenly an' gives him a hell of a smack across the chops.

He don't hardly move his head though. He puts out his hand with a quick thrust an' grabs her arm. I hear her yell with pain, an' I know he's got some sorta grip on her that must be hell for a dame as soft as this dame.

He says, 'I always pay back – with interest. Let's go.'

He does something to her arm an' she screams again, but it's just a scream. I'm scared as hell she'll yell my name which she has heard from the late Rudolf when I came in, but she's got nerve, this Malwa. As far as my presence is concerned she's dumb as an oyster.

I watch them go out an' hear 'em move toward the stairs;

then in a few moments I hear the heavy steps of the ape and see him pass the door. He is carryin' Jeanette in his arms an' he's grinnin' down at her an' she's beatin' his great chest with her hands, but she might as well be slappin' the Rock of Gibraltar.

She's still gagged an' she can't say the things she wants, but I bet my sweet life if she could she would be callin' him names she didn't think she even knew.

I come out from behind the curtains when this vision has passed an' the gorilla is on his way downstairs. I think to myself I am havin' one helluva day.

I reckon this old dark house with a shot corpse in the linen room and a ape an' a snake somewheres downstairs with two purloined dames is no place to spend a long vacation. I think it is about time there was some law an' order about the joint because, whether it has anything to do with the murder at old Roy's or not, a first-class shootin' has been did, an' I got plenty of excuse for ringin' up Brownie to bring along a coupla sets of handcuffs.

I gotta urge to finish the job myself even if it means two more grave plots, though, as far as I am concerned you could dump both these heels in one hole at a cut rate. But I gotta remember I am a small, weak woman, an' these two thugs downstairs are experienced gorillas. If anything slipped up, I wouldn't like to think what is going to happen to Jeanette Mackie an' Malwa, let alone me.

I begin to nose around for a phone though how the heck I am goin' to use it without the boyfriends downstairs hearin', I don't know. I pretty soon find there's no phone upstairs. I take a peek over the stairs and it's all dark. I begin to go down.

I got my shoes in my pocket remember, an' when I feel the boards firm I move pretty slick holdin' to the bannister. When I'm right down I hear voices from a room where there's a light showin' under the door. It is this lounge room I told you about where Sidoli keeps his liquor.

I hear a bit of a scuffle an' the big belly laugh of the ape,

Pete. The door comes open a bit an' I see him standin' at the entrance but lookin' back into the room. I flatten against the wall an' wait. I am so damn close to him you'd think he'd smell me. I make up my mind if he sees me I'm goin' to let him have it an' take my chance with Sidoli.

But I'm lucky. He don't look round. He is having fun. I hear the tinkle of glass, an' I guess Sidoli is pourin' hisself a drink. He is sayin', 'Ring up the joint, Peter, an' tell 'em I have a slight influenza an' I won't be back.'

The ape says, 'Okay, chief. That's the stuff. You been workin' too hard.'

Sidoli says, 'Yep! I been workin' too hard. I need some relaxation.' I can imagine him lookin' at the dames he's got herded into his damn corral. He goes on, 'Tonight we're goin' to have a little holiday, Pete.'

The ape slaps the panel of the door with his paw. 'Now you're talkin', chief. I getcha. A Roman holiday like I read you about. Remember? Play games like them Emperors wit' their three-ring circus. My, my! Did those boys know life?'

Sidoli says, 'Cut along, Pete. The ladies are waiting.'

The ape slaps the door again with his fist as if this snake inside has shot off some first-class wise crack. 'The ladies are waitin',' he repeats, and laughs fit to bust hisself. He goes off to the back of the house makin' sounds like he was seein' Donald Duck. He's such a goddam yes-man and so full of what's in his dirty mind he don't look my way.

An' me, little Rosie Bosanky, I'm so dam het-up at what I think these filthy palukas will do I'm not takin' any more chances in findin' a telephone. I think if I can catch this Sidoli bending, I can make him tell the gorilla who has gone outside how to behave. I edge up to the door an' see Sidoli pourin' himself a drink. I push the door open with my foot an' step in.

'Hold it, Sidoli,' I say.

He looks up, damned surprised. He's got the decanter in one hand an' his glass in the other. The girls is huddled together on the settee at the end of the room.

Sidoli says, an' he's standin' like a statcher an' only his lips move, 'Why, who have we here?'

'That can wait,' I say, an' I'm damned if I quite know what to do next. I don't know whether to plug him now an' make some good apology to Brownie, or wait till I hear the ape comin' back, an' then I would have a better excuse.

Sidoli goes on. 'Well,' he says, 'it's nice to see you whoever you are though, as you can see, we're already stocked up.' He makes a slight gesture towards the dames with his glass.

Jeanette gets up. 'Shall I take his gun, Rosie?' she asks.

I've been so occupied in my mind this is the first time I've noticed that they've taken her gag out. I can tell by her voice that she's still a bit dopey. She's only got back enough sense to know what's goin' off.

I'm wonderin' what Sidoli will do when she gets close to him. I bet he knows a trick or two. He'll probably grab her an' hold her in front of his measley carcase. I'm wonderin' whether I can risk tellin' him to chuck his gun out because, even if I make him turn round first, this snake is so quick on the draw he may beat me to it.

I'm wonderin', too, how long the ape will be in sending his message to the gamblin' joint. I ain't got to wonder long because Malwa gives a scream and next moment a great hairy paw has grabbed my arm from behind an' another has smacked down on the gun itself an' knocked it on the floor at Sidoli's feet. He puts the decanter an' glass down on the small table an' stoops down an' picks up the gun. He unloads it an' tosses it into a corner, contemptuous. I am so damn mad I could cry.

Peter gives his belly laugh an' his breath is like poison gas on my ear. 'Just as well I changed to evenin' shoes, chief,' he says, an' I know now why I didn't hear him. He's wearin' a pair of floppy carpet slippers.

Sidoli says, 'Very suitable, Pete.' He nods his head at me. 'Friend of yours?'

The gorilla swings me round an' gives me the once over.

'Sure, I know her,' he says. 'It's Rosie Bosanky, the dame who's got her pitchers in the papers over that Roy Adams case.'

'Ah, yes,' Sidoli says, softly, 'I think I heard something about it.' He picks up the decanter an' glass an' pours a drink an' brings it over to where this gorilla is holding me. He says, 'Take her coat off, Pete. Ain't you got any manners?'

The ape gets it off an' throws it over a chair in the corner an' Sidoli leers. His eyes give me a good undressing while this Pete holds me like I was a slave being offered up at a black market like you see in the art gallery any wet Saturday afternoon. The gorilla says, 'Goes in an' out the roundabouts, don't she, chief? Oh, boy! Oh, boy!'

There is then a long silence like we was the congregation in the House of Lords. Then, when about a million years seems it has gone by, Sidoli says, 'Let her go, Pete,' an' the gorilla unhands me but stands near ready to grab.

Sidoli offers me the glass of liquor he has poured.

'Congratulations, Miss Bosanky,' he says in that oily voice. 'Won't you join us? Just to make the occasion more festive. Because' – he leers round at Jeanette an' Malwa – 'it *is* going to be festive, isn't it, Pete?'

The gorilla laughs. 'You said it, chief,' he says. '*Festive*. Oh, boy, can you pick them words? *Festive*?' He makes a smacking sound with his thick lips. I bet if this ape spoke his mind on to a record an' you put it on you would get the silence of the tomb.

I take the glass an' I give Sidoli a sour look. If I made a fair average chart of this punk this is how I would give him a percentage:

Good points .........................Nil
Lack of character ................100 per cent
Deceit .................................100 per cent
Bad looks .............................100 per cent
General lousiness ................500 per cent

I say, 'I can do with a drink, Sidoli, but I ain't goin' to drink it, you big bum. When I drink water, I drink it by myself to keep my innards clean. When I drink liquor, I drink it with my pals. I drink it with clean people. People I like, an' I don't like you, Sidoli. I think you're a louse. You're a low-class, weak imitation of a big shot who's gotta rely on his laughs from a half-baked paluka like this gorilla you got yessin' you. To hell with you an' all like you.'

I throw the liquor in his face an' toss the glass away. He don't even move his head, but he steps back a pace or two so I bet some of the stuff has got into his eye, which is all to the good if there's to be any shootin'.

The gorilla says, 'Shall I slap her round, chief?'

The whisky is runnin' down Sidoli's chin an' on to his soft collar. He's gotta tone like he's talkin' through ice blocks when he speaks. 'Amuse yourself, Pete.'

The gorilla opens his big mouth an' he says again, 'Oh, boy! Oh, boy!' like he was bitin' chunks outa the air. I don't know what's in this paluka's mind, but I gotta good idea it ain't goin' to be healthy for me nor nice for dames like Malwa an' Jeanette to behold.

When he makes a move, I suddenly let the old frame go limp. I let every blame muscle I got take a holiday, an' I crumple up an' sink slowly to the floor like I was the last gasp of one of them rubber roosters you blow up an' then let the wind out of. But I've took damn good care when I collapsed in an ungraceful bundle to know just where my hands is, an' one of them is busy with the little weapon I got strapped near my knee.

I hear Malwa cry, 'She's fainted.'

Pete the Paluka stands over me. He has to stoop down. He grabs me by the waist line with his two hands and begins to lift. I am hangin' as loose as a rag doll which has come unstuffed. When my legs are swingin' clear from the floor, I let him have it. I give a back kick with my right with all I got, an' he gets it where he don't like it a little bit.

It's a trick my pappy has taught me for just such an emergency. When his eyes told him I was developin' in a way which, with my red hair and all, was likely to make me fair game for the sheiks, he tells me, 'Rosie,' he says, 'when you are grabbed by some bloke you kinda like you gotta use a neat balance between head an' heart. I can't help you. But, if you are grabbed by some paluka who you hate like poison, you gotta have some defence. There is the knee defence an' there is also the toe an' heel defence which can only be done by those dames with trained bodies. We will now proceed to Exercise No. 1, an' try an' remember for God's sake that this is a rehearsal only, and don't make it too damn realistic.'

Well, what I have give this gorilla Pete is Exercise No. 2, an' you can tell it is a very realistic exercise because he drops an' has let out a yell of agony an' collides with the floor where he is rollin' in a groanin' heap.

Almost before he is there I have shot at Sidoli. He gets it in the right wrist which is good shootin' because I am in a position for trick shots only. I am only just in time an' we are all damn lucky because as I told you this snake was quick on the draw an' had pulled his gun almost simultaneous with the gorilla's yelp.

The gun has slithered across the floor. Jeanettte is comin' to all right because she now makes a flyin' leap at it. I go up to Sidoli an' I point my gun just below where he would have a navel if he was a human. The gorilla is still groanin' on the floor.

I work fast. I say, 'Jeanette, that ape is in great pain. It would be kinder to have him unconscious.'

I told you this dame was quick on the uptake. I think she is a great kid goin' through what she has an' not even knowin' she's gotta job an how much it pays. She leans over this groanin' ape, and usin' the butt of Sidoli's gun, she gives him a welt that is so loud I woulda winced only I daren't take my eyes off Sidoli himself who is in such danger he might be undergoin' a navel engagement at any moment. The ape stops groanin', which makes things more peaceful.

I say, 'Malwa, in my coat they have so rudely tossed in the corner there is a gun I took from poor Rudolf who is now restin' in peace in the linen room.'

I see Sidoli's eyes flicker when he realises I am on to this, but he don't say anything. He is thinking damn hard. He is thinking how the hell will he get outa this mess. He now has to do three murders which is a tidy issue because, if only one of us dames gets away, he won't have a chance in life. The police'll catch up to him all right, because, in this country, once they gotta real knowledge that a guy is worthy of a scaffold, they are pretty damn quick to oblige him, an' there is no messin' about with ninety-nine years in gaol, which is more than any crook could serve unless he was Methuselah.

If, however, Sidoli can finish his triple murder, he will delay the issue a bit and maybe gain enough time to make a getaway while the friends of the deceased are wonderin' where in goodness name they can be.

I do not like the idea of this triple murder, an' I do not think Jeanette an' Malwa would like it either, an' I bet we are in one mind in favour of stopping it. We have a pretty good chance because we are three dames to two guys, one of who is unconscious an' the other wounded in the hand an' the blood spoilin' his pale grey suit. Us dames also have one gun each, so we are highly mechanised. Also, if the unconscious guy comes to his so-called senses he can be made unconscious again very easy.

I tell Malwa to hop up to the room next to her late prison where I have seen some rope lying which would be very suitable for tyin' up rattlesnakes, an' she is back in no time which is good, because the silence while I am holdin' the gun at Sidoli's abdomen an' Jeanette is sittin' on the gorilla ready to smack him into the realms of Morphia if he starts to get restless is quite embarrassing.

Malwa ropes Sidoli an' she is not too damn gentle about it. She ropes him so good an' proper you would think he was bein' parcelled up to send to cannibals in the equator. When he is well trussed, we push him into a round sitting room chair which has sides to it an' spaces very convenient for further ropin'.

We can now relax. I tell Malwa that, somewhere there is a phone, an' will she find it an' ring a number I give her an' ask Inspector Browne to come at once to this old dark house because Rosie Bosanky has something to tell him. She goes out an', while we are waitin', I ask Jeanette how come.

Without takin' her attention from the gorilla she is sittin' on, she says she'd gone through the old hoosis with the phoney door a second time an' found the stairs. She was part way up when a door on the landin', she never woulda dreamed was there, opened, an' Sidoli came through.

He spotted her at once. She made a dash back to the hoosis and got through the fake door behind the calendar, but he followed her an' caught her, an' I bet this is the first an' last time in her young life, Jeanette will be captured in such a place. He then lugs her upstairs, an' Pete arrives an' they give her a drink.

The drink was doped of course because she's got no more recollections till she wakes up an' finds the gorilla she is now reclinin' on has her in his arms an' is carrying her along a passage, only a few minutes ago. The poor dear still thinks she is in some premises near the famous old hoojah-kapippy.

Malwa comes back to say she has found the phone. She has rung up Brownie who is in bed an' he says he won't leave it till Miss Bosanky comes to the phone in person. I send her back to say Rosie is too damn busy with a pistol stuck in the guts of the snake who killed the guy they found dead in Roy Adams's mansion an' asks to be excused.

I learn he says to her, 'An' who the devil are you?' an' she says, 'I'm Mrs Adams, Roy's wife.'

'The hell you are,' he yells, an' she tells me she can hear him leap outa bed. She guesses he will be along.

I reckon out how long it will take Brownie to get his pants on, and etcetra, an' have the boys out, an' I think we still got time for a little amateur theatricals which Sidoli is not goin' to enjoy.

I tell Malwa I gotta ask her to do a bit of menial work because I want Jeanette to carry on her job of sittin' on the gorilla. She says, 'It's quite all right, Rosie. Anything you say.' Which shows a nice spirit.

I tell her what I want, an' she is surprised, but she has got such class she don't say nothin' but goes out. In a minute she is back. She has gotta safety razor an' a shavin' brush an' a basin with some soap an' water like I told her an' a brush an' comb.

Sidoli is keepin' on sayin' nothin', but his eyes has got an uneasy look.

I say, 'Now, Samson, this is the nearest close-up in your sweet young life you will ever get to bein' a bible personality.'

Jeanette's eyebrows go up because she has had an early bringing-up in a Scotch kirk, but Sidoli snarls, 'Quit the double-talk. Tell me what you want.'

I am like a cat plying with the famous mouse. I tell him, sweet as pie, I don't want anything, only that he should close his ugly mug and listen. 'Samson,' I explain to him, 'was a big-shot till a dame gilletted him.'

He winces at this news because he is no bible student, and the word I have used has given him a very unsavoury impression.

I tell Malwa, if she can bear it, I want her to shave off the snake's sideboards which she does. I tell her now I want she shall snick off his moustache.

Sidoli begins to get it. His lips go back an he gives a sorta snarl like any full grown wolf woulda been proud of.

'By God, you Bosanky bitch,' he says, 'I'll make you pay for this.'

It is a rude expression an' one I do not like. Malwa is horrified, too, to hear such language, an' she sticks the soap brush in his mouth.

After that I do the talkin' while Malwa, bless her, acts the lady barber but not too damn gently. I think if it was real life instead of a bit of melodrama in a old dump of a two-storey house she would never get a tip in all her born days.

I say to Sidoli, 'You called me a Bosanky so-an-so, an' that's true enough an' it woulda been a damn sight better for you if it wasn't. You gotta poor memory, you louse, or maybe you done so many murders you can't remember 'em all.

'I can guess what you're thinkin' about me, an' you'd be sayin' it too if Mrs Adams weren't ready to choke you with that brush. But I'll tell you what I think of you an' that's what my pappy thought of you an' all your lousy sort.

'You're cowards, everyone of you, even before you've stolen the money to buy a gun. You're cowards because you're afraid to work like decent guys. You wanta live easy by takin' off the honest, decent guys the money they've sweated for.

'You got vanity a hundred per cent., too. You begin by bein' a school bully an' you kid a lotta little boys into thinkin' you're a hero, an', when you grow up a bit, you can't bear to have no one around you that don't yes you like this unconscious gorilla on the carpet.'

'And none of you is clever, either. It's only in books you got any good ideas. You work out a clumsy idea like puttin' a greasy heel like the late Wessex into the bed of the lady who is now shavin' you, an' writin' an anonymous letter you hope'll get her husband hanged.

'You even go to the length of gettin' some couple to stay at a pub in Brighton to lend a bit of technicolor to your story. Why, you crazy thug, there ain't one dame in a million who wouldn't know the whole idea was phoney after one little peek at the corpse you put in Malwa's bed, because Malwa is a lady, an' that's a thing you and your kind would know nothin' about.'

Malwa by this time has got the snake's moustache off. He is very changed, but not for the better.

The gorilla Jeanette Mackie is sittin' on begins to emit groans. He says in a thick voice, '*Sidoli*,' an' Jeanette raps him, which is safer. You could never dream, to see her sittin' on this ape's belly so prim an' proper, with her skirt nicely pulled down over her knees, that she's got it in her to do a job of work like smackin' a gorilla down with the butt of a gun. I think I have a very good staff who will climb trees at the dead of night and sit on the stomach of lousy yes-men.

I say to Sidoli, 'So he calls you Sidoli?' I gotta lotta sarcasm in my voice. 'Sidoli me foot!' Only I don't say *foot*, I am so damn mad with this louse. I tell Jeanette an' Malwa I am sorry about my English, but I got hard feelings towards this guy, who is now clean shaved, an' they both got such class they say, 'Don't mention it.'

I tell them why I got hard feelings. Not only because of what he's done tonight. Not only because I believe he has stuck a knife into a gent who was double-crossing him, which in some ways could be counted a good deed; not only because he tried to make poor old Roy take the rap; not only because he kidnapped Malwa an' shot her relation, Rudolf the Smelly; not only because he runs a tobacconist's shop which I think is a dope centre, but because he ain't Sidoli at all.

He's Stalozzi, the snake who shot my pappy – a man who he had never seen before in his life – because he was the only man in that there cafe who was game enough to stand up for his idea that it weren't decent to allow a wop gun man to do a murder an' then walk out like he had every right to do it.

'You're a lyin' bitch,' the snake says. 'I never killed any Bosanky.'

Malwa forgets to shove the soap brush in his mouth, she is so interested.

'All that comes of not payin' attention, louse,' I tell him. 'You killed my pappy all right an' it made the headlines, but, because he was an Englishman in New York the papers played up his real name which you would, in your ignorant way, call Bosanquet to rhyme with cigarette. Now do you get it, snake?'

He gets it all right but he pretends different. 'My name ain't Stalozzi,' he says, dogged.

'Okay, okay,' I say. 'Have it your own way. The finger prints'll prove it.'

Malwa has now quite finished her job. I test the way this so-called Sidoli is tied. I give Malwa the gun an' show her where to point it so he'll feel most uncomfortable. I then take the brush an' comb she has brought and I do this snake's hair in a new way. I put the parting in a different place. I've looked at this thug's picture so many times I could do my job in the dark.

While I am engaged in this fancy bit of hair-dressing, Malwa offers to relate the story of her life since she left Roy's mansion. I say better not make it too fascinating because you have to remember Jeanette Mackie has to keep her weather eye on the prostrate gorilla, an' this so-called Sidoli we have got tied up has more likely got oil in his veins than blood and, unless he has got a gun pointed in his stomach without a cease, he is very prone to slip out of his bonds, an' then we will all be in a state of flux again.

So Malwa says very well she will just give a slight synopsis, an' this synopsis, when you boil it all down an' fill in the gaps, is as follows.

She leaves Roy's mansion and tootles off to the place where this Hotel Palatial is her favourite haunt, an' who should pop up in the vestibule like a horror out of a opium dream but our old friend Rudolf Barenski who, I should say, would be the last person in the world anyone would want to meet on a holiday.

Malwa figures he musta been layin' in wait outside the mansion an' has then tracked her to this Palatial joint. Like the dirty blackmailer he is, he pretty soon puts the claws in. But this is where he gets a jolt, because Malwa tells him, only more ladylike, to go fry his face. She puts it straight to him, she has decided to cut out the old tactics and that she is sick and tired of handing over old Roy's valuable cheques for goodness knows what purpose.

Rudolf says, 'Okay, Madam. Then, with great reluctance, I shall have to write a chatty little letter to your husband.'

He is putting up a bluff, I guess, because I gotta intuition he is the sort of a crook who would think twice and then hesitate before putting his head in a noose an' get a black eye into the bargain. He has got enough sense in his thick skull to know that, even if what he is going to spill to Roy is true, it is another thing to make Roy believe it. And, even if this same Roy believed it, he would have too much class to let a goat like Barenski think he did.

I think Plaster Hair has gotta spine like a jelly fish who is a bit run down. I bet, too, he is making what is known as a bold front an', all the time, he is thinking the game's up an' the goose who lays the golden eggs has gone dry.

So he makes a few more empty threats at Malwa but, when he sees he is really washed up as a blackmailer with her for a customer, an' that she has come down to this Palatial joint just for a holiday an' to pick up enough fresh ozone to fit herself for the task of going back to Roy and tell him the whole story, this Plaster Hair emerges down some dark hole an' hatches out a new plot for making another inroad on Roy's cheque book, which you would think, he is such a heel, was given out by the bank just for his benefit.

This plot is this. He will sool Sidoli (so-called) on to Mr and Mrs Adams, spilling him a yarn how he could very easily kidnap Malwa and have Roy pay an amount to get her back again. You can see at a glance how low he has sunk when, in the twinkling of an eye, he can switch over from a blackmailer to a snatcher. If I was Bernard Shaw I would make a wise-crack about this class of louse which would be bandied about in future history an' make him a stench in your nostrils.

Plaster Hair will put it to this snake, Sidoli, that Malwa is the type of dame a man would pay a lotta dough to get returned to him if he thought she was in the hands of rough fellows who had no idea of etiquette, an', even if they had, they wouldn't use it.

Malwa is sitting in the lounge-room of this Palatial joint reading a good book when a woman breezes up. She is a woman who has grey hair an' glasses and she sits down alongside Malwa and looks round uneasily to make sure no one is quizzing.

She says in a whisper, 'Are you Mrs Adams?'

Malwa admits it and then she sees this old dame is very excited. The o.d. is saying, 'Oh, Mrs Adams. I don't know how to tell you. Someone has kidnapped my husband.'

Malwa puts down her book an' says, surprised, 'Why tell me? Why not go to the police?'

The dame presses her hands together and leans on the table, putting her face close to Malwa's, and says, 'I got to come to you, Mrs Adams. They *made* me. Oh, dear!'

'Who made you?' Roy's wife asks.

'The men,' the old lady tells her. 'Those dreadful men. Oh, I am so frightened. If I don't do exactly as I have been ordered they'll kill him.'

Malwa, who is no mug, is wondering why she has been cast for a role in this gangster drama, so she says, 'I'm sure I don't know how I can help you. I don't even know who you are. Why come to me?'

'Because,' the grey-haired old dame says, 'they got your husband, too.'

Now this is a news-flash that makes Malwa sit right up an' take a lotta notice, because you can bet your sweet life she straight away gets a ready-made vision in her mind of old Roy lured to some foul lair with a grating over a cob-webby underground window and a candle stuck in a disused beer bottle while a lotta low thugs play rummy.

It is not a nice picture because Malwa knows Roy is not used to candles stuck in even wine bottles, an' never in his born days has he set foot in such a filthy lair except to see it in the movies. She puts her book away and says very calm, 'You'd better tell me everything.'

The woman says she will. She says her name is Mrs Wessex and her husband is a man who would always get a welcome in any good bank because he has a habit of making a lotta money. These crooks have got wise to this and they have, therefore, got hold of Wessex while he was coming home from church an' taken him to a distant lair. They have then got in touch with his wife an' told her what she has got to do.

She has got to go to the Palatial Hotel an' find a Mrs Roy Adams an' tell her that her husband has been kidnapped, too, and is quite well at present, but there is a old-fashioned razor being kept handy alongside his stretcher an' it ain't to shave him with. She – this old lady called Wessex – has got to tell her to pay her way out of the Palatial at once and, then, the dames has to take a car which they will find waitin' in front of the hotel, and they will be whisked off to where their husbands are lying in wait against their will. The two wives will then be told just what they will have to do to prevent themselves becoming a coupla widows at a very early moment.

'They told me,' the old lady says, wringing her hands, 'that if I made one false move that would bring the police about their ears they would do a most dreadful thing to poor Wessex which would make him next door to irreparable.'

Malwa by this time has a bosom full of anxieties on account of the hint Mrs Wessex has given her of old Roy wearing a very haggard air and perhaps no clean collar, with his poor, frightened eyes staring at this sharp razor that has come into the picture.

Put yourself in her place with a husband worth £60,000 p.a., who she has, in her silent way, just begun to find the good points of to an extent that she is now practically in love with him, an' what would you do? Take the grey-haired old lady's word for it, or scream 'Police' and chance old Roy getting slit? She looks at the old lady whose husband is a fellow captive an' she decides she has gotta believe her.

She pays her bill and takes her bags and tootles off with this Mrs Wessex and, sure enough, there is a big car waiting. Someone inside it pushes the door open an' in they pop.

There is a big guy at the wheel an' another guy in the back of the car sitting near the door. Mrs Wessex plants herself near the other door an' is very quiet an' pensive while they travel a number of miles. It is very darkish and, in the gloom, Malwa can't see very well, but she can feel the old lady shaking an' heaving, and she thinks she's crying, and she is sorry for her.

The man alongside her says, 'Stow it, can't you?'

The old lady puts her handkerchief over her mouth, but in a little while she is off again and, suddenly, Malwa gets it and knows she has won this year's blue ribbon for being the prize mug. The old girl with the white hair isn't crying at all. She's laughing.

All at once she says, 'It's no use, Sid. I can't help it. It was so funny. The way she fell for it and all,' and she lets herself go, laughing like she was seeing her best friend in a distortin' mirror.

This Sid, who you have guessed, is this alleged Sidoli, is mad but he can't stop her; but he can stop the car. He tells the old dame to hop it and, still laughing, she opens the door an' gets out an' it looks to Malwa, by the blackness outside, they are a long way from anywhere where she is likely to have any friends.

The old dame says to Malwa, 'Ain't you goin' to kiss gran'ma goodbye?' and Sidoli calls her a nasty name. Malwa now knows she is in a mess, and she makes a move to get out of the car but Sidoli grabs her arm an' twists it in some foul way an' slams the door.

He says, 'On your way, Pete,' and this is the office to me that the driver has been none other than the celebrated yes-man over who Jeanette is now waving her magic gun. I guess this Mrs Wessex is a frame-up, an' her white hair is a wig, an' she has borrowed the spectacles, and, when she is stripped of these an' in her right mind about clothes, you would find she is just a mass of lipstick an' mascara got up as a facsimile of Mother Machree, and, when you boiled it down, you would find she was one of this snake Sidoli's fancy bits from the low, high-class gambling joint.

I make up my mind, as Malwa relates it, to catch up with this dame one day an' tear her hair out whatever colour it is.

As they skid along, with the gorilla at the wheel and the rattle snake in the rear, Sidoli tells Malwa all the nice plans he has thought up for her, some of which is to put her into some old dark house and then tell her husband, Roy, all the games they are going to play with her unless he pays a ransom that would make a miser sick even to think about.

So you see, it is all cut and dried. Sidoli leaves her in the old house like he has promised in charge of a oily sheik whose name, to her astonishment, turns out to be Wessex, but who, she thinks, in her innocent mind, is too young to be a husband to that antique old fraud who brought her the fatal message.

Malwa puts it to this Wessex, very cunningly, that he is a mug for letting them use his name because, now, she has a clue, and, if ever she gets out of her predicament, she will hand his monniker to the police an' he will never hear the last of it.

He says, 'Can you beat it? There's about a hundred thousand names in the telephone book, and that stinkin' doll has to pick on Wessex!'

Malwa then sees he is a man who is apt to be scared easy

and maybe is the weak link in the chain, so she puts it to him wouldn't it be a far, far wiser plan to have £500 all for himself than go on being a simple cook workin' for a snake like Sidoli who wouldn't give him £500 in ten thousand years even if he lived that long.

He says he has sometimes thought that hisself only the snag in it is that there is no £500. Malwa then tells him she knows where such a sum may be had for the asking, and, if he will tell Roy where she is, she will tell him how he can get the dough.

Wessex says he will do it. He will do it, he says, because there is a fellow called Barenski mixed up in this deal who is a pain in the neck to any decent crook, an' he is always afraid he will rat on his best pals an' get them put in a dock. He says he doesn't care to be associated any more with men like Sidoli either, who, once they had collected the dividend, would just as soon put a bullet in you as not.

He says he has decided to turn over a new leaf and he will collect this money to help him do it, an' then tell the police where they can find Malwa and, at the same time, lay their hands on Barenski an' Sidoli an' the gorilla, Pete. After which, he says, he will make a quick getaway to a place he knows in the middle of Ecuador; or, better still, he will take a single ticket to Sidoli's old home-town which will be safer because, when Sidoli left there, they had thanksgivings in all the churches an' swore a sacred oath, if ever he came back, they would have a big vat of oil ready for him to be boiled in and would use sharp hayforks to find out was he getting done.

Malwa tells Wessex the money is in the philately drawer, an' he tells her she is practically as good as free an' tootles off. From what I have seen of this guy, even in a dead state, I think he was right about making a quick getaway to a foreign clime, but I don't think he had any idea in the world he would tell Roy. His whole idea is to get the money out of the drawer at Roy's mansion, after which he would put a great lot of distance between him an' Sidoli an' let Malwa stew in her own juice.

And now, I guess, Plaster Hair comes on the scene again, and it is as plain as last year's hat he has somehow got suspicions of Wessex and, like the low heel of a yes-man he is, he has worded Sidoli and, together, they have watched their fellow-crook an' followed him to Roy's mansion where they have caught him red-handed with the money honest old Roy has won at the races. There is a bit of an argument which enlarges to a fight an' Sidoli sticks the paper knife in the neck of his boon companion.

He then gets rattled because what started out to be a private snatch has turned out to be a public murder, as you might say. He gets a crazy idea of putting Wessex in Roy's pyjamas and shoving him in Malwa's boudoir an', all the while, I bet he is frightening the life outa Rudolf by explaining the legal aspect of the case is that he is just as guilty of sticking the knife into Wessex because he was present at the deed an', if he doesn't keep his mouth shut, he will be swung off from the same scaffold.

But now, with my gun tickling his tummy, it looks to me like Sidoli will later on be a lonely soul on the gallows unless something can be pinned on this low gorilla Pete. My idea is that if you had said Pete had a vacant mind you would be in the realms of exaggeration and, now that Jeanette has been at him, I really don't think there would be anything left worth while taking to a scaffold.

I am thinking, while Malwa is finishing her story in its synopsis form, that things have come to a fatal climax with Sidoli, Barenski, Wessex and Pete, which goes to show that the old proverb saying your sins will find you out is a very true saying if you are not careful to keep your wits about you.

This roped thug, to who I am giving the finishing touch to his new hair-do, suddenly goes a shade paler an' I know he has heard the dread sound of cops racing up the drive. Malwa gives me the gun an' goes down to do the honours. In a minute I hear them running up the stairs. Brownie is in the lead, an' he comes right over to me.

'Rosie,' he says, 'you poor kid,' and he slips his arm round me as if I might be goin' to faint. I say, 'I think you have met Miss Mackie.' He is very surprised to see Jeanette sittin' on this Pete ape because he has once met her at a party with me an' thought what a nice girl she was. He orders a cop to take Jeanette's place. 'Who the hell is this?' he asks, nodding at the tied up snake.

'He calls himself Sidoli,' I say. 'He runs a gambling joint.'

'Nonsense,' he says. 'I know Sidoli. He's gotta moustache an' side levers.'

Malwa gives a honeyed giggle.

'That's him just the same,' I say. 'I reckon he an' another guy went to Roy Adams's mansion an' one of 'em killed a guy there. His name was Wessex. I ain't sure which one did it, but it don't matter.'

'It doesn't matter?' Brownie snorts. 'The hell it matters!'

'It don't matter, Brownie,' I say, soothing, 'because a while back he destroyed the guy who went to the house with him.'

I no sooner have said it than I hear a noise like someone has stumbled down some steps. We all look round an' a copper throws the door open wider. We can see the stairway, and, half-way down it is a guy who is covered with blood. He has blood on his face an' on his hands an' on his clothes. He is in one helluva mess.

He is clingin' with both hands to the bannister. We all watch him, sort of fascinated for a moment, and then a coupla cops rush up an' ease him down. It is Rudolf an' he ain't dead. For once in his life the snake has not done a perfect job. Rudolf is dyin' on his feet, but he manages to get it out.

He points a shaky hand at where Sidoli is tied up though there is so much blood on his face I should think he could hardly see him.

He says, 'Stalozzi, you bastard! You thought you killed me, but I've come back to hang you. You shot me tonight like you killed Wessex –'

He is by now a complete corpse an' they carry him over to the settee.

I have a squiz at Sidoli, so-called. I think I can see his hair slowly turnin' grey. Brownie is shoutin' orders, an' cops is runnin' to the telephone an' up an' down the stairs, an', while everyone's so busy, I manage to sit down by old Rudolf's body an' ask Jeanette to cover me up. She does it, an' I ease the deceased of his pocket book. I have to be very careful because of the blood. When I have got the pocket book it is easy to take out the half of the ten-pound note which he has got there an' which would only be wasted if it got to the hands of the coppers because it would maybe spend the rest of its history in a police museum. I put the pocket book back.

Brownie is lookin' closely at Sidoli an' has just made up his mind he is really the guy he knows under that name when in breezes that handsome devil Clancy with none other than poor old Roy who they have urged out of his warm bed.

Clancy takes one look at the louse in the chair an' he says, 'Well, I'm damned. *Stalozzi*!'

An' now Brownie is not quite sure who the snake is, so much corroboration is bein' bandied about. He's gettin' irritable. I leave it to Clancy to explain, though I am wonderin' how he knows, because I am watchin' the coppers get the gorilla on his feet.

The big feller stands swayin' for a moment, an' then he realises what is happenin'. He makes a dive for his pocket, an', my God, a girl can't think of everything! His gun is there an' I see hell an' damnation ahead till there is something that looks like a animated blurr leapin' through the air.

I hear a crack, an' old Roy has given the gorilla as sweet a upper cut as ever I see. Oh, boy, am I pleased! Because this is what I always thought about Roy, that he is a lad with class who has got hisself so filled with repressions such as British Colonial stamp philately that he does not know that there are some dames, even if they have the look of born an' bred angels, who require to have their men live life in the raw.

For a moment, because Roy is lookin' so sheepish at Malwa, I think he is goin' to apologise. I catch his sleeve an' he bends down an' I whisper. I put it in a few words. They are words he has never heard in his life before but the smack he has given the gorilla has warmed his blood. A bit of colour comes into his cheek. He looks round at Malwa an' I whisper, 'Now or never.' He decides on now.

He lifts his head an' I see he's gotta square chin. I think he's goin' to give the Tarzan cry but, instead, he rushes over to Malwa. He grabs her up in his arms an' carries her upstairs. Half way up I see her arm go round his neck, an' I bet he gets to the top like a man in a dream. Maybe, in her late prison, she will tell him her past Bombay life but, if she don't, what the heck? The blackmailin' Rudolf is defunct, anyway.

I look round to see this devil Clancy makin' a play with Jeanette. She leaves him an' comes over to me an' says she's gotta give me back the money I gave her because there's been practically no expenses except for the special delivery letter an' a bus fare. She is not puttin' down for her tea because she would have to eat anyway, an' Mr Clancy has been kind enough to say he will give her a lift back to town.

I am glad to see it is like I thought an' this Jeanette is not the sort who would monkey round with a expense account an' put down threepennorth of tacks ninepence. I think it is another good *tray* in her character.

Brownie is waxing more officious an' orderin' everybody around, and I take him into the second-best bedroom of the house where the late Wessex an' the more recent Rudolf have been mutual club mates an' I give him the evidence of the hair oil an' the corn plaster. He says again I oughta get slapped on the pants for holdin' back evidence such as the plaster I found in Malwa's bed on the toe of the corpse Harold. But I tell him I don't want to be dragged into this too much, an' would he mind sayin' that he found everything hisself. He says he don't mind.

He says, too, thank God he was in time to save me from such a fate as would be mapped out for me by this Sidoli who he has captured. He has had his eye on this bird for a very long time, he relates, an' he is glad at last he has been able to bring it to a dead-end.

He gives a big laugh. 'You see, Rosie,' he says, 'I'm so glad everything has come right I can't help making quips.'

This so-called quip, it seems, is in the word 'dead-end'. He explains Sidoli will be *dead* at the *end* of a rope. Hence '*dead-end*'.

I tell him why doesn't he write a book of his jokes an' get it placed in all the big museums, and he says yes, sometime he will sit down an' compose it because, when he is in a mood, they simply teem out of his brain and, if a man didn't have some relaxation from his work, life would be just one damn routine after another.

I am very glad when he has got back to a more serious strain again because, by this time, I am feeling nearly at a dead-end myself an' not up to the mark enough to stand too many more jokes.

Brownie says, 'D'you know sumpun, Rosie? I wouldn't be the lease surprised it works out that this Sidoli guy is mixed up in the dope racket I told you about.'

I ask, innocent, who is the copper to who the cheap doll gave the packet of dope, and he tells me it is a young feller by the name of Pat Mulcahey. He's only been married six years but already he has five children and he has an ambition in life to give so many Mulcaheys to the world that in the end there will be nothing else but. I give a sigh because I can see a blight has been cast on what I had been counting on for a very nice slice of future romance.

In a little while I find myself with Brownie in his little two-seater, an' he is saying, 'So Sidoli is really Stalozzi who bumped your poor pa off! Well, well, wonders will never cease! Though, mind you, I had a intuition.' He pats my hand. 'You take my advice, Rosie. No matter what they say, in this game you gotta use a lotta intuition. You bear that in mind, kid.'

It is now nearly dawn. When we are some way up the turn-off road I ask Brownie will he pull up. I tell him I want to pick some flowers.

He says okay, an' I make my way to where I left young Buck an' his all-night taxi. I find it. He is there in the front seat, a rug round his bottom half, in a innocent youthful sleep. He looks like a young Greek God. His lips are a bit wet with the dawn dew, an' his white teeth are just showing. I get quite poetic lookin' at him in the fresh early mornin' air, an' I feel like the guy who said in the picture book, 'Not Angles but angels,' only this is an angel who has grown up. He looks *good*.

He don't hear me. I climb up on the runnin' board an' lean over, an' I give him my friend's special. Then I stand back an' wait. He wakes up suddenly an' in a very irritable mood, an' he has no longer got the principles of an angel.

'Hell an' damnation,' he says. 'Who woke me? I was havin' one whale of a dream.'

I give him some more of the late Rudolf's lucre which I will get back out of old Roy's bill of costs. This is a good business because I sorta get paid twice. I think I will see Roy early in the mornin' because I have learned this in life, that, for a young girl of a modern type, it is always wise to strike while the iron is hot.

Ronald Gaylord nearly burst into tears when he found out what he'd been missing in the old dark house of which he was practically the Dr Livingstone since it was he who discovered it. I've made it up to him by promisin' to take him to see old Rudolf in the morgue. I will also have a pass from Brownie an' take him to see a condemned cell for Christmas.

Young Jeanette Mackie says she will accept the job to be my offsider; so now she has a position in life where she can kiss who she likes at last. When she comes to the office next day after we have washed up this Misplaced Corpse case, I ask her how does she like my hat which I have bought from La Fifine, the French piece. She puts her head on one side and says, after a bit, 'Um – y – es. It goes with you. How much did you pay for it?'

I have a flash of guilty conscience because this Jeanette Mackie has a mind like a female Harry Lauder in his most frugal moments, so I make a lie of it an' say, 'Four guineas.' I hear a slight cough and look round and there is Ronald Gaylord standing at the door with his freckles and another too-small hat. I know he has heard, the little blighter, because he gives me a wink which Jeanette does not witness because, when I mentioned even four guineas, she has raised her eyes to heaven.

Clancy, it turns out, is a loan out from the New York police, an' that is why he had such a good knowledge of Stalozzi after Mrs Adams has shaved him. He ain't never been in the North West mounties at all, the liar. Just the same, I bet I would still like to hear his memoirs, but he has now proved a fickle swain an' has got his eye on Jeanette which, unless he can see a altar steps and a wedding march at the same time, is like tryin' to thread a needle in a haystack.

On account of it being an alleged solemn occasion, though, as for me, I don't call it an occasion so much as a celebration, I wear a very sombre outfit an' black silk stockings. The dress is a black dress but it has a fashionable cut, an' I have also a black hat which is a hug-me-head with a cute feather.

Brownie is there, an' holds my hand on account of it being a kind of funeral an' he is representin' my old man who died a hero all because of this punk Stalozzi, who is to make a brief farewell performance before us. Brownie has said did I think I oughta go to such a ceremony? An' I say yes, because I know damn well my pappy woulda walloped the tail off me if I should miss such a thing, especially when he has a connection with it.

Across from me there is a slim guy who, they tell me, is a French detective. He is dressed in a dark blue serge suit which is cut to his figure without giving any effect of a cis, an' he has a tie with a tiny stripe which has got class an' a lotta chic. He has got hair that has got a little wave in it which makes a girl feel like, if she stroked it, it might send a electric shiver up her arms to the back of her neck an' down her spine, too, an' he looks to me like he was a lad who, whatever path he was leading you, he would pave it with good inventions. He has the look to me that he would have a technique which would be a new type to a dame of my category.

I catch this guy's eye, an' then I look away quick an' I cross my leg, careless. I see he is gettin' an eyeful, an', after that, he can't hardly keep his mind on the execution.

This Stalozzi, so called Sidoli, makes his entrance, and, believe me, if he used to have a pasty make-up, now he looks like raw dough that has had a powder puff run over it. They say to him has he got any remarks to make an' his lips move but he can't make 'em work, an' I can tell by his eyes he's frightened as hell, the low heel; an' I wish his face could be put on a fillum so it could be distributed for all budding gangsters to see so they would know what cowards such so-called men as Stalozzi really are.

While I'm wishin' that all the guys he has bumped off an' all the young dames he has traded in could rise up an' give him one helluva raspberry for a *bong voyage*, someone whisks a cap over his ugly mug an' he does a sudden drop which they say is only seven feet, but I bet what he's got for a soul goes on a long way past that, an' down, an' down, an' down to where they are waitin' with hot pitchforks to give him a sample of what he's done to folk up above.

Brownie is patting my hand an' sayin', 'There, there now, bear up,' the poor old goat, while I am wonderin' whether it would be the right etiquette to hand the hangman a tip; an' then we are outside in the sheriff's office havin' solemn drinks. Brownie is called away an' this French guy I spoke about sidles up.

'M'lle Rosie Bosanky?'

'Yep,' I say. 'To who may I have the honour?'

He gives a bow an' hands me a card an' it is a card for a 'Andre Castelaggio'.

He says: 'I am in zis countree but two day, an' already I find zee mos' charming woman in the world.'

I like it this way. I think it is like a soldier who could make love in the jaws of death, puttin' it to me in the midst of this office of a hard-boiled official who has just hung a man.

I say: 'Smart work, Ondray.'

He puts his lips near my ear, an' I feel his breath wiggling my ear-ring. He says something very low. I mean it is low in the sense that you can hardly hear it. To me it sounds like a finish to a perfect day.

He adds a bit more in his native dialogue which he speaks with great speed an' vim, an', my God, I think, it is Charles Boyer got loose.

It sounds to me like he is saying, 'Mamwahzelle on shon-tay voolee voo monjay avec m'wah cess swah? Tray sholee on shontay, voolee voo, voolee voo, *voolee voo?*'

This *voolee voo* is the French habit of saying, 'Will you?'

I say I will.

THE END

Archibald Eric (A.E.) Martin was born in 1885 at the Scotch Thistle Hotel (now the Cathedral Hotel) in Adelaide. He grew up in the small South Australian country town of Orroroo, where his father had the Imperial Hotel, and attended Prince Alfred College in Adelaide. After he left school he worked for a time on the *Adelaide Critic*, where he met C. J. Dennis. The pair founded the notorious parish-pump paper, the *Gadfly*, and at eighteen Martin not only co-owned a weekly newspaper, but also wrote for it satirical prose and verse of such quality that readers were often left guessing whether Dennis or Martin was the author.

A cast of talented youths gathered at the *Gadfly*, including its society columnist Alice Rosman ('Aunt Tabatha'), who later became a successful romantic novelist; political journalist Geoff Burgoyne, who set up a Labor paper in Western Australia; Beaumont Smith, entrepreneur and maker of some of Australia's earliest silent films; and artists, illustrators and cartoonists Ruby Lindsay, Will Dyson and Will Donald.

The *Gadfly* folded in 1909 and in 1912 Martin left for the fairgrounds of Europe, where Houdini became his mentor. He brought back to Australia 'The Wonder Show', a circus featuring freak acts such as 'The Fat Man', Edgar Crane, who weighed in at fifty-two stone, prize-fighters and stars. The show opened in Adelaide in a heat-wave that followed it to Melbourne. Martin was left broke after he'd paid the artists' passages home. He moved to Sydney to work as advance publicity scout for Beau Smith's 'Tiny Town', a touring sideshow of midgets.

In 1915 Martin and Smith took the play of *Seven Little Australians* to New Zealand. Martin returned to Sydney and worked as publicity agent for First National Pictures and then for the Fuller brothers' vaudeville show. In the early 1920s he became the publicist for J. C. Williamson, and worked for them until about 1934, promoting many great acts, including Anna Pavlova.

He took some time off during the 'twenties to travel to Europe, where he bought the Australian rights to movies such as the German health-and-skin flick *The Golden Road* and one about venereal disease. Martin, or the authorities, or perhaps the two in collusion, were careful to alert Australian audiences that a qualified nurse would be in attendance at the single-sex viewings.

Later in the 1930s Martin established The Woman's Weekly Travel Agency, which offered overseas package tours, until the war forced its closure. He then wrote and published magazines for soldiers and children's comics, often working with the artist Brodie Mack. He also wrote books of place-names for the New South Wales Bookstall Company.

His career as a novelist was not launched before he was well over fifty, by which time he had racked up a wealth of life-experience. In 1942 the *Australian Woman's Weekly* announced a £1,000 prize for an unpublished novel. Encouraged by one of his sons, and needing money, Martin set to work and wrote two in six months: *Sinners Never Die* and *Common People*. Consolidated Press considered each worthy of the award, but finally plumped for *Common People*. (*Sinners* features an Orroroo postmaster who opened people's mail, and Consolidated Press was fearful of offending the Australian postal authorities.) Both books were eventually serialised and published in Australia.

A.E. Martin's son, Jim, is unsure how the books were

picked up by the American publisher Nimmo. *Sinners Never Die* was released in the States to fabulous reviews, being listed as among the 'Ten Best' in 1944 by every respected reviewer. Both books were later published in Britain and in 1955 *Common People* was filmed in the UK as *The Glass Cage* and released as a Hammer production.

*The Misplaced Corpse* was published in Australia in 1944 by the New South Wales Bookstall Company but was never published overseas, unlike Martin's other mystery novels, *Death in the Limelight*, *The Curious Crime* and *The Bridal Bed Murders*, all of which had US and UK editions.

Martin was one of very few Australians to have short stories published in the US *Ellery Queen* mystery magazine, and also wrote radio plays and serials for George Edwards productions. He died of cancer in 1955.

Many of the characters in Martin's novels were drawn from his life in shows and circuses. The hero of *Common People*, Pel Pelham, manager of Henri Sapolio, World's Champion Starving Man, and protector from crooked cops of an array of side-show freak acts, is doubtless an autobiographical figure. In *Sinners Never Die*, a sleepy outback town is brought to life, and its senses, by the arrival of the Great Boldini, a touring Italian magician and hypnotist. Martin always said, however, that the nineteen-year-old, red-headed narrator of *The Misplaced Corpse*, private-eye Rosie Bosanky, was created purely from his imagination. She was his favourite character and it saddened him that the book was published only in Australia and went to just one edition. The New South Wales Bookstall Company, which published the book, was in its death-throes in 1944, and Rosie is probably a more suitable heroine for the 'nineties than the 'forties. They were, as Rosie says, 'a war-time period', during which young women were supposed to have their nose to the grindstone, not gadding about using their natural assets to solve murder mysteries and acquire green felt hats.

Rosie Bosanky's first editor headed his admirably discreet prefatory note, FOREWORD AND WARNING. If he feared that readers might find her alarming in 1944, how will they view her almost fifty years on?

The immense popularity of Peter Cheyney's ingenious Lemmy Caution thrillers should have prepared A.E. Martin's readers for a present-tense vernacular first-person narrative. Actual comparison with Lemmy Caution suggests that his ersatz American lingo, larded as it is with dames, mugs and palookas, offered little more than a launching tickle to the more sprightly Bosanky. Caution attributes much of his homely wisdom to Confucius, but Bosanky nods only once to him in upsaging the Chinese cautioner: 'Like Confucius said in his less ribald moments, a Paris gown may entice a man around a block but what's inside it will lead him round several hemispheres'.

Far be it from us to recommend Rosie's linguistic vandalism, but there is a great deal of difference between butchering a shark and gilletting a catfish. Rosie's apparently casual approach to the conventions should not be lightly nominated hit-and-miss when it is really miss-and-hit. The style is set early when we are told about Brownie's inability to 'run down to a satisfactory climax'. Elsewhere we find much evidence to show that, like Sterne in *Tristram Shandy* and Joseph Furphy (Tom Collins) in *Such is Life* before him, Martin is a brilliant exponent of learned wit. That so much of his learning is that of the 'common people' (to borrow the title of his first novel) should not blind us to what is really going on here.

Take, for instance, Rosie's passing reference to young Ronald's 'most verbatim description of me, which makes it sound I was like one of those so-called Persian gazelles who were whisked out of warm beds on their bridal nights by visiting Jinnies just to please the whims of some Arabian Knight'. The use of 'gazelles' is surprisingly precise. Although it looks like a mistake for 'damsels', even Persians would not in Rosie's warmest imagination share their bridal beds with real gazelles.

What Martin is really alluding to is ghazals (sometimes spelt 'gazels'), which flourish abundantly in the *Arabian Nights* and are highly formal couplets, often erotic, and often offering verbatim descriptions of beautiful and ingenious oriental Rosies.

Take also the passing mis-reference to a little known French writer and courtesan, Ninon de Lenclos (1620-1705): 'I think it woulda been a night which a girl could write down on the tablets of memory, an' it would do her a bit of good in her old age, like this Nina Lenclose, who was a French bit an' was chased all through the palaces of Europe, even after she was fifty.' Made famous by an inaccurate letter of Voltaire, to whom she bequeathed a thousand francs to buy books, Ninon is also remembered by the saying, recently refuted by Germaine Greer, 'Old age is woman's hell.'

If *The Misplaced Corpse* were to become a school or university textbook, it would need abundant annotation. Our hope is more modest, that it will reach a sufficiently large intelligent readership with a sense of humour to become a cult classic.

That Rosie Bosanky is a hard-boiled heroine goes without saying, though she does say it herself: even today, when it is *day rigure* for women detectives, they don't come with harder boils than Rosie Bosanky, if she will let us suppose for one minute that anything more forward than a freckle would dare break out on her lily-white skin (corns she specifically disowns). Consider her at the corpse's bedside: no young girl had probably been quite so nonchalant in the face of death since Susannah in *Tristram Shandy* heard about the passing of young Bobby and immediately concluded that she would thereby inherit her mistress's green satin night-gown. In 1944, Rosie was perhaps the first Australian female private investigator, at least in a book-length story, and she would have had to be hard-boiled even to think of taking on that famously unsuitable job.

The big question over Rosie's claim to priority seems to be not that there is a queue of unknown challengers (anyone who invokes Phryne Fisher is cheating), but that she appears to be operating in London. We say 'appears' because a case can be made for her working in Sydney. She seems to picture herself situated between America and Paris. The allusion to Brighton proves nothing, of course: there are suburbs called Brighton in Adelaide, Melbourne and Sydney. Street names are suggestive of London and horse-races of England, not to mention the *News of the World*, but Martin has been very careful not to alarm nervous readers by providing a definite location.

That Rosie, in spite of her education in New York by her police detective pappy, thinks of herself as Australian is evident in her language from the first page. That her text is also peppered with American and British slang only illustrates the devastating effect on Australians of two world wars and the talkies.

There is a lot of basic Australian in *The Misplaced Corpse*, some of it not in the *Australian National Dictionary* yet, some of it postdating, some antedating, the recorded usages of particular words. The Australian phrase 'in the nuddy' appears earlier here than in the *Australian National Dictionary*; 'tabbies' (presumably a diminutive of Australian 'tabs', meaning young women), suggests that the word continued in use until at least the 1940s. Several words and phrases are in neither the second edition of the *Oxford English Dictionary* nor the *Australian National Dictionary*. Usually these will not give the reader any trouble. But sometimes the reader may be misled: when we come across a pimp in chapter seven, for example, she is likely to be a good Australian police informer, not a working girl's best friend. Those people who cannot work out what a 'hoojah-kapippy' is should not be reading books for grown-ups.

The text is something of a hurdle for proof-readers. As series editors, we have made a very few obvious corrections (a crooked Silodi becomes a crooked Sidoli, for example). We have not thought fit to change 'scran' to 'scram', even though we are not familiar with 'scranning', and 'scram' appears in the text. We have seen no need to correct 'sheik' to 'sheikh'. Even Orwell used the first spelling (the term comes from the films based on E.M. Hull's 1919 novel). The punctuation is still not sprinkled to our perfect satisfaction. We can only hope that we have not inadvertently introduced any new Bosankyisms.

MICHAEL J. TOLLEY AND PETER MOSS

**WAKEFIELD CRIME CLASSICS**

Peter Moss and Michael J. Tolley, general editors of the Wakefield Crime Classics series, are colleagues at the University of Adelaide. Late in 1988, they began assembling a series of Australian 'classic' crime fiction and soon realised that the problem was not going to be one of finding sufficient works of high quality, but of finding a bold enough publisher fired with the same vision.

This series revives forgotten or neglected gems of crime and mystery fiction by Australian authors. Many of the writers have established international reputations but are little known in Australia. In the wake of the excitement generated by the new wave of Australian crime fiction writers, we hope that the achievements of earlier days can be justly celebrated.

If you wish to be informed about new books as they are released in the Wakefield Crime Classics series, send your name and address to Wakefield Press, Box 2266, Kent Town, South Australia 5071, phone (08) 362 8800, fax (08) 362 7592.